THE
TEACHER'S
SECRET

BOOKS BY LAUREN NORTH

My Word Against His
She Says She's My Daughter

All the Wicked Games
Safe at Home
One Step Behind
The Perfect Betrayal

THE
TEACHER'S
SECRET

LAUREN NORTH

Bookouture

Published by Bookouture in 2024

An imprint of Storyfire Ltd.
Carmelite House
50 Victoria Embankment
London EC4Y 0DZ

www.bookouture.com

ISBN: 978-1-83525-138-6
eBook ISBN: 978-1-83525-137-9

For Tara

PROLOGUE

I look down and there you are. Both so still. Frozen almost. It's on my lips to tell you there's nothing to fear, but that's a lie. The boy's arms are locked around you in a tight embrace, reminding me of the baby monkeys on the nature programmes, clinging to their parent as they swing from tree to tree, high up in the canopies.

I try a reassuring smile, but your boy whimpers, so I place a finger to my lips instead. Without a word, you tighten your hold on him. No more is needed. You know what will happen if you make a sound.

The air in the van is stuffy. I can smell the terror on you. Sweat and tears and something primal. Fight or flight. Neither is an option now.

I wait for your whispers and your pleas, that pathetic begging. But all I hear is silence. You're learning fast.

I allow myself a moment of pride in what I've done, and then I slide the door of the van shut and climb into the driver's seat. I check the time, thinking of the air in the back and the next part of my plan. Adrenaline skips through me. There is much to do, but this – the taking – is the best part.

Traffic is light, but I drive carefully, humming a tune I heard on the radio this morning. Relaxed. Casual. Stress and speeding would get me caught, and I'm too smart for that. I think of the air in the back again. The stuffy heat, the dizziness. How soon before you're gone?

Soon.

Very soon.

TUESDAY: FOUR DAYS MISSING

ONE

LEXI

'Good afternoon. It's lovely to meet you all,' I say with a wide smile.

The hall of Leedham Primary School is packed. Seven rows of children sit cross-legged on the floor. Teachers sit at the sides, one eye on me, one on their class. And at the back, row after row of parents on bright-green plastic chairs. I don't know much about designer clothes, but I know what money looks like, and this parent group have it. It's in the shine of blonde highlights, the effortless fit of a blouse, the sharp, crisp cotton of a shirt.

I've never seen a primary school quite like this one. It's Tuesday afternoon, the end of the school day. Outside, the sun is warm in that way late-spring days can be when the wind drops and the day holds all the promise of summer. The children must be desperate to escape to the park for ice creams and play, and yet they sit perfectly still. Hands in laps.

I saw a film once, starring Nicole Kidman and Daniel Craig. It was about aliens invading our bodies, removing free will and giving us all the same thoughts, the same purpose. That's what I think when I look at these children. Not a grazed knee or a hair out of place. There are only ten weeks left of the school year and yet every single blazer still looks brand new. How is that possible?

I'm being unfair. I'm sure they're all lovely kids, but I prefer to see grass-stained polo shirts and scuffed shoes at this age.

Oliver Walker, the school's head teacher, clears his throat and moves a step towards me. His hair is a tad too long for a man in his mid-forties, but I can see already it's part of his Hugh Grant charm, which I'm sure everyone falls for.

'We're very lucky to have Miss Mills joining our Year Four class from tomorrow morning, although we're grateful to Mrs Woodcock for taking care of the Year Three and Four classes together yesterday.'

He beams out at the hall, catching the eye of a woman in the front row of parents. She's wearing a green polka-dot maxi dress and has a pair of expensive-looking sunglasses perched on top of a sleek black bob. It's Anika Jones, the head of governors and the woman who gave me the tour this morning, proudly pointing out the iPads in every classroom and the state-of-the-art electronic display boards in the hall, because 'sugar paper can look so messy'. The officiousness of the tour was interspersed with a more breathless, half-whispered explanation about Mrs Walker, the Year Four teacher, and her son. As if I hadn't already seen it on the news.

'We're all so very worried.'

'And to disappear on the way home from school too. The police don't have a clue what happened.'

'Little Archie is only eight.'

Oliver clasps his hands together. 'Well, I think we should give Miss Mills a warm—'

Before he can continue, a hand shoots up from a pupil in the fifth row. It's a girl with auburn hair tied in a pristine French braid who I recognise from the introduction to my new class earlier.

Oliver frowns, tilting his head a fraction to one side. 'We

don't normally have question time in assembly, Jessica, you know that. But perhaps you have a question to help us get to know Miss Mills a little better?'

Jessica places her hand back in her lap and takes a steadying breath, aware of the attention now on her and seemingly unafraid. 'Mr Walker,' she says, 'have Mrs Walker and Archie been found yet?'

There's an audible intake of breath from the rows of parents at the back, followed by a murmur from the children and a hissed 'Shush' from Gemma Rowley, the Reception class teacher in the front row, who'd given me barely more than a distracted 'hello' on my tour earlier.

A silence draws out. All eyes are on Oliver. He stands, frozen, mouth hanging open, eyes wide with the unmistakable deer-in-headlights look about him.

'I...' he starts then clears his throat. 'My wife...' A cough now as though the thought, the words, are lodged in his throat. His reaction is no surprise. It is, after all, not just a teacher and a little boy from his school who are missing. It's his wife and his son – his family – who disappeared on Friday. And the fact he's in school right now is either commendable or strange. I'm not sure which yet.

There's a rustle of clothing, a wave of fidgeting spreading across the hall. I spot Anika Jones looking as though she's about to stand. Oliver must see it too as he shakes his head, and somehow – and I'm not sure how, considering how pale he is, how panicked – he gets hold of himself.

'Jessica, that's not the kind of question we ask in assembly,' he replies.

I immediately like Jessica. It has taken the bravery of a nine-year-old girl to ask the question we've all been wondering. I know from watching the news this morning that it's been four days since Cate and Archie walked out of this school together on Friday afternoon, and never made it home. The solemn voice of the reporter echoes in my thoughts. *'Police are concerned for the whereabouts of a forty-two-year-old woman and her eight-year-old son, who went missing on Friday in the Leedham Vale area.'*

I wait for Oliver to gather himself and carry on. He doesn't. Instead, a tense silence falls across the hall. I wonder if I should step in or let him flail. The latter would be so easy to do, but I really need this job. I've barely worked more than a handful of days in the past few months and I don't want to think about how close I was to living in my car when the substitute teaching agency called about Leedham Primary yesterday.

'We don't know how long the placement will be for yet. They've said it could be weeks. Will that be an issue?'

I couldn't get the words out fast enough to tell her it wouldn't.

Anika's words from this morning ring in my thoughts. *'Leedham is a very special school. We're a family, and it's important to find staff, even temporary staff, that are the right fit.'*

If I'm going to keep this job, then I need everyone to like me – parents, children and teachers, including Oliver. So I rescue him.

'How about,' I say, smiling again, first at Jessica and then across at the sea of faces, 'I tell you what my favourite colour is? Can anyone guess?' I touch my hair, pulling a corkscrew curl straight before letting it ping back into place.

A little boy in the front row grins at me, pointing to my hair. 'Red,' he says.

'Well done,' I say, ruffling my curls. My hair is not the burned-orange natural hair colour people describe as red sometimes, but bright red. Rebellious Red, according to the hair dye box I bought last week.

'I also really like cats,' I continue. 'Hands up who has a cat.'

I ask and answer a few more questions. Favourite food (pizza), favourite chocolate bar (Toffee Crisp) and finally my age (twenty-six). The atmosphere lifts, and Oliver regains his composure, shooting me a grateful look.

'OK, children,' he says with a clap of his hands, 'it's home time. Walk nicely back to your classrooms to collect your things, and we will see Miss Mills in the playground before school tomorrow morning.'

The classes stand row by row and file out. I step to the side and smile at each of them as they pass. From the corner of my eye, I spot Oliver slump against the wall and rake a hand through his hair. He looks broken. Not a single sighting since they left school on Friday. What is he doing here, at work?

I look around at the teachers and teaching assistants getting to their feet. Plus Oliver. Plus the parents at the back now whispering quietly to each other. I wonder if maybe someone in this room knows what happened to Cate and Archie. The police are appealing for witnesses. No one has come forward so far, but in a small community like this, people are always hiding something. Everyone has a secret.

I should know.

TWO

OLIVER

Oliver drops into his office chair and sighs. Today has been hard. Harder than yesterday, facing the pupils and parents for the first time since it happened. Harder than Saturday even, when he first called the police and told them Cate and Archie hadn't come home, and Sunday when the detectives arrived and asked him a million questions.

He misses the ease of his life a week ago. He misses his son. He even misses Cate. She always knows what to say to calm him down. It isn't just him either. Cate knows how to read people. She can make anyone laugh. She has a quick wit and an eye for when to use it. She really is so bloody perfect. Or should he say *was* now?

The thought threatens to engulf him in a black sea of guilt. He fights to shut it down before it drowns him. He didn't mean for this to happen. Whatever comes next, he has to cling on to that one fact.

There's a light tap of knuckles on the door before Karen's head pops around the frame. The school secretary gives him the same pitying look she saves for the children when they're sent home sick. He should never have let Anika strong-arm him into

an assembly to introduce the substitute teacher. He's certain
everyone noticed when he almost lost it. Thank God the substitute teacher stepped in.

Lexi Mills.

He only met her for a second as the children piled into the
hall. She's not the usual sixty-something, part-retired substitute
Anika usually gets in. The red hair is a bit too much, but the
children already love her. That much is obvious. There's something else about Lexi niggling at the back of his mind, but Karen
is already talking and the thought is lost.

'Oliver, the police are here to talk to you.' Karen raises her
eyebrows behind the thick frames of her glasses.

'Really?' He sits up. 'Send them in.' His heart feels
suddenly too big, the sides knocking against his ribs with every
pounding beat. Karen gives him a final look, less pity, more
curiosity, and he wonders if he sounded too nervous or too
upbeat. He doesn't want to seem like he isn't keen to talk to
them, but maybe he went too far the other way. Christ, holding
it together is exhausting.

She disappears in a swish of material from the shapeless
summer dress she always wears. A memory catches him off
guard. They'd been in The Bull for Friday drinks. Friday voices
– buoyant and loud. Cate's laugh as she and Karen had
swapped fashion disasters from their teenage years. He remembers laughing too, feeling happy. It must have been last summer,
before everything started to go wrong.

Oliver stands as the two detectives appear in the doorway.
He should offer his hand to shake, but he can't, and so, as he did
during the two previous visits from the detectives searching for
his wife and son, he keeps his hands by his sides, resting against
his legs, hiding the cut on his palm that's starting to throb in
time with his racing pulse.

DS Jen Pope steps into his office first. She's wearing a
different shirt today. The first two times he met with her –

Sunday and yesterday – she was wearing a white shirt that was too tight around the fat of her stomach. She'd caught Oliver staring and scowled at him. Today, the shirt is blue. It brings out the colour of her eyes. She's pretty beneath the exhaustion and the puffy eyes; no make-up and hair scraped into a ponytail. He'll say that for Cate – she never let herself go. Even at home, when it was just the three of them, she made an effort.

But the detective is smart. He can see her taking everything in. Not just the words he says, but how he says them. It puts him on edge. He prefers the detective constable – DC Rob Hacker – he's young and eager, and handsome too; Oliver has no qualms admitting that. Mixed race, dark eyes and black hair, short and gelled, with designer stubble cut with a sharp edge. Sharper than his mind, Oliver hopes.

'DS Pope, DC Hacker. What can I help you with?' he asks, immediately regretting the question. He should have asked if there's any news. Stupid of him. They notice too. He can tell by the way DS Pope cocks an eyebrow, exchanging a look with Hacker. 'Have you found them?' he adds quickly and far too late.

'No. I'm sorry, Mr Walker—'

'Oliver. Call me Oliver please.'

She gives a slight nod. 'We don't have any updates for you at this time. We wondered if you had a moment to go over some of the things you told us on Sunday and yesterday. We went to your house, but one of your neighbours said we'd find you here.'

There's no question, but she pauses, and Oliver finds himself needing to fill the silence. 'I couldn't stay home doing nothing. It would've driven me crazy. Easier to be working. What did you want to ask me?'

From outside his office, the photocopier hums into life, sounding more like a jet plane about to take off than a machine printing out letters about the summer sports day. Pope turns a fraction; looks at the photocopier and Karen now standing beside it, doing her best to pretend she isn't listening.

'Perhaps it would be better if we had this conversation at home,' Pope says. 'We'd like to get a few more photos of Cate and Archie for the media too.'

'Right. Of course.' Oliver grabs his wallet and keys from his desk and motions to the front entrance. If he's lucky, the last of the parents will have left the playground by now. Or, at the very least, please let them be standing out of view.

The school is a one-storey, purpose-built L-shaped building on a large plot of land, surrounded by a dark-green metal fence. At the stubby end of the L are the main front doors, reception area, Oliver's office and the staffroom. Along the length of the L runs the school hall, and parallel to that, on the inside of the L, are the classrooms, library and study areas. The classrooms have two doors: one into the school hall and one facing out into the playground, and the playing field beyond it.

It's the playground doors that the children use most, as parents congregate outside them to collect and drop off their children. But there's only one main gate in and out of the premises, and it's this gate where the stragglers of parents stand and chat long after the bell has gone. This gate where he will be seen with the police if he's unlucky, which, of course, he is. He wouldn't be in this mess if he was lucky.

His heart is still banging against his chest, and it's a struggle to breathe normally, to act normal, as they step into the warmth of the late-spring afternoon.

And yes, there they are. A gaggle of women with pushchairs and children tugging at their mothers' dresses and jackets, pleading for an ice cream or to just go home while their mums swap the latest gossip. They'll be talking about Cate, no doubt. And him. Keeping his right hand tucked in his pocket, he makes a show of lifting his left in a cheery wave. *Nothing to see here*, he wants to call to them.

When he turns again, DC Hacker is standing by a silver Mondeo. 'Shall we?' he says, already opening the rear door for Oliver.

'Sorry,' Oliver coughs, masking the 'no' forming on his lips. He feels the eyes of the parents burning into the back of his head. He can't get into the back of a police car and be driven away. It would look like... like they're arresting him; like he's done something wrong. 'Do you mind if I meet you at the house? It's only a five-minute walk and I'd like the air.'

There's a pause. He's sure Hacker is about to tell him to get in the car, but DS Pope nods. 'No problem.' Her head tilts to one side again. Oliver recognises the action as Pope's way of assessing him. 'It will give you a moment to collect your... thoughts, I'm sure.'

She says 'thoughts' like she's thinking 'lies', and he has the sudden urge to explain, to tell her that the village is a hotbed of gossip, and there's no way he can be seen getting into the back of a police car like he's done something wrong.

Actions speak louder than words, he tells the children in assembly at the start of every term. But in this village, appearances are more like a foghorn, compared to the whisper of reality. He knows that better than anyone.

But Oliver says none of these things, and instead gives a stupid thumbs up to Pope and Hacker, a final wave to the parents watching him and walks away. He read once that liars overexplain, adding more detail than is needed, tripping themselves up. The truth doesn't need a story, he keeps reminding himself as he runs through the lies he's already told the detectives.

THREE

JEANIE

There is a commotion on Jeanie's street. The detectives are back to talk to that head teacher. Jeanie stands at her living-room window, stepping a little to the right, finding the patch of carpet that's almost worn through, the place with the best view of her neighbours' houses through the net curtains that keep her own hidden.

It's not one of the rich roads. The hoity-toity, as Jeanie refers to them. Those ugly bloated mansions with the pale brick and ridiculous black gates. It's not one of the old roads either. The coveted Tudor properties that the tourists stop to take photos of.

Jeanie wouldn't like that. To watch is one thing. To be watched is quite another. But no one stops to stare at Jeanie's house, smack bang in the middle of a modest road of fourteen houses. It's a quiet street with a cut-through at the end to the village playing field for those who know to use it, and not many do, preferring to drive their fat 4x4s and use the car park off the high street.

The Walker house is on the corner by the turning into the

road and is a larger plot than the others. And don't they know it. One of those houses where the garden circles the property with a white picket fence they jet wash and paint every April. Jeanie's view of the Walker house is slightly obscured by the laurel bush in their front garden. She clicks her tongue to the roof of her mouth. A single 'tsk'. She must get on to Andrea and Marcus on the parish council again. It's grown the last few weeks and is violating the village bylaws for the third time this year. Shrubbery in front gardens must not reach above one metre in height. Jeanie doesn't agree with all the silly rules of living in Leedham, but she likes that one. She likes to be able to look into people's gardens and windows, and overgrown laurel bushes do get in the way.

Still, the overgrown laurel is preferable to the white-and-orange monstrosity of a campervan that the Walkers keep in their garage until summer, when they leave it on their driveway for weeks on end – an ugly blot on the street, and another council violation.

Jeanie adjusts the sight on the binoculars and zooms in on the house just as he appears on the road. Oliver. She's never warmed to the man. Something about the way he's always touching his hair. Men really shouldn't have such nice hair. He's one of those 'I'm better than you' types. A future parish council leader if ever she saw one.

She watches Oliver fish out his keys, open the front door and usher the detectives inside. Oh how she'd love to know what they're talking about. She's often wondered how difficult it would be to sneak a little microphone or nanny cam into a neighbour's house. Wondered but not acted. It's a step too far, even for her.

There's nothing to see on the street now. The Fishers opposite Jeanie at number eight won't be back from work for another two hours. It's Tuesday. So she'll be off to her Pilates class while he cooks the dinner. Later, they'll have sex on the kitchen counter. Every Tuesday without fail they do this, and every Tuesday Jeanie watches through her binoculars. Fascinated, not by the act itself – she's not a pervert – but by the routine. Tuesday night. It's so mundane. And yet there's nothing mundane to Jeanie about sex on a kitchen counter. Not that she'd know anything about that. She's only had sex in a bed, lying flat on her back, feeling like a beached whale.

Her experience of sex is boring.

She was boring, according to the handful of lovers who came and went in her twenties and early thirties.

Jeanie is edging closer to her fifties now, and even though she knows that's still young by today's standards, she's quite happy to embrace middle age. Cutting her greying-brown hair close to her head and not giving two hoots about the bulge of her stomach. Eating chips whenever she likes and toast for breakfast with lashings of butter and jam. Expensive little glass jars of chocolate puddings from the supermarket every night. And aside from the occasional splash of mascara for work in the council office in town, three days a week, she doesn't bother with make-up either.

The gold clock on her fireplace dings 4 p.m. The Woodham boy will back from high school soon. An hour alone to stare mindlessly at his computer before his mother comes in from work and tells him to turn it off.

Jeanie looks back to her armchair – the empty wine glass from lunch and the waiting *Times* crossword she needs to finish. Clue five down is bothering her. Guttersnipes. Four letters. It's on the tip of her tongue.

The sound of movement upstairs – a floorboard creaking. She finds her gaze pivoting to the swirly Artex ceiling. A moment later, Buster arrives in the room, stalking towards the armchair and curling into a ball on her newspaper. Jeanie is about to move away from the window and join the cat when the police cars arrive. The white ones with sirens and the strip of blue-and-yellow chequers along the sides. One, then two, then three. A little convoy that park in a row two doors down from Jeanie's house.

A flutter of worry works its way through Jeanie as they climb out. Six officers in stiff black uniform, walking two by two towards the front doors of her neighbours' houses. She hears the firm tap of knuckles on wood at number seven. Gail Pilston opens the front door, hand clutching at her chest, and ushers them inside. She'll make a show of being flustered, but Jeanie knows the minute they're gone, a WhatsApp message will appear on the neighbourhood watch group, spilling every detail. Jeanie doesn't particularly like Gail, but at least she can be relied upon to be indiscreet.

Two police officers move on from number nine. They'll have to come back at the weekend if they want to speak to the Heckley family, whose girls stay at the nearby boarding school during the week while the parents live in London, all four coming back at the weekends to spend two days avoiding each other.

She watches two male officers stand in the middle of the road for a moment before turning to face her house. The flutter intensifies until a siege of moths rattle in her chest – fluttering wings, firm bodies, crashing against each other and her insides, searching for an escape they won't find. She thinks of all that she knows, all that she's done. She thinks of the little box room at the back of the house with the door she keeps locked. Then she pulls her phone from her cardigan and finds his number. She can't avoid it any longer. It rings only once.

'It's me,' she says, not bothering with any kind of pointless pleasantries.

'What is it?' he asks, not bothering either.

'The police are here. They're knocking on doors.'

'Have you spoken to them?'

'Of course not,' she says, trying not to snap. 'I'm not stupid.'

'Good. Just keep out of sight of the window,' he says as though he knows exactly where she is right now. 'They'll give up soon enough.'

'What should we do?'

'Stick to the plan. Like always.' He hangs up.

Jeanie pulls the phone away from her ear and slips it back into her pocket as the knock comes. A firm thud of knuckles – thump, thump, thump – and then the trilling ring of her door-bell just for good measure. And even though she's watched the officers step by step as they've moved towards her front door, even though she knew what was coming, the sound still makes her jump, causing a yelp to escape her throat.

She freezes; tries not to breathe. Did they hear her?

Silence rings in her ears. Slowly, very slowly, she moves away from the window. Voices fill the silence then the crackle of a radio. If one of the officers thinks to step on the border of her peonies and press his face to the glass, she'll be seen.

Jeanie keeps stepping back until her heels find the skirting board, then she shuffles a little to the right, hiding herself behind the open living-room door. Another step and she'll be in the hall, her silhouette seen behind the glass of the front door, but here, in this space, she's hidden.

She holds her breath for a moment before realising how stupid that is. They can't hear her breathe. The doorbell rings again, a short, sharp burst, and as Jeanie's heart races in her chest, she wonders if they know she's inside. She closes her eyes to the dizzying panic and waits for them to leave.

They'll be wanting to ask about that mother and child who've gone missing. Jeanie has watched the Walker family come and go for years. That stupid campervan Oliver loves so much; the barbecues they have with friends every summer. The arguments they have when everyone has gone home. Oh yes, Jeanie has seen it all.

But she won't tell the police a damn thing. Scum, the lot of them.

Scum. Jeanie smiles to herself and thinks of her crossword on the armchair.

FOUR

LEXI

I drive my old Citroën out of the school and turn towards the
village, passing gated houses on a tree-lined street then a row of
Tudor properties painted white or pastel pink. I round the bend
and the high street appears before me – one long road leading
up to a huge stone church.

Leedham is one of those English villages with the quaint
high-street shops that sell nothing of any use. I pass a homeware
store with a window display of overpriced mugs the size of
bowls. By the time I reach the end of the high street and the
church, and turn into the car park of The Bull pub, I've passed
four gift shops, four cafés and one café-gift shop.

Every building has the same matching racing-green awnings
and black chalkboard signs on the pavement advertising ice
creams and afternoon teas, and I can imagine the village will be
overflowing with tourists at the weekend, come to picnic on the
rolling hills of Leedham Vale, while children paddle in the shal-
lows of the river that winds around the back of the village.

I park in the far corner near a long single-storey building in
black wood. There are five doors painted red, each with a
plaque on the door and a name in swirly writing. *Guard House*,

Honeysuckle Den, Servant's Delight, Wisteria Home and last – on the far corner near a broken fence and a sycamore tree with branches hanging over the building, my new home for however long I'm here – *The Old Stable.*

There's a gravel car park leading to a pub garden. One white Fiat and a dark-blue van are parked near the back doors to the pub.

The Bull is another Tudor property – dark beams racing across white walls, and a roof that looks like it's seen better days, but inside it's all freshly painted walls and shiny wood floors as I make my way through a restaurant to a bar area with over-stuffed leather chairs, and three men in the corner clutching at pints of half-drunk ale.

They look at me as I walk in but say nothing. I meet the eyes of one, sitting a little away from the others. He's in his fifties, I guess, with midnight-black hair, grey at the edges and cut close to this head. He's tall. Even sitting down I can tell he towers over people. Six foot four or five maybe, and broad too.

I offer a smile that's not returned. I look away, assuming Leedham will be one of those places that doesn't welcome newcomers.

A girl appears from behind the bar. She looks eighteen or nineteen, and has long false eyelashes and a pretty smile. 'What can I get you?' she asks.

'Hi, I'm Lexi. I'm renting The Old Stable.'

She gives me a curious half-smile before shouting out for, 'Paul?'

I hope the landlord hasn't changed his mind.

The rental – a one-bed apartment – wasn't easy to find. They never are when I'm looking for short stays at cheap prices. There's no point committing to anything more permanent. One week or two, three at most, before I have to leave again. And this time of year, in this village, everywhere was booked. But I called the estate agent yesterday, and he called the landlord of the pub.

Paul appears a moment later – a large man with a shaved head, a tight, black shirt and a blue striped apron over a large belly.

'Hi.' I smile my sweetest smile. 'I'm Lexi. I'm renting—'

'The Old Stable. You certainly are. Welcome.' He grins, causing his cheeks to bunch. It's endearing, and after fewer than a dozen words, I know instantly that I like Paul.

'I'll say sorry now,' he continues. 'It's in a state. I hope Jake warned you about that. I'm waiting until the end of the summer to do it up like the rest of the block, which is why it's not listed this year. It will be a lovely self-catering unit like the rest of them when it's done. Are you sure you don't want a room in the hotel instead? I can do you a good rate? Anything to help the school.'

'Thanks, but I'm sure it will be fine.'

He pauses, taking me in. The red corkscrew curls, the spray of freckles across the bridge of my nose, the long-sleeved white blouse and navy skirt that floats around my legs. I half expect him to offer the hotel room again, but he nods instead. 'Just don't write me a bad review, all right?'

I laugh. 'Deal.'

'I'll show you where it is,' he says, unhooking a key from a corkboard behind the bar.

As I turn to follow Paul through the pub, something makes me glance back at the lone drinker. He's staring back at me, his face still expressionless. There's something about him that makes me want to hurry away.

We walk across the car park and back to the single-storey building and stop outside The Old Stable.

'Like I said,' Paul begins, unlocking the door and pushing it open, 'it's in a bit of a state, but it's clean, and I put fresh bedding on this morning.'

A strong smell of damp wafts out, and as I step into the dimness, I spot a yellow stain covering one wall.

'The shower next door leaked.' Paul makes a face. 'I really think you'd be happier in the pub.'

'Honestly, it's perfect,' I lie. It's not the worst place I've stayed, but it's probably close. Still, desperate times and all that. So much substitute teaching is just for a day here or there. The money might be good compared to a day on a full-time contract, but it still doesn't go far. I need this job and doubt I'll find anywhere cheaper in the nearby town, and a hotel room won't work. Besides, something tells me Leedham is the kind of village where you have to be here, among the people and the beauty of it, to really be accepted.

'Nosey Parker.'

The voice is so familiar and so real in my head that it's a fight not to whirl around to find its owner. I sense Paul staring at me and flash another smile.

'It would be such a big help to stay here. Thank you.'

'No worries. And hey, I tell you what – I'll chuck in breakfast in the pub too. We start serving at six thirty. I do a mean full English, if you can't tell that already,' he adds, patting the curve of his belly.

'Deal,' I say, laughing. 'I'll get my things then.'

Paul hands me the key, and we walk side by side towards my car.

'So you're taking over Cate's class?' he asks.

I nod.

'Bet those kids will be missing her right now. You'll never meet a nicer woman or a lovelier family. Salt of the earth is our Cate. And Oliver and Archie too. They're good people. We're all heartbroken by what's going on.

'We're all racking our brains, trying to understand it, you know? If it was anyone else, I'd say they'd taken themselves off for a little TLC, but not Cate. She loves this village. There's nothing she wouldn't do for the people in it. I swear she's always raising money for someone or something in Leedham.'

We fall silent as the gravity of Paul's words sink in. Cate didn't leave by choice. She disappeared on the way home from school. Eight-year-old Archie is missing too. She has a job, a husband and a life here. It's not the kind of life you walk away from. And Leedham isn't the kind of place you walk away from without someone seeing something, I think again.

'Well, if you need anything, just give me a knock. I live over there.' Paul points to the other side of the road and a cute, dollhouse-like cottage with teal window shutters and a matching front door. 'Not much of a commute.' He laughs. 'And honestly, don't hesitate. We're all really proud of the school and will do anything to help.'

'Do you have a child there?' I ask.

He laughs again; the sound is so jolly, so open. 'No. Molly behind the bar is our youngest and she just turned eighteen. We're well past all that, but we help raise money and look after the school where we can. You wouldn't know it from looking at me, but I'm a decorator and handyman by trade, before the pub came up for sale a few years back, so I do the odd bit of maintenance when they need it.'

'Sounds like they're lucky to have you.' I point to my car. 'I'd better get unpacked.'

Paul nods, giving me a cheery wave goodbye.

I open the boot and stare at everything I own. It's not much, but then there's an art form to moving around, zigzagging across the country, wherever the work takes me, keeping one step ahead. A new hair colour, a new me with every school. It's how I've lived for the last year, after Brighton and the police investigation and the looks the parents of Haventhorpe Primary gave me.

Packing is key. Marie Kondo would be proud. I only need the essentials. My Nutribullet blender for my spinach-and-fruit smoothies; five outfits – all long-sleeved – for when I'm in school; two sets of casual weekend clothes, two pairs of shoes, one going-out outfit – tight black jeans and an emerald-green top that hugs my body. Although I can't remember the last time I bothered to unpack it, let alone put it on. It's only ever for the occasional teacher's birthday drinks I'll get a last-minute invite to. Or a Christmas party if I happen to be in a school at that point in the year. I always go. I make polite conversation and share in a bottle of wine. Staying long enough to be polite, friendly, to not draw attention.

The only other thing I need is my boxing kit and punch bag – a large, heavy, black base and long weighted tube that sits on top. It's the reason a hotel room wouldn't work, and it's the bag I'm dragging into my new home when Paul's words surface in my thoughts.

'You'll never meet a nicer woman.'

When the bag is inside and resting on its base in the middle of the small living room, when the door is shut and I drop onto a lumpy sofa, I pull out my phone and find the latest Sky News report about Cate. Five hundred words of nothing new, but there is a different photo this time: Cate in a square-necked, red linen dress, her arms wrapped around Archie, both of them laughing at the camera.

I wonder where they are. I wonder what happened. I think of the news reports I saw over the weekend. Cate is married, she has a son, friends, a community around her. And yet she and Archie were missing for nearly twenty-four hours before even her husband, Oliver, noticed.

Who would know if something happened to me? Who would sound the alarm?

I have no one. No ties. No contracts of employment. If I disappeared tonight, the school would assume I'd simply changed my mind. All they'd do is call the agency to find someone new. I wouldn't be a headline; I would simply be gone.

The thought is unnerving; I get up and put the key in the door
and hear the bolt click into place.

As I throw on my workout kit and strap on my gloves, I look
to the jagged line of the scar on my right arm, which I always
keep covered. A dozen memories strobe through my head at
once. Tyres screeching, the spray of broken glass, piercing
screams. Sirens shattering the still of the night. Running and
running, never stopping to see who's still chasing.

I shut it all out and throw myself into my workout. I start
with a warm-up. Left jabs then right jabs, shifting my feet and
stretching my arm out a little further each time. An hour later,
I'm covered in sweat and breathing hard, but the memories are
shut away, and my mind returns to the disappearance. They've
been missing four days with no sign. Where are they? What
happened to them?

FIVE

OLIVER

Oliver steps out of the sun and into the cool of his hallway, instantly catching the smell of home – coffee grounds and the fabric softener they use; the lingering scent of Cate's perfume on her coat hanging by the door. He has a sudden urge to reach out and run his fingers over the fabric, to rewind time and do everything differently.

They loved each other once, but he can't quite hold on to the memories. All he can see is what they became; what he did.

'Can I get anyone a drink?' He turns to the detectives as they step in behind him, aware of their close proximity and the beads of sweat on his forehead. He wants to tell them he's sweating because of the heat and the fast walk, but he doesn't. 'Two sugars, DC Hacker, and decaf for you, DS Pope – is that right?' He knows it is. He always remembers the little things about people. It's what makes him good at his job; it's why the children and parents like him so much.

'We're fine, thank you, Oliver,' Pope answers for both of them.

'I'll just get myself some water. Please go through to the living room,' he adds, waving them towards the room at the back that overlooks the garden and the football goal where he kicks a ball around with Archie sometimes. Not enough times, he thinks now, with another stab of guilt that slices straight through him.

He steps into the kitchen for a glass of water, a final moment alone. He hates this room. He hates the giant grey island in the middle of it with the sharp corner edges that he catches his hip on every morning when he's still half asleep. He hates the eight-ringed, four-door range cooker that cost a fortune and only ever gets used properly at Christmas. This kitchen is Cate's domain, not his.

There's a cup on the side, which he left there this morning. He could have put it in the dishwasher. He could've put it in the sink, but instead he left it by the toaster with the spray of breadcrumbs from breakfast he didn't bother to wipe away either.

Cate always wanted things to be tidy, and for a long time, her 'everything has a place' mentality worked. It kept the house clean, but, more than that, her organisation and planning kept them on track as a family. Until Oliver began to feel like it wasn't just the bread knife or the coffee pot that had a place they had to be kept in; that he did too.

Oliver grabs a glass and pours himself some water from the huge American-style fridge freezer. His hand trembles as he gulps it back. The cut continues to throb. He straightens the collar of his shirt and steps into the living room.

As far as anyone knows, he's done nothing wrong. The thought doesn't make him feel any less nervous.

'No water?' Pope asks as Oliver sits down on the stubby end of the L-shaped leather sofa, positioning his body to face them. He leans forward, trying to attain an open, ready-to-help position.

He forces himself not to look at his hands, now clasped

together in front of him, the tremble hidden along with the cut. He gives an easy shrug. 'I drank it all in the kitchen.'

There's a pause. Oliver searches for something more to say, but there's nothing. His gaze roams the room. Grey walls, grey cushions. How has he only just realised that his entire house is grey?

'How are you holding up, Oliver?' Pope asks.

He nods, a slow movement. 'As good as can be expected, I guess.'

'If it would help to have a family liaison officer here again, then—'

'No,' he says quickly. Too quickly. He didn't like the woman they'd sent on Sunday. She'd hovered around him, making calls and giving him nonsense updates. All that faux sympathy when really she'd been watching him, feeding everything back to DS Pope. It had made him second-guess every word and every movement. 'Thank you, but I'm fine. There's no point anyway as I'm at work all day. I need to keep busy.'

'I see.'

Another silence. The racing of his heart is making him feel sick. It's suddenly all too much. He fights the desire to cry and then wonders if tears would help.

'So,' DC Hacker says as he glances to Pope and receives a slight nod, 'we appreciate that we've already gone over the events of Cate and Archie's last known movements, but it helps us to hear them again. Sometimes small details can emerge which make all the difference.'

'Sure. Where do you want me to start?'

'Can you talk us through everything you remember about Friday afternoon and when you last saw Cate and Archie?'

He grits his teeth, forcing back the truth and focusing on the lies he's told so far. Every time he speaks to Pope and Hacker, it feels like another one is added.

'I saw Cate at lunchtime in the staffroom with the other

staff. I was on lunch duty, so I only popped in to make a quick cup of tea before heading outside.' The words have taken on a wooden, practised feel. He takes a breath and tries to pad it out. 'We have dinner ladies, but I like a member of staff to be outside with the children every day as well. It helps the teachers get to know the children who aren't in their own classes, and every other Friday, I take my turn.

'I watched...' He pauses; swallows. Tears fill his eyes. More guilt and another what-has-he-done moment that he fights to keep from playing across his face. 'I watched Archie play football with the other boys in his year. When the bell for afternoon lessons went, I walked straight to my office. I had to organise some staff training and was on the phone to the council for a lot of the afternoon.

'School finished at three, and the staff left soon after. We usually stay for a few hours after the children go home, but I encourage everyone to leave earlier on a Friday. I finished about five o'clock. I was last to leave, and so I locked up the school and walked home.' Oliver stops then, biting back the words threatening to rush out. Give enough detail but not too much, he reminds himself.

'And Cate didn't say goodbye to you at the school?'

'No, but that wasn't unusual. If my office door is closed, or if I'm on the phone, she won't disturb me.'

'And were you on the phone?'

'I... I'm not sure. I'd have to check.' Oliver pushes a hand through his hair before remembering the cut he's trying to hide and the tremor, the outward sign that he's barely keeping it together. He drops his hand and clasps them together again. 'I'd have to check. I certainly didn't think anything of her leaving without saying goodbye. Like I said on Sunday, Archie had a class party at the swimming pool in Colchester. Cate was probably rushing around to make sure they weren't late. She doesn't like being late to things. It stresses her out.'

He remembers driving with Cate early on in their relationship. They'd been on their way to the wedding of one of her cousins and had got utterly lost in the hills of North Wales when a road closure had sent them on a diversion. Cate had planned everything so meticulously, from the time they'd leave, where they'd stop for breaks and when, and where they'd change into their wedding clothes. She'd written it all out and titled it 'Welsh Wedding Itinerary', and the moment it had gone wrong, she'd burst into tears.

He'd pulled over to comfort her and somehow they'd ended up having frantic sex on the back seats, right there on the quiet lane. They'd made it to the wedding forty minutes late, sneaking into the back of the church like giggling teens. Oliver doesn't recognise either of those people anymore.

'The silver BMW in the driveway – is that your car, Oliver?'

The change of tack throws him for a moment. 'Yes. It's our car. Cate uses it as much as I do.' Now would be the moment to mention the campervan. He hopes the omission won't come back to bite him. It's not like they specifically asked how many vehicles they have access to.

Thoughts of the campervan cause a knot to form in his gut. He needs to do something, but he's not sure what. He doesn't like the growing suspicion he senses from DS Pope. They were never supposed to think it was him.

Not for the first time, Oliver wonders if calling the police was the right thing. Sometimes, at night, when sleep won't come, he wishes he'd left it longer. Given himself more time to fix everything, but other times, he wishes he'd called on Friday night. It already looks bad that he waited until Saturday afternoon.

'What did you think when you saw your car on the driveway when you got home?'

'I... didn't think anything. I assumed Cate had car-shared with one of the village mums. She does that a lot.'

'What did you do when you got home?' Hacker's question is fired out.

'I had a shower and then I had a couple of beers and cooked myself some dinner and watched some TV,' he says, feeling like he's stuck in the middle of a tense game of tennis. Him on one side, them on the other. Every time he answers a question, hits that ball back, it comes flying at him even harder.

Hacker opens his mouth to ask another question, but Pope leaps in first. 'You didn't mention the shower before now. Do you always wash when you get home from work?'

'Oh... I... No,' he admits, trying to keep the grimace from his face. They've tripped him up, but he can't stumble now. There's too much at stake; too much to lose. 'I was hot, I guess.' Oliver's pulse drums in his ears. He catches the gleam of something in Pope's eye.

'Even though you were alone in the house and had no plans for the evening?'

He shrugs again. 'I like showers.'

'What did you watch?' Hacker continues.

'Excuse me?'

'What did you watch on TV that night?'

'Oh... nothing really. I just flicked around a bit. I watched a bit of a quiz show and then a *Seinfeld* rerun, I think.'

'When did you start to worry that something might be wrong?'

'I wouldn't say I was worried, but I was surprised that they weren't home by nine. The pool party was due to finish at seven thirty, but I thought they'd gone for an ice cream or back to someone's house. Cate is popular among the mums. She's always getting invites to go places and makes an effort to say yes to as many as she can. The village community is important to her. To both of us.

'It was around nine that I tried her mobile, but it went straight to voicemail. I guess I fell asleep on the sofa, because when I woke up, it was morning, about six a.m. I assumed I'd slept through Cate and Archie coming home. As you can see, we're at the back of the house here. If they'd come in late and gone straight to bed, I wouldn't have heard them.'

'Was it normal for you and Cate not to sleep in the same bed?' Pope cuts in.

'No.'

'No?' She raises an eyebrow.

'No, we had a good marriage if that's what you're asking.' Oliver can see where this is going. His mouth is dry, and there's a heat creeping across his face.

'Sorry, Oliver,' she says like she really means it, 'but I'm really struggling to get my head around this. You see, I'm always falling asleep on the sofa in the evening. Practically every night, in fact. And every night my husband wakes me up and tells me to go to bed. So I guess I'm finding it a bit strange that you thought Cate had come home and not done that.'

He forces himself to nod. To swallow. 'Yes, I guess you're right. I didn't think too much about it. I probably assumed Cate had found me snoring, which I do after a few beers, and left me to it. In the morning, I went straight out for a run. I'm training for a half-marathon and always run early on Saturdays. My running kit was still in the dryer so I didn't even go into our bedroom.

'I got back at eight and made myself some breakfast. Archie had a tennis lesson at ten, so about eight thirty I went to wake him up. And that's when I realised they weren't home. I called everyone I could think of. I called the hospital and some of her friends. One of them was Felicity Kim, who was hosting the pool party. That's when I found out Cate and Archie hadn't gone. I knew then that something was wrong, and that's when I called you.'

'So by the time you reported your wife and son missing, you hadn't seen them since lunchtime on Friday?'

'No.'

'It's a long time to wait,' DC Hacker comments as though they're talking about a queue for a supermarket checkout.

'I've just explained all that.' He looks to DS Pope and follows her gaze to the two clenched fists of his hands. He moves, stretching out his fingers before realising his mistake. The cut. The plaster. His eyes betray him, shooting straight up to Pope's face, and of course she sees it all – the injury to his hand and his reaction to her seeing.

'What did you do there?' Pope asks, nodding to the plaster.

'Nothing.' The word comes out in a rush. He sounds like the surly teenage version of himself when his parents asked him what he'd been doing all night long before he understood that people like Cate existed, and so did places like this – somewhere he could make a difference, where he mattered. He sighs inwardly, preparing another lie he'll have to remember. 'The bread knife slipped while I was cutting some bread.'

'When was this?'

'Friday.' The truth feels like it's burning in his face. He's just gone over every detail about Friday and didn't mention cutting his hand.

'Friday?' Hacker asks.

Oliver nods.

A sudden tension crackles in the air. They sense the lies. Oliver can tell by the look that passes between the detectives as they stand and make their way to the door.

'Thank you again for your time, Oliver. We'll be in touch as soon as we have an update. And if you remember anything else about Friday that you've forgotten to tell us, please call.'

The second the door closes and the detectives are gone, Oliver leans against the wall and allows his legs to give way and his body to drop to the floor. Already the lies, the story he's telling them, feel slippery in his thoughts. Is it only a matter of time before everything catches up with him – the bad things he's done and can never take back?

He stays like that for a long time. He thinks about the holes appearing in his story and the next steps the detectives might take.

Maybe it's not too late. Maybe there's something he can do to save himself.

SIX

I pull my hood over my head and step into the night. There is no breeze, and the air is cold but not biting. I like this time best. When it's gone midnight and the ornate black streetlights have all been switched off and the village is shrouded in darkness. When it's just me and the occasional fox looking for some dinner, or a cat on the prowl. When there's no one to ask me to do one more thing; no one to see me lurk in the shadows.

I push my hands into my pockets and turn left along the road. I could tell myself this is just another walk, no particular destination in mind. But that would be a lie. I walk the same loop each time; stopping outside the same houses, the ones I like, breathing in the still air and thinking of those inside. Sometimes I catch glimpses of the occupants. A light on in a bedroom. A figure at the window closing the curtains. No one sees me. Not until I want them to. Like I did with you when I stepped out of the shadows and showed you the real me.

And yet, tonight, I find myself on a new route. I'm not sure why. It's like a feeling I have. No, that's not right. It's more like a calling; a need.

I pass the pub and turn into the car park. The Bull's lights are all out now. The curtains closed. Some nights, Paul will let the stragglers stay on for one more drink. Some nights, a group will nurse their last orders in the garden for hours after the doors have been locked. Some nights, I am among them.

Tonight it is quiet.

The car park is gravel, and I step lightly, slowly, pausing after each crunching scrape beneath my feet. At the tree, I stop and run my hand over the scraping, rough bark.

Above my head, the night is clear, the sky scattered with a thousand and more stars. I watch the flashing lights of an aeroplane. From nearby, an owl hoots. I watch the dark windows of the holiday lets. I watch The Old Stable and think of the inside of my van. A fizzing starts in my chest.

For now, I must wait. It's too close to you.

But soon I will find a new occupant.

THURSDAY: SIX DAYS MISSING

SEVEN

GEMMA

Gemma Rowley straightens the line of her pencil skirt, smooths out the ends of her long, blonde ponytail, pushes down the panic threatening to send her spiralling into the world of the unhinged and steps into the playground.

The morning is fresh and carrying the scent of cut grass on the breeze. There's a nip to the air still, and most of the parents are wearing their Burberry jackets with the classic plaid lining or bright yellow Joules rain macs – their own uniform of acceptable drop-off clothing. By pick-up, they'll be in their dresses and sandals. The noise is the usual babble of children calling to each other, playing tag around their parents, pushchairs and the toddling younger siblings that will be sitting on the rug in her Reception class in a year or two. Parents huddle in groups near the classroom doors, waiting for the bell to ring and their days to start.

From across the playground, the twins – Etalie and Eddie – now in Year Two, race towards her, both speaking at once.

'Miss Rowley—'

'Miss Rowley—'

'Do you want to meet our new puppy?'

Gemma loves that she's still the favourite teacher for most of the children here. She loves that all the children come back to see her often. Like Faith in Year Six. When she was worrying about her SATs, it was Gemma she came to. And Archie still came to see her at least once a week. She remembers the troubled frown of the little boy and the problems he whispered about through hiccupping sobs; so different from the smiling photos plastered across the news. She shivers at the memory of Archie and pushes it to the back of her mind. Thinking of that little boy is sure to send her spiralling back to the frenzy and the fear and the WTF thoughts smacking her awake in the middle of the night, the taste of bile in the back of her throat.

'Miss Rowley?' Eddie calls out again.

It isn't a competition of course – favourite teacher; best teacher – and yet it matters. There are many things she does to stay at the top – a place she needs to be if she wants to move out of Reception and into another class when an opening comes up – and one of those things is saying yes to the children's requests. 'I would love to meet your puppy.'

They charge across the playground back to their mum, Gemma following behind. She likes Etalie and Eddie's mum. She's one of the normal parents. Her hair in a messy bun. No nanny, no false eyelashes. Gemma says hello and coos over the little sausage dog in the mum's arms, pretending desperately to want one, but she isn't actually a big fan of dogs – or cats for that matter. She prefers horses. There's something majestic about them. There's nothing like the power she feels when she's cantering across the open land.

Nothing like the cost either, which is why, at the age of twenty-seven, she's still living with her parents half a mile away from the school. Andrea and Marcus, she should say. They stopped being Mum and Dad when she was fourteen and told her they'd prefer it if she called them by their names. They had their image to think about, cultivated over years of co-chairing the parish council, dinner parties on Saturday nights and compulsory attendances for all three of them at every village event, even now.

Except it's not an image. It's who they really are, and having a twenty-seven-year-old daughter, single and living at home, isn't part of the deal. They haven't asked her outright to move out yet, but the humourless jokes about expecting to get their lives back when she turned eighteen – always finished with an, 'Oh we're only kidding, darling' – have morphed into significantly less subtle Rightmove links her mum sends her every week.

But the room-shares and the single-room flats she could afford are nothing like the high ceilings of the Tudor property her parents own – modernised and light, heated floors, and huge fireplaces. Plus they have a paddock and a stable for Ginger, her horse, who she thought, at eighteen, would be so much better than having a car. Not to mention space for the horse transport van she bought a few years later, which lives tucked away behind the stables.

Gemma has some savings, enough to rent a flat in the nearby town, but then she'd be back every day to look after Ginger – a fact Andrea and Marcus don't seem to care about. Besides, she doesn't want dingy and small. She wants grand and beautiful. It's what she deserves.

She's seen it too – the perfect cottage, the one she wants. There's even a livery across the road for Ginger. She just has to keep going a little while longer and her plan will work out. It has to, even if it feels like she's clinging on to it with the tips of her fingers.

The panic circles once more and she says goodbye to Eddie and Etalie and weaves around the huddles of parents back to the line of dumped coats and book bags outside her classroom door. She checks the time. Just five more minutes until the bell rings.

She's passing a group of three mums from the Year One class when she catches Cate's name. Gemma pauses. Listens.

'Poor Mrs Walker and Archie. I still can't believe it.'

'Has anyone heard anything?'

'No. But did you see the reporters at the front gates on Monday?'

'Anika Jones was straight in there. Front and centre for the camera. Dabbing at her eyes and acting like they were best friends. You know they hated each other, right?'

'Did they? I had no idea.'

'It was something to do with the PTA elections last year. A mum in Mrs Walker's class wanted to stand as chair, and Mrs Walker encouraged her to have a go, but Anika scared her off.'

'God, that was nothing short of a hate campaign,' the third mum jumps in. 'Poor woman. I didn't blame her for moving schools after Anika got everyone to ignore her. Didn't she accuse her of having an affair with one of the dads too? Even the kids picked up on the vibe and started bullying her little girl. I heard Mrs Walker had a right go at Anika about it, but it was all too late by then. Poor Mrs Walker felt completely responsible because she'd encouraged the mum to stand.'

'Anika acts like she owns the school. It's not right. She's head of governors and chair of the PTA. It's gone to her head.'

'Yeah, but I'm not above kissing her arse to keep the kids happy.' The three women laugh. 'This is the best school for miles, and they keep the intake low every year.'

'True. Just don't cross Anika, or you'll probably end up being driven out of the village.'

They laugh again, then one of the mums looks up and catches Gemma's eye. A blush creeps over her face, but Gemma pretends not to have heard the cattiness. She can't publicly agree, but Cate isn't the only one who can't stand Anika. The mums are right. She has too much power in the school. Oliver lets her walk all over him because she raises the money and controls the budget for all the little extras – the subsidised uniform, the classroom iPads, not to mention the school trips every year.

'Any word on Mrs Walker, Miss Rowley?' one of the mums asks, stepping back to include Gemma in the group.

Gemma shakes her head. 'I only know what's on the news,' she lies, ignoring the pang of guilt. Cate isn't here anymore. It's one less person to compete with. And yet, Gemma didn't expect to feel quite so bad about it. Once upon a time, she'd looked up to Cate. The older woman is everything Gemma isn't – married, a mother, adored and loved in the village. But Gemma knows things about the Year Four teacher no one else does – things she didn't tell the police when they questioned her on Monday.

'Did you see Mr Walker in assembly yesterday?' one of the mums continues. 'He looked devastated.'

'I can't believe he was even in school.'

'Bit weird, don't you think? For him to still be coming to work when his wife and son are missing? They say it's always the husband...'

From the corner of her gaze, Gemma watches Lexi walk across the playground towards them. Hard to miss her with that bright-red hair. Honestly, who does she think she is? The floating floral skirt and white pumps, the knitted cardigan in pale yellow – it's all so hideous. If a banned uniform list went out for teachers at the start of the year, like it does for the pupils, Gemma thinks Lexi's outfit would be on there.

Gemma knows what the other teachers think of her. They think she dresses in office-wear because she's on the prowl for a single dad. They can't see that wearing smart clothes stops the smaller children from treating her like their mum, from wiping their noses and sticky fingers on her. She is their very first teacher. Through her, most of them take their first steps towards independence. It's an important job, but God, she's had enough of toilet accidents and snotty noses.

She lifts her chin a little higher as Lexi approaches. It's obvious the children already like Lexi. So do the staff. She's bubbly and smiley, and is winning everyone over, but Gemma can't see the appeal yet.

'You think Oliver might have...' The mum's voice trails off.

'No way. He's too soft. I know they say it's always the husband, but not this time.'

'Hi,' Lexi says with a wide smile. 'How's everyone doing? Were you just chatting about Mrs Walker? Any idea what happened to her?'

The group shake their heads, but Lexi continues regardless. Gemma wonders if she can sense the apprehension hanging in the air. Doesn't she realise that you can't rock up on day two and join in the gossip?

'Did anyone see Cate and Archie on Friday?' Lexi asks. 'The news reports say she never made it home.'

One of the mums glances behind her before turning back and leaning in. 'My husband, Steve, does the pick-up on Friday. I did ask him if he saw anything, but he barely looks up from his phone. I swear he'll come home with the wrong kids one of these days,' she adds with a grin that makes the others laugh.

'What I want to know,' another mum says, 'is how do they know it happened on the way home? How do they know she didn't make it home and something happen after that? Karen told me at yoga last night that Oliver stayed late after everyone left on Friday. So how do they know someone wasn't waiting at the house for them?'

'But who?'

'A lot of weirdos out there. God, I hope they're all right. Cate is so kind. She'd do anything for anyone. The way she helped get my Freddie's reading level up last year was nothing short of a miracle.'

'And she raised all that money for that former pupil who needs the cancer treatment in America.'

Gemma fights not to roll her eyes. Talk about rose-tinted glasses. Have they all forgotten that Karen in the school office was the first one to suggest the fundraiser and did a load of the work too? From what Gemma saw, all Cate did was post about it on the village Facebook group.

Gemma is about to say something, a breezy comment about Karen's role in the fundraising, but she's stopped by the trilling of the bell. Children rush to their lines, scooping up bags and coats. The group of mums disperse, hurrying to say goodbye to their children.

Gemma moves too, off to shepherd her class into the school. The mum's question lingers in her thoughts. How do the police know Cate and Archie went missing on the way home?

She hadn't thought of that. There's a lot she hadn't thought about when she'd started down this road. But it will be worth it in the end. It has to be. She closes her eyes and tries to picture the vision she has for her life. It's fuzzy, out of focus.

Six days.

Six days they've been gone.

Archie's face and the secrets she's keeping float across her thoughts. The middle-of-the-night panic threatens again. She takes a breath. She's got this. Her life might not be the life she wants right now, but if she stays the course, she'll get there.

EIGHT

LEXI

'Miss Mills? Miss Mills?' The voice carries across the emptying playground. The bell has gone and most of the parents have disappeared out the gates. My class are filing into the classroom – a perfect line. I've been standing in the playground for the parent drop-off for the last thirty minutes, talking to children and parents while running over the class names in my head as the children jump and play around the brightly painted lines.

No one expects a new teacher – substitute or not – to remember their child's name on day one. But day two is a very different matter, and after spending an hour memorising faces and names last night, I think I've nailed it.

I turn and find Anika striding towards me. She's dressed in the yummy-mummy uniform of activewear – bright-red leggings and a matching cut-off top, showing a strip of toned skin. Her make-up and hair are flawless. I think of my own sweaty face when I'm punching the bag. I can't imagine Anika going anywhere near a gym today.

'Sorry, Miss Mills. Can I grab you for a minute?' she says, pushing her sunglasses onto the top of her head. 'It's just, I didn't want to talk to you about this on the tour on Tuesday as that was me with my governor hat on, and I'm wearing my mummy hat today.'

I nod as though I have a clue what she's talking about.

'I wear a lot of hats, lols.' She actually says 'lols'. I've never heard anyone say it out loud like that before. It's usually tacked onto the end of a message or email, softening the sentiment of whatever's being said. Anika adds a tinkling laugh.

'Anyway,' she continues, 'I'd really like to talk about Sebastian.'

I smile. 'Of course.' Maybe if it was a year ago, I would've told Anika to make an appointment for the end of the day, not caring that she's the woman who hired me and could as easily fire me. My job is to teach the children, not to pander to the parents. But I am not that person anymore and I can't lose this job.

'From what I've seen so far, Sebastian is a really great kid,' I say, thinking of the little boy who sits at the front of the class-room, dark hair combed and gelled. And the look of frantic concentration on his nine-year-old face yesterday when I set the first piece of work.

'He is, isn't he?' Anika beams at me, and I take in her flaw-less skin. She must be in her mid-forties, twenty years older than me, and yet there isn't a single line or wrinkle. Everything about her screams money. 'And with his diabetes as well, honestly, nothing holds him back.

I remember Karen explaining Sebastian's diabetes to me on Tuesday. The digital reader on his arm that alerts Anika's phone to any fluctuations in his blood sugar, and the insulin kept in the fridge in the staffroom just in case.

'I'm sure you've noticed already that he's very smart.'

I give a non-committal nod. These poor kids. It's really not their fault. Helicopter parenting is the norm now. Parents hovering over their children, watching their every move and swooping in to help at every turn. They want their children to be smart, creative, resilient, independent and completely reliant on them all at once.

But in a few moments, when I step into my classroom and close the door, and it's just me and my twenty-four children, I'll see their personalities shine through. The extroverts, the future leaders; the steady ones who will turn up every day no matter what, and the risk-takers, the ones who could earn a million by the age of twenty-one and lose it just as easily. That's why I like children – they're so full of potential, so unburdened with the darkness the world throws at us.

'I'm so glad you agree,' Anika says. 'Cate – sorry, Mrs Walker – would set him extension work to do after he's completed the work set for the... other children.' She lowers her voice and whispers 'other' like she doesn't want anyone else to hear, even though we're alone in the playground. 'Sebastian mentioned that you let him organise the library books when he finished his literacy yesterday.'

'Yes. Breaks can be important too.'

'Of course, and he gets plenty of breaks at home. So if you could set him extension work instead, that would be wonderful.'

'No problem.'

'Thank you, Miss Mills. You are a lifesaver.' She steps away but stops. 'Oh, before I forget, you wouldn't mind sending me another employment reference, would you? Just email it over to me or Karen when you get a second.'

'A reference? I've been sent by an agency. All my references have been checked by them.'

'I know, but between you and me, the parents at Leedham Primary really like to know their little darlings are in the safest possible hands, especially with the current situation. Cate is a very popular member of our little community.' She gives a shuddering breath. 'We're really good friends, and Archie and Sebastian are very close, even though Sebastian is almost a year older and very mature for his age. He's devastated Archie is missing. He's cried himself to sleep every night this week, poor thing.

'It's nothing to worry about,' she continues. 'We've got the references from your most recent substitute positions, but we really need one from your last full-time role. I assume that won't be an issue?' Anika looks at me, and I get the sense that she might be frowning somewhere beneath the layers of Botox I'm sure she's had injected into her skin.

'No problem,' I lie. Inside, I seethe at this woman and her nicely-nicely way of checking up on me and telling me how to do my job.

For a moment, I wonder what would happen if I gave Anika my favourite jab cross. A quick pow-pow using all of my shoulder on the cross, knocking out a few of her perfect white teeth and breaking her nose. Not that I ever would, but it doesn't stop me thinking it.

Instead, I smile my brightest, most understanding smile. 'I'll email the details later. I should probably get back.' I give a quick wave before hurrying into the classroom.

The children are already sitting at their desks, some chatting, some completing the anagram I put on the board this morning.

I throw myself into maths and then literacy. Mrs Kelp, the teaching assistant, takes a group out to a side room to work on their spellings, and I set Sebastian his extra work. Just two extension questions he can tell his mum he did. And then he can go back to the bookshelves at the back of the class.

It's only when the bell for breaktime rings, and the children rush out to play, leaving me alone with my thoughts, that Anika's words come back to me. I was so focused on Anika's 'lols', and her pushy way of telling me how to do my job, that I didn't register the danger in her request. The governors want the reference from my last full-time role – Haventhorpe Primary in Brighton.

A hum of worry begins to wind itself through me. I'm a good teacher. I'm patient and kind and funny. I see all the quirks and potential of the children I teach. I'm the right person for this job. But I can't give Anika that reference.

Haventhorpe Primary School know too much about me. They know what happened a year ago, before I left Brighton and became a substitute teacher. They know about the police and the investigation. They know what I did. If I give Anika the name of the school, if she asks for a reference, it will all come out. I'll be fired. I'll never get another job.

I can't let that happen.

I think about running away. It's what I'm good at. I could pack my bags and call the agency, hoping another school will come up that will accept the agency's references. But work is thin on the ground this time of year. A day here, two days there. It's not enough.

Even my Year Four class can do the maths on this. Holiday rental prices on a teacher's salary, even with the day rates of being a substitute, and finding run-down places like The Old Stable, it doesn't add up. After paying the first week's rent to Paul, my bank account is teetering into an overdraft I hate to use. Thank goodness I get paid weekly.

Besides, there's something about this school, this community, which doesn't feel quite right. I can't explain the disquiet rippling through me. There's something unsettling hanging in the air, an intensity no one talks about.

I huff a short laugh and shake my head. What am I saying? That I want to stay because I'm worried about the children? Sebastian with his anxious frown, and Jessica Hill with her confidence and just the right amount of sass; cheeky Benjamin Arnolds with his big imagination and terrible handwriting.

I'm being ridiculous. Of course there's a strange atmosphere in the school. A teacher and a child are missing.

I'll delay Anika for as long as I can. I'll wait for her to ask again. And then I'll tell her the school have posted it. And really, they need me too. It won't be good for their 'precious darlings' to have me leave now. The worry settles. Not disappearing but not expanding either. I can drag this out for a few weeks. That's all I need. Surely Cate and Archie will have been found by then.

I reach for my phone and the news sites I've been refreshing every spare moment. I've read all the articles, but I click on them again anyway.

TEACHER AND SON MISSING ON WALK HOME FROM SCHOOL

WHERE ARE CATE AND ARCHIE?

WOMAN AND CHILD MISSING IN LEEDHAM AREA

How can a mother and child disappear from a place like Leedham without anyone seeing anything? What happened to them?

NINE

OLIVER

Oliver avoids the playground this morning. All those parents. Even the children. They're all staring at him like he's an animal at the zoo, a circus freak. Pretending he's the broken husband soldiering on has sapped the last of his energy. He doesn't know what he is anymore, but he's not that.

This morning, when he'd given up trying to sleep and had stumbled into the bathroom, he'd barely recognised the man staring back at him from the mirror. There's an angry red stye on the lid of his left eye that itches to the point of infuriation. He can feel it twitching as he strides through the gates and heads straight for the main entrance.

He steps inside the building, cutting off the shouts of the children from the playground. The reception area is empty, but there's a steaming cup of milky tea sitting on the desk, so he guesses Karen is somewhere nearby. Probably in the staffroom, or in the playground tracking down the parents who still need to sign whatever form is being handed around this week.

Oliver has a sudden desire to turn and flee, to hurry back to his house. He can feel the world closing in – like the Fortnite game he and Archie play together sometimes when Cate isn't there to disapprove and say he's too young. The timer in the corner of the screen, the shrinking of space, the pressure to kill first.

Thoughts of Archie are a punch to the guts – winding, leg-weakening. It's a fight not to double over. He's made so many mistakes, but he didn't mean to hurt anyone. He didn't mean any of it. All he wants is his boy back.

But he's messed up in the most colossal, unspeakable way, and all that's left is damage control.

Oliver fiddles with the ends of his hair. He can't get it to sit right. He even used Cate's hairdryer this morning, but it's still lying flat. If his family are gone, if his charm has left him, and his looks too, then what's left? He pushes the thought aside. Pity isn't going to get him through this.

The week has slipped away from him. It's Thursday already. Tomorrow will be seven days since Cate and Archie didn't come home. He's done everything he can to divert suspicion. Reporting her missing to the police and calling everyone he can think of. Old friends and distant relatives, and her parents of course. It took five attempts before they finally picked up the phone. They told him they'd be on their way home just as soon as the world cruise they're on docks and they can get a flight back. Wally and Lisa are the most stuck-up, interfering people he's ever had the displeasure to meet, and he seriously has to do something before they get back.

The heat he feels on him now will be a winter chill compared to the fiery fury they'll unleash on him. Of course they assumed it was all his fault.

'Oliver, good morning.'

Karen's sing-song voice startles him out of his thoughts, and he finds himself still standing in the entrance hall.

'Morning, Karen. How are you?' He coughs, the floral scent of her perfume catching in the back of his throat.

'Yes, I'm well, thank you. I wasn't sure if we'd see you

today.' Her words come out quick and flustering. 'What have you done to your hand?'

He follows her gaze to his raised hand and the white bandage now wrapped around his palm. There's no point trying to hide it now the detectives have seen it. And besides, the plasters weren't doing any good. The cut beneath the bandage is an angry red that throbs through the night, keeping him awake. He's pretty sure it's infected despite the antibacterial cream he's coated on it every night. Oliver hates how obvious the bandage is, but it's better than anyone seeing how bad the cut has become. 'It's nothing. I wasn't concentrating while I was cutting some bread.'

'You must take care of yourself, Oliver. We'd all understand if you'd rather be at home—'

'No,' he cuts her off. 'I want to be here. I want to be doing something.' His words land with more tension than he means. He grits his teeth and swallows back his anger. 'But thank you, Karen. You're a lifesaver.'

She smiles – placated, he hopes.

Oliver ignores the beckoning quiet of his office and moves straight to the photocopier. This is why he's come today. If there's still a chance to get out of this and salvage what's left of his life, this is it. The thought makes every beat of his heart jolt through his body. He wants this to be over, and he can't think of a quicker way.

He unfolds the piece of paper he worked on last night and lines it up to the ruler that runs down the side of the copier. His finger hovers over the numbers. How many copies does he want? How many is enough? He taps in one-zero-zero and presses enter. The machine whirs into life. A single piece of paper is sucked into the machine from a tray on the top. And then the humming stops and an error message appears on the screen. Oliver feels the last trickle of energy seep out of him. He could cry. He could break down right here, right now. Not because his wife and child are gone, or because he's pretty sure the police suspect him of being involved, not because of the guilt or because he can feel himself teetering on the edge of losing everything, but because of Error 832.

'Everything all right?' Karen asks, stepping up behind him.

'Fine, fine. I wanted to photocopy something, but—'

'How many copies did you want?'

'A hundred.'

'Ah, that would do it,' she says. 'The photocopier doesn't like to make more than fifty-one copies at a time. It's been like this for years. Don't ask me why fifty-one is the magic number. It just is. Trial and error has taught me not to question it.'

'That's ridiculous,' he replies. He remembers how much they splashed out on new playground surface – the squishy kind to protect the children when they fall – then forking out an extra five grand for the multicoloured snakes to be painted on it. Even the number of pencils, rubbers and glue sticks they buy every month seems astronomical.

With Anika running both the PTA and the governors, the budgets are completely out of hand. She's simultaneously raising the money and spending it. Cate had been trying for a while to get one of the parents to replace her on the PTA. He didn't retain all the details, but it clearly hadn't worked.

'Why haven't we replaced it or got it fixed?' he asks.

'I've submitted a request for a new one more than once, but the governors always turn it down. I'm told the money is better spent on things that directly impact the children, and,' she adds in a lower voice, 'are seen by the parents.'

He sighs for what feels like the millionth time that morning. 'So I need to do it in two batches then?' There's a crack to his voice, betraying how close to the edge he feels. He clears his throat, willing himself to get a grip. A moment later, Karen's hand touches his forearm.

'Let me do this,' she says. 'It's my job.'

Oliver starts to protest, but what's the point? She'll see it soon enough. He steps aside and watches Karen lift the lid and retrieve the poster he made. She shrinks back at the words in large black print across the top.

HELP SEARCH LEEDHAM VALE FOR CATE AND ARCHIE
SATURDAY 10 A.M. – MEET AT THE PLAYING FIELD

Oliver's gaze is pulled to the photos underneath. He picked the one of Archie in his football kit, grinning at the camera. It was taken last summer when his adult teeth had come in at the front, too big for his little mouth and making him look a bit goofy, but his hair is windswept and sticking up at the sides, the way Oliver likes it best.

A nausea burns at the back of his throat. His little boy.

Karen gasps, a hand flying to her mouth. Tears brim in her eyes. 'The police think she's out there somewhere? And little Archie too?'

Oliver gives an 'I don't know' headshake. He doesn't want to tell Karen that this is his idea. His search. His plan. The detectives have told him to sit tight and wait for their updates, but how can he do nothing? Don't they see the tension building through the village? Gossip is spreading faster than an outbreak of head lice. He knows the parents, the staff, the whole village are looking to him. Some with pity and sympathy, but others with suspicion. Organising the search will show he has nothing to hide surely?

'But it's been nearly a week,' Karen continues. 'Do they think—'

'I don't know. I just don't know. But it's worth a try, isn't it? I can't keep waiting around like this.'

Karen dabs at the corner of her eye. 'Let me get this sorted for you. I can make the copies and pop them around the village. I'll send an email out to the parents too. The whole village will turn out in force. If they're out there, we'll find them.'

A wedge cuts into his throat. He forces out a 'thank you' before slipping into his office and closing the door. He sinks into his chair as the world closes in around him again. This had better work.

TEN

LEXI

I glance behind me, checking the hall is empty before stepping quietly to the closed door of Oliver's office. It's gone 4 p.m. on Thursday and I'm pretty sure Karen and the teaching staff have left for the day. I saw Steve Bishop, the elderly Year Six teacher, leave with Ruby Jung, the Year One and Two teacher. They car-share to one of the nearby towns. And Bella Woodcock, the Year Three teacher, already mentioned needing to leave early for an appointment.

I'm not sure about Gemma Rowley from the Reception class, but the school has an empty feel to it and I'm sure it's just me now. And Oliver.

I'm curious about the man I've not seen properly since the assembly on Tuesday. His wife is missing, and his son... his eight-year-old boy. So young. So innocent. Is he scared? Is he crying for his daddy? Is Cate with him? All day the questions have been spinning in my head.

It doesn't matter how many times I tell myself that it's got nothing to do with me, that I need to keep a low profile here – and I can't do that if I'm sticking my beak in, like Donna always said, in her big-sister know-it-all voice – the same questions still come.

I knock gently and hear a muffled, 'Come in,' before opening the door into a small tidy office. The blinds are drawn, and the air is stuffy with the smell of body odour and... onion, I think, spotting an empty packet of crisps in the bin and fighting the urge to stride straight to the window and throw it open.

Instead, I step across the threshold and smile. 'Hi.'

Oliver stares at me with a blank sort of frown as though we've never met before. His pupils are large, gaze glassy, as though he's been staring at his computer screen for eight hours straight.

'Lexi,' I offer. 'The substitute teacher.'

Oliver rubs a hand over his face. There's a red spot on his left eye, which looks sore. He has the look of a man who hasn't slept for a week, but beneath it all are the lingering good looks of the man I saw in the photos shared across the news sites, beaming beside his missing family.

He clears his throat. 'Sorry. My mind went blank there. I meant to come find you at lunch to check how you're doing, but I... got caught on a phone call and lost track of time. Are you settling in OK?'

'Yes, it's all fine. Cate is so organised, it's easy to step into her shoes.'

Oliver's face visibly pales, and I cringe inwardly at my poor choice of words.

'You have no idea how organised she was,' he says.

Was.

The past tense rings in the air. He flinches and looks like he's going to correct himself but says nothing. Does it mean something that he said 'was'? Another question poking at my thoughts.

'What can I do for you, Lexi?' he asks.

'I'm sorry to disturb you, but I wanted to give you my

timesheet for this week and ask if you could sign it tomorrow at the end of the day please?' I say, handing over the slip of paper that I could probably have given to Karen tomorrow morning to sort.

Oliver nods and swallows, his Adam's apple bobbing up then down. He looks like he might be about to cry or throw up. I take another step into the office.

'Are you all right?' I ask. 'I mean, obviously you're not, but is there anything I can do?'

'No. I'm fine.' Oliver grabs a pen from his desk and scrawls a signature on the bottom of my timesheet. 'I'd better do this now in case I forget.' He hands the slip back before turning his attention to the computer screen. From the corner of my eye, I see the dark-blue logo of Facebook and a collage of bright photos – all of Archie.

Is Oliver a man who cares so little for his family that he comes to work instead of waiting at home for updates from the police? Or is he someone so devastated by what's happening that the waiting at home alone is too much and he has to keep busy?

'Thanks,' I say, moving to the door, but Oliver holds up a hand in a 'hang on' gesture before picking up a piece of paper from a stack on his desk. It's face down, so I don't see it until it's in my hands and I'm turning it over. **HELP SEARCH LEEDHAM VALE FOR CATE AND ARCHIE** is written in bold lettering.

'In case you have time to come,' he says, already turning back to the screen.

'Of course. I'll be there.' And then before I can stop myself, the question is out. 'What do you think happened to them?'

In the silence that follows, the only noise is the hum of the computer fan and a fly buzzing lazily at the window.

'I...' Oliver's voice trails off. He turns his head slowly, like it's being physically pulled to look up from the computer screen. But then he does and our eyes connect. The glaze passes and there's a flicker of something, like he's seeing me for the first time.

'Have we met before?' he asks.

I frown. 'In assembly?' It's a stupid comment, but I don't know what else to say.

He shakes his head. 'I mean before that. Where did you teach? Where are you from? I have the weirdest feeling we've met before.'

'I don't think so. I was in London before this,' I reply, ignoring the specifics of his question.

Oliver continues to stare for another long moment. 'Why are you asking me what I think happened to my wife and my child?'

There's something in his eyes that sends a tendril of disquiet through my body, and I'm suddenly aware that I'm alone in this building with a man I don't know, whose wife and son are missing, and the more days that pass, the less likely it seems they're still alive.

You have no idea how organised she was.

'I'm sorry,' I say. 'I didn't mean to overstep.'

There's a pause. He doesn't respond, so I start moving back towards the door. 'I'll see you tomorrow.'

Oliver's eyes linger on me for another moment before turning back to the computer screen. He reaches for the mouse with a hand covered in a white bandage and starts scrolling. A part of me is rooted to the spot, wanting to ask him about that bandage, but another part – a bigger part – can feel the adrenaline in my veins and wants to turn and run.

I shut the door, face hot, pulse fast, and grab my bag before hurrying out of the school. For the strangest moment in that office, it felt as though Oliver was looking right through me, like he could see all of my secrets and the past I'm running from. The thought sends a shiver of fear racing through my body.

ELEVEN

JEANIE

Jeanie walks with a certain amount of purpose out of her house and towards the cut-through to the park. Not too fast to be hurrying. Not too slow to be waved down by Gail or one of her other neighbours wanting to chat. It's one of those rare outings where she wished she had a dog. No one ever stops to ask a dog walker where they're going or where they've been. She quite likes the idea of getting a dog. Something snappy that growls at passers-by and children on scooters. But dogs crap a lot, and Jeanie has a sensitive nose and has no desire to pick up dog mess wherever she goes. Besides, there's Buster to consider. The cat isn't technically Jeanie's, but he might as well be for the amount of time he spends in her house.

She checks her watch – a gold-looking bit of tat she picked up from the market a few years ago.

She doesn't like leaving the house when there are so many police coming and going on the road. She knows they'd have no cause to kick down her door and discover what she's hiding in the locked box room, but it doesn't make it easier to leave.

She hates them all with a passion that makes her grind her teeth and want to scream out loud. Jeanie wishes they'd all go away. As if any amount of asking questions is going to find that teacher and her lovely boy.

And, quite frankly, they're all too stupid to scrape away the veneer of the life she's built as the village spinster and coordinator of the neighbourhood watch to see the truth of who she really is. Still, she is nervous. She wouldn't have gone out today if he hadn't told her that it was urgent.

'Will you do it?' he'd asked. No please. No thank you. But then it wasn't really a question. They are both in far too deep to change things now.

The park is a large open square with tennis courts and a cricket pavilion in the top corners, and a playground and public toilets at the bottom beside a small car park. There's a tree-lined path cutting through the middle, which Jeanie walks down, heading in the direction of the village high street. It's quiet. A lull, she expects, before the schoolchildren descend and then the older kids and their footballs and music and vapes, and who knows what else.

She'll be fine until she gets to the little supermarket on the corner. Until then she can say she's popping out to get some milk. But after that, she'll have to make something up. She can say she's looking for a gift for a friend or some other tat. Come to think of it, she could do with another plate. She only has two left.

A fine sheen of sweat dampens her armpits and prickles her forehead. She wonders if it's her age – that damn change. It feels like she spent her twenties being asked when she'd settle down, her thirties being asked if she wanted children and her forties being warned how awful her life was about to become. Her responses have always been short. In her twenties, she replied: 'I have no desire to share my life with someone, wash their stinking pants and cook their dinner every night for the rest of my life.' Her thirties, it was a simple no. And in her forties she's always said she has plenty of time before all that. But time has caught up with her.

In her darker moments, she wonders if she was too hasty in her answers. A relationship and marriage would never have worked for her, but a child? She thought no, but little Archie has shifted her thinking. A sweet boy; a sensitive soul that reminds Jeanie of her mother – a woman soft and kind with none of the brittle edges Jeanie inherited from her father.

No doubt it's simpler than all that. This heat, this worry, is about her destination. It's making her jittery. She tries not to think about what's in the canvas shopping bag hooked over one shoulder.

She really is too hot in her cardigan and raincoat. There's a chill in the wind, but when she steps out of the park and onto the high street, the wind drops and it's suddenly too warm. The sweat is no longer a sheen but a dampness on her face. She wishes she'd driven now. But it's only around the corner, and she wouldn't want anyone on the parish council or the neighbourhood watch to see her drive. Not after petitioning for a pedestrianised high street and moaning about all those parents at the school who tear through the village in their cars twice a day, when most of them could just walk. Children have no idea what it is to walk to school anymore. Besides, she hates to drive after her glass of wine at lunch. After that last time she'd got behind the wheel. She'd only had one glass, plus a little top-up. Not even an extra half, she's sure, and they'd come out of nowhere. It was them in the wrong. They hadn't looked properly before stepping out, and Jeanie had slammed on the brake and jolted forward in the seat. The memory of that moment and what followed makes her feel queasy.

After the supermarket, Jeanie makes a show of nosing at the displays in the gift shops. There's a plate she quite fancies – cream with coloured spots on it. But it's expensive, and really, what's the point? It will end up broken like all the rest.

On and on she goes. She glances over her shoulder before turning down the side road and to the building she needs. Three sharp knocks. No one answers. Good. Jeanie does what she has to do and hurries back to the high street.

'Jeanie.' She jumps at the sound of her name, spinning around to find Heather Morrison striding towards her. She's wearing her usual Barbour jacket and her beige wool fedora hat with the pheasant feather in the brim. It looks like something out of a fancy-dress box, in Jeanie's opinion, but Heather does love to dress the part of village busybody.

'I thought that was you,' Heather continues, her voice high and clipped in that way hoity-toity people always speak. 'Where have you been?'

'Nowhere,' Jeanie is quick to reply. 'I was... just looking for some new plates.' The lie feels quite ridiculous now it's out, but it's too late to drag it back in. She dabs discreetly at the sweat forming on her upper lip, and thankfully Heather pushes on.

'I've just come from Andrea Rowley's house,' she says. 'Have you heard about this search that's happening on Saturday? The parish council are in full organisation mode. I could do with another pair of hands to post flyers door-to-door. We want the whole village out in force.'

Jeanie feels a kernel of anger inside her. 'What search?' she forces herself to ask, hating being the last to know.

Heather gives a tinkling laugh. 'When did you last check your phone? It's all over the neighbourhood watch group, and Andrea has posted on the parish council Facebook page too. We're searching the vales for Cate and Archie Walker. It was Oliver's idea, but you know how Andrea and Marcus like the parish council to support village events, especially since their daughter Gemma works at the school too. We're all getting involved.'

The anger fizzles, doused by a tidal wave of sheer cold

dread that makes her shiver inside her coat. A search of the vales. They can't. They mustn't.

'Are you all right?' Heather asks, a frown forming between two spidery thin brows.

'I... Yes, I'm fine.' She's not. She's far from it. A dizzying lightness hits her head. 'It's just all so upsetting, isn't it? That poor woman and child,' Jeanie adds, her voice shaking.

'It really is,' Heather replies. 'Well, I must get on. Lots to do. I'll drop some flyers over to you tomorrow.'

Jeanie nods. 'Yes, do.' She'll dump them straight in the bin, but it won't matter. It's already on the village Facebook page and WhatsApp group. Of course people will come. If not for the Leedham community spirit, then for the spectacle and curiosity of it all. If she was the cursing type, now would be the moment for every expletive she knows.

The dread expands – a physical push that leaves her feeling like she might be sick. The urge to double over is almost too much. She has to stop the search. There must be something she can do. Her thoughts charge from one stupid idea to the next. Already she knows it's futile. Everything is in motion. She closes her eyes. Hot, angry tears prick at the edges.

How many people will come? Two hundred? Three hundred? All those eyes, all those miles of ground covered. Someone will find the terrible, terrible thing she did.

Her phone is in her hand before she can stop herself. She's shaking so hard it takes three goes to tap his number.

'It's me,' she says when he answers. 'We have a serious problem.'

TWELVE

LEXI

The envelope is sitting on the doormat as I open the door to The Old Stable. I step over it and drop my bag on the sofa. I don't shut the door. It's better to leave it open until I've adjusted to the smell of damp clinging to the air. After an hour in the apartment, I'll barely notice. And I really don't mind the smell or the size of my temporary home. The one room with its kitchen and dining table at the front, and a two-seater sofa, TV and coffee table at the back. I don't mind the white walls, scuffed and stained, or the generic prints of hillsides on the walls. I don't mind the narrow door at the back that leads into a bedroom and a bathroom off to one side.

But I do mind the gloom of the place. There are only three windows. One in the kitchen, looking out to the car park. One in the bedroom, facing a dilapidated fence, and the third is in the bathroom in mottled glass. All three are blocked from most of the daylight by the large sycamore tree in the car park, thick and leafy branches hanging over the building. The gloom is a bad mood that sinks into my skin the longer I stay inside these walls.

I switch on a small lamp with a frilly cream shade that casts an orange glow around the space and remind myself that it's not for long. That soon I'll pack my bags and be on my way again. At least, I think I will. It's been six days since they were last seen. The same thoughts from Oliver's office return. Can they really turn up safe and well now?

I pull out the poster Oliver gave me and stare at the grainy photos of Cate and Archie. Do people really believe the mother and son can be trapped somewhere in the vales?

After leaving Oliver's office and the school earlier, I walked down to the river and along the banks. It's not exactly a vast wilderness. The fields are open, the paths well trodden. There are herds of cows and sheep, farmers checking in regularly, dog walkers, ramblers, families with picnics. Even if they got stuck in one of the small woodland areas, someone would have heard their shouts for help. And none of the news reports suggested that Cate and Archie went for a walk or took a different route home.

I drop the poster to the kitchen counter and remember the envelope. I pluck it from the doormat, assuming it's a note from Paul – next week's bill that he's pushed under the gap. The envelope is thick paper – expensive – with no name on the front. I peel open the lip and pull out the single white piece of card.

I make a noise, an exhale of disbelief, a yelp. I drop the note, but the words still burn behind my eyelids.

STOP ASKING ABOUT THE MISSING TEACHER OR YOU'LL BE NEXT.

Fear clutches at my sides, claws digging in. My eyes scan the apartment. It's empty of course, but then I spin to the open door and slam it shut. The white door is made of sturdy wood, with no windows or peepholes, and no Yale lock either. The only way to lock it is to put the key in and turn the deadbolt. I fumble in the fabric of my skirt, snatching for the key until the cool metal is in my hands and I'm shoving it into the hole and locking the door.

Where has this threat come from?

Who would do this?

My mind races back over the last few days. All the people I've spoken to since arriving in Leedham. Anika and the other parents. Karen and my TA, Mrs Kelp; Gemma and the other staff at the school; Paul the landlord. And then I think of Oliver.

'Why are you asking me what I think happened to my wife and my child?'

I've heard the rumours circulating the playground. The half questions about him that no one wants to believe let alone finish, and yet still they ask: 'You don't think...'; 'It couldn't be...'

But why threaten me?

I've never met Cate. But something about her has got under my skin. It must be taking over her class, and the tragedy of a mother and a little boy never making it home.

'You'll never meet a nicer woman.'

'Salt of the earth is our Cate.'

'She'd do anything for anyone.'

The disappearance is all anyone can talk about. I've only been in Leedham for two days. Why am I being threatened like this?

I glance out of the kitchen window. There are only a handful of cars and a blue van in the car park. Nothing suspicious, and yet I step away, feeling watched and on edge.

You'll be next.

Next for what?

I thought Leedham was a safe village. The beautiful landscape. The picturesque high street, bustling with tourists so much of the time. The kind of place where nothing bad ever happens. But when the tourists pack up their picnic blankets, dump their rubbish in the overflowing bins and drive away, then it's quiet. The roads empty. Suddenly that thought doesn't feel so reassuring. Because, really, it doesn't matter how safe a place is if you meet the wrong person and there's no one around to help.

THIRTEEN

LEXI

The gloom closes in. It's not yet evening and I'm trapped inside these walls. A familiar longing pulses through me. The desire to run is a physical pull, just as it was a year ago. I've been running ever since. Never staying in one place for more than a few weeks at a time. Except I can't keep running. I need money. I need this job.

I stare down at the note on the floor as questions spin in my head. Who sent it? What happened to Cate and Archie? What do I do? My heart starts to race. I'm dizzy, anxious.

And so I do the only thing I can think of. The one thing that will calm me down. I pull out the small Bluetooth speaker from my suitcase, connect it to my phone and blast my favourite Tabata interval-training playlist. The fast beat of the music fills the silence as I throw off my teaching clothes and pull on my shorts, sports bra and trainers. By the time I'm back in the living room again, I'm in control.

I move through my routine, my punches to the bag getting harder and faster with each round. Jab, cross. Jab, cross. Hook, hook. Uppercut, uppercut, jab, cross. My fist slams against the punch bag in time with the music.

I move, dart, duck, punch, and I don't stop until my shoulders ache and my muscles are weary, and I'm too tired to think anymore.

The playlist ends, and I pull one arm across my chest, stretching my right shoulder and then my left. I'm about to unstrap my gloves when my phone starts to ring. I step across the room and stare at the screen, expecting a call centre or one of the supply teaching agencies I'm signed up to, or even a rare call from my mother. It's none of those.

The Brighton area code stops me dead. What do they want? How did they get this number? I changed it after leaving Brighton, wanting nothing more to do with that place.

A burst of childlike terror shoots through me. Like I'm seven again – a little girl – when my parents would go out for dinner and leave Donna to babysit, and she'd sneak out to meet her boyfriend and I'd be all alone. That fear of a monster, a kidnapper, a murderer, lurking out of sight in the shadows, pumps through my veins.

Instantly, I'm drawing back, away from the ringing phone, as though the caller might reach a hand up and grab me.

The world disappears as the memories fly out at me – bats from a cave. I'm frozen. Unable to move. To stop what I know is coming – the memory that haunts my dreams. The screams, the pleading. I never wanted her to die, but I couldn't save her.

I thought I could leave the feelings behind me when I drove out of Brighton. I thought if I kept moving, kept smiling, kept pretending I was fine, it would come true, but there's no escape from the fear and fury and guilt. It's hot poison burning my veins, pulling me back.

The ringing stops. A temporary reprieve. They'll try again of course. They won't give up.

One question pushes the rest out of my head. They found my number, but do they know where I am?

FRIDAY: SEVEN DAYS MISSING

FOURTEEN

GEMMA

In the early-morning sun, Gemma runs the brush over Ginger's body. Firm, even strokes; rhythmic, hypnotic. She loses herself in the task, and with each sweeping movement it feels as though she's brushing away her own anxiety and the stress of the last week.

She wonders about Cate. She wonders where she is right now. Have the last seven days gone in a flash or a lifetime?

The skin on her chestnut mare shivers under her touch and Gemma is sure the horse can sense the panic that's only one breath away from overtaking her. The life she wanted so badly is slipping further and further from her grasp. It isn't fair. It isn't right.

Somewhere nearby, a woodpecker hammers its beak against a tree, and in the distance, Gemma can hear the soft rumble of cars and the early commuters. She should get on too, she thinks, continuing to work her way around Ginger's hind. Gemma's nose tickles and she sneezes, once, twice, three times, making Ginger shift her legs and swing her head around.

'Hey.' She smiles as their eyes meet. Gemma stops her groom to step closer to Ginger's neck. 'It's just hay fever. You were the one that wanted to ride through that long grass, remember?'

Ginger replies with a snort before pressing her nose into Gemma's shoulder. She laughs and pulls out her Polos from the pocket of her gilet. From the corner of her eye, she spots the wheelbarrow and fork, the hay bale that still needs to be moved, and all the jobs she has to complete this morning before getting ready for school.

'Come on,' she says. 'Have this and then go eat some grass. I have lots to do.' She unbuckles Ginger's bridle, pats the mare lightly on the bottom and watches her walk regally towards the field of dewy grass that sits to one side of her parents' house at the edge of Leedham.

'To be a horse,' Gemma whispers under her breath before grabbing the old metal wheelbarrow and steering it inside the stable. She throws herself into the work, relishing the ache to her back as she forks piles of manure and spent hay into the barrel.

She's halfway through lugging the bale of hay into the netting container hanging from the wall when the detectives appear in the doorway, blocking the light and causing Gemma to whirl around in surprise.

'Oh. Hi,' she says.

It's the same two that questioned her on Monday morning, pulling her out of a phonics lesson to ask her what she saw on Friday afternoon. The answer was nothing at all, but somehow she doubts this conversation will be as simple. The thought sends a bolt of adrenaline coursing through her. She has to protect what's left of her future. And she promised she wouldn't tell, even if that means lying to the police.

'Hi, Gemma,' DS Pope says with an apologetic smile. 'Sorry to disturb you so early.'

She looks less tired today, Gemma thinks, although there's still an air of bone-weary exhaustion to the woman that Gemma recognises from the mums in the playground hurrying in their children while a newborn sleeps in a pushchair. It clicks then. DS Pope is a mum. A new mum, she guesses, spotting a pale-white stain on the bottom of Pope's trouser leg that looks like hurriedly wiped away baby sick. She wonders briefly if this is a good thing; if Pope will be distracted and miss something.

DC Hacker steps alongside Pope, looking overdressed compared to his superior. He smiles, and she waits for the flicker to cross his eyes, the look she sees in most men, from the dads at drop-off to the boys her own age she meets on her rare nights out with friends. The look where they're wondering what it would be like to take her to bed.

It's the blonde hair, a boyfriend once told her. *It's like the colour of caramel or something. That and your great arse,* he'd said, laughing. It's the make-up too, she's sure. The way she's careful to accentuate her cheekbones and eyes, covering dull, blotchy skin. But the look doesn't come. Instead, Hacker's gaze is already moving to the open notebook in his hands. 'We thought it would be easier to talk now than at the school.'

'Sure,' she says. 'Do you mind if I carry on with this at the same time?' She nods to the hay bale. 'I'm running a bit late already.'

'Of course,' he replies.

She turns back to the bale, glad for the distraction.

'We're talking to people now,' Pope begins, 'to build a picture of Cate's life. What can you tell us about your relationship with her? You were close, I think.'

'We were friends. I'm not sure how close we were. Cate was good friends with a lot of the mums and people in the village. I never really found a way into that village group.'

'Why not?'

Gemma shoves the last block of hay into the net and pulls off her gloves. 'As far as I can work out, it's because I don't have children, I'm not married and I'm not in my forties. The women don't seem to like a younger, single woman hanging out with their husbands. I think they see me as a threat.'

'Did you talk to Cate in the staffroom on Friday? What frame of mind was she in?'

'I didn't, no. I was on playground duty at break, and I run a worry workshop with the kids on Friday lunchtimes.'

'A worry workshop?' Hacker looks up from his notebook, pen poised on the page.

'I know it sounds silly, but the kids love it. They can come to my classroom at lunchtime on Fridays and write little notes about anything that's on their minds. They place it in the worry monster, which is this colourful teddy with a zipped mouth, and then I take out the note and we can sit and talk about it if they want to, or they can go back outside to play.'

She's proud of her worry workshop. It's nice to spend time with the older children, and it will look good for when Steve Bishop retires from his Year Six class, and she can step into the role. *If* he retires, she thinks then. He's been telling them he's leaving for at least three years, and she really, really doesn't want to teach the Reception class again in September.

For a brief moment, Gemma wonders about Cate's class and what will happen long term. Then she thinks of all the plans she's made, the things she's done. She shuts the thought down before the detectives see it on her face.

She brushes the hay from her jodhpurs. 'Shall we start walking back to the house?' she asks.

Hacker and Pope step away from the stable entrance and they fall into step beside her. In the short time she's been inside, the sun has inched up in the sky. She pulls out her phone, cringing at the time before firing off a message to Robyn, her TA, to tell them she's been held up.

'And this worry workshop, is that for any child in the school?' Pope asks.

Gemma nods. 'It's usually little things. So-and-so won't play with me, or it might be something about a sports event or music exam. These kids lead full-on lives.'

'And did Archie ever visit your workshops?'

Her steps falter for a second. She feels her cheeks flush. How does she reply? It takes her a beat too long to decide and in that pause she gives them the answer. It's too late to lie. 'Yes.'

'What worries did he share with you?'

'He... he said his parents were fighting a lot.' Gemma has the sense of digging herself a hole she won't be able to get out from. Inside, she screams. It's too late to backtrack or lie, but she tries. 'A lot of children say that though. You know what kids are like? They have big imaginations.'

They reach the back of her parents' house. Through the window, she can see Andrea in the kitchen, already dressed in her charcoal-grey Stella McCartney suit, drinking her usual cup of black coffee before leaving for the solicitor's where she and Marcus are partners. They've never said it, but Gemma senses they're disappointed about her career choices just as keenly as their disappointment at her single status and living situation. Hardly much to brag about to the village crowd who treat them both like the king and queen of Leedham.

Andrea taps her watch and makes a face, and Gemma nods. 'I'm sorry, but I'm really not sure what more I can tell you. I should get ready for work.'

'Of course,' Pope says. 'Just one more question for now. You've spoken about Cate, but what about Oliver? He's your boss – you must know him well. What do you think of him?'

She shrugs. 'He's nice enough. He's a good boss anyway. He made sure the more experienced staff gave me a lot of support when I first joined the school three years ago. It was my first job after training. It might not sound like much, but it makes such a difference.'

'And what about outside of school?' Pope asks.

'I see him and Cate socially sometimes if there are birthday drinks or a village event. We chat a bit, but he's my boss, so I wouldn't say we're friends or anything. Like I said, I try not to spend too much time talking to married men.'

'I see,' Pope says, although Gemma isn't sure she does. There's a strange balance to living in a small village like Leed-ham. Gossip is currency regardless of how true it is. Something she's all too aware of.

Gemma opens the back door and leads them into the mudroom, as her mum calls it – the airlock-like space between the garden and the kitchen where they hang their coats and store footwear. The place beyond which Gemma is forbidden to enter wearing her horse-wear. She pulls off her riding boots and gilet before they all step into the kitchen. From the other side of the house, the front door opens and her parents call a 'see you tonight' goodbye to her.

'Why are you asking about Oliver?' she asks. 'You can't think he had anything to do with Cate and Archie going missing?'

'We're exploring all possibilities at this time,' Pope says, giving nothing away.

All?

Gemma doesn't like the sound of that. Just how much trouble will she be in if they find out she's been lying? Not to mention why. She needs the detectives out of her house. She needs to think.

'Look, if there's nothing else right now, could we talk another time?' Gemma asks. 'I really need to get ready for work.'

Pope nods. 'Thank you, Miss Rowley. We're going to the school now to continue interviewing the staff, so if we have any other questions, we'll be in touch. And if you think of anything else that Cate or Archie said to you, please get in touch. Even the smallest things can seem insignificant but might help us to build a picture.'

'Of course. I'll have a think,' she lies. She's already said too much.

'We'll see ourselves out,' Pope says.

Gemma hurries up the stairs, taking them two at a time. The front door bangs again as she strips off her clothes and steps into the shower. It's only as the prickly heat of the water hits her skin that she lets out a single sob. She cups her hand over her mouth. The panic is quicksand. The more she fights it, the greater its hold.

She shouldn't have mentioned Archie's worry. But how much weight are they really going to put on the hearsay of an eight-year-old boy? Pope said they're considering all possibilities, but they don't know the truth about Gemma. No one knows. No one could possibly know, and that's the way it has to stay.

FIFTEEN

Cleaning day. Never my favourite. But it must be done, and done right. I work slowly, methodically, with my soapy sponge and my bucket.

You were never one for cleaning, were you? Not the type. I could spot that a mile off. No need to clean when there were others to do it for you.

I lift the sponge, sloshing warm water and suds onto the flatbed of the van. My jeans are wet at the knees as I crawl across the empty space. It isn't really dirty. There's no mud, no mess, but it's the unseen that I'm cleaning. Your DNA. Yours and Archie's.

His name rattles in my thoughts before clenching the muscles down my back and across my body. I shouldn't have used his name. It's easier to think of him as nameless. The boy.

My back aches, but I'm almost done, and it wouldn't do to be late for work, not when the police are in the village again. Two cars spotted outside the shop and reported on the village WhatsApp group before 8 a.m. I do hate that chat group. All those stupid people nitpicking over stolen bins and missing cats. And

*you, always nagging for cakes and donations to whatever
fundraising target you had that month.*

*But the group is useful too. Like when there's a party on in
the cricket pavilion and I know the streets will be too busy at
midnight to walk unseen. And like today, the message about the
police doing door-to-door again, expanding outward to the rest of
the village.*

*Not to mention the talk of the search. It's worth scrolling
through the reams of inane speculation for the little gems of
detail. Take Phyllis Martin and her message last night:*

> *Oh my. I'm just home from visiting my daughter in Spain and
> seen the news. I think I saw Cate and Archie on the day they
> went missing. They were running towards the river by the
> Upper Street footpath. Should I tell the police?*

*The message prompted a hundred or so replies and another
round of gossip and speculation.*

*A flicker of worry moves through me. It's unusual and
unpleasant. The question appears in my head before I can stop it.
The one where I wonder if I went too far with you.*

*I've seen the true crime shows. I understand escalation,
going that bit further each time – for the thrill as much as the
knowledge that they can. I thought myself above all that pop
psychology, but maybe I'm the same.*

*The worry returns as I swap the sponge for the scrubbing
brush, pushing it hard into the wood floor of the van. My
thoughts draw back to you again and again. How perfect you've
always seemed to those around you. Me included. How your
smile lit up a room, how you drew me in, burrowed your way
under my skin – a leech or a toxin – forcing me to take risks I
wouldn't usually take. Risks I'm paying for. But you're mine
now, and that makes it all worth it.*

When the scrubbing is done, I pick up my torch. It's small but powerful – a bright white light that shows up all the little specks of dirt I might have missed. On the first sweep I see nothing. On the second, something catches my eye. A glint of metal. A screw holding down the plywood? No. Something else pushed into the corner where the metal shell of the van meets the floor, barely visible, almost overlooked.

I move fast, a magpie swooping, and I wonder, like I always do when I think of the black-and-white birds, if they really are as attracted to shiny objects as the old wives' tale says. I hope so. I understand that attraction, that need to take what isn't mine. I reach out and pinch the object between my thumb and forefinger, drawing it up and into the torchlight.

It's a pearl earring. There's the smallest smudge of blood on one side, dark and dried. It's yours of course.

I see it then – the sudden burst of my anger. The struggle we had. It was taking so long to get you in the van. My heart was hammering, and I had one eye on the street, knowing that, at any second, someone was going to come around that corner and we'd be seen, and it would all be over. Everything I'd built and worked so hard to protect. I didn't mean to hurt you then. I didn't mean to hurt either of you.

But I had. And I'd do it all again if it meant you were mine.

Forever and always. That's what my father would whisper to my mother just before he swung his arm back and smacked her across the face, before every punch landed in her gut. 'Forever and always, I will do this to you.'

But I'm not like my father. I have control. I must have control.

The worry disappears. I have my plan. I'm always one step ahead.

I slip your earring into an envelope. Perhaps Phyllis Martin's message in the group chat wasn't so pointless after all. They're searching the vales for you and your boy. It would be such a shame to disappoint them.

SIXTEEN

LEXI

The threat of the note is still on my mind as I walk to school on Friday morning. I called Ipswich police station last night and left a message for the detectives in charge of Cate and Archie's case. No one has called me back yet. The note is in my bag, tucked inside a plastic food pouch I found in one of the kitchen cupboards. If I don't hear back from them today, I'll drive to the police station after school.

A fuzzy exhaustion clouds my thoughts this morning. I barely slept, my mind racing over the phone call from Brighton and the note. The words scratching like a sharp nail on my insides.

I still can't understand why I've been targeted. Yes, I asked about Cate and Archie in the playground yesterday. It was all any of us could talk about in the staffroom too, and of course, I asked Oliver last night. I think of the times I've refreshed the news app on my phone, rereading the same articles about the teacher and son. Maybe I have become a little obsessed, but I don't see how anyone could've noticed.

I shiver despite the blue sky and the sun and the warmth already building in the late-spring day. There's a deserted feel to the village this morning. A single car is parked outside the small supermarket on the corner by an old Tudor building painted pink and selling cakes and ice creams and old-fashioned sweets in large jars – rhubarb and custards, and white mice, fizzy cola bottles and the chocolate buttons with the sprinkles on top, reminding me of the times Mum would drop Donna and me off at the cinema and she'd sneak me in to watch twelve-rated films, long before I should've done.

I round the corner to the school and think again of how vulnerable I felt last night – the empty apartment, the desperate fumbling to lock the door. Is that how Cate felt when she was walking home with Archie?

I let the questions about them circle; I let myself grip hold, fixate, because then I don't have to think about my ringing phone yesterday and what it means that my past is catching up with me.

Somewhere in my fitful sleep I thought again about running. A new hair colour, a new phone number. How easy it would be. And yet it's more than the need of this job that's compelling me to stay. I don't know Cate, I don't owe her anything, but her disappearance feels personal now. Taking over her class, stepping into her shoes, and now someone is warning me to back off. I have to stay, don't I? I have to help if I can. Someone has targeted me. I feel too close to this to leave, even with the threat of the note and the fear it's unleashed. I just hope I can help before the events in Brighton catch up with me.

I'm so lost in thought that I almost don't notice the man sitting on the bench by the war memorial. I recognise him from the pub on my first day – the lone male. He's staring at the shop opposite, and he has the look of a person waiting for someone. I feel his dark eyes on me as I walk by. Any other day and I might have given a cheery greeting or a smile, but the fear from the threat and the phone call keeps me quiet, and I dip my head and keep walking. Only as I'm nearing the corner to the school do I glance back. He's still there. Except his head has turned. He's no longer looking straight ahead but to the side at me.

Even with the distance between us, there's an intensity in his gaze. I have the strangest feeling that I saw him yesterday on my walk to school too. I think back. There was a blue van parked on the high street with a figure inside. I didn't pay any attention at the time. I think I saw the same van parked in the pub car park last night too. Was it him?

The school gates come into view, and I force all thoughts of the man and threat and my past away. By the time I step into the playground before the morning bell, my smile is bright and welcoming. I look around at the teachers and parents. Oliver is here today, standing off to one side with Anika. He's wearing a smart suit and a red tie, but it does nothing to distract from the dark circles around his eyes and the sallow colour of his face in the bright sun.

I catch the curious glances from parents and the bent heads of whispers that follow as they look at him and then quickly away. Speculation hums around me like the trilling stridulation of crickets in summer. I look at Oliver. What does he expect to find at tomorrow's search?

'Miss Mills,' a voice calls out, shaking me from my thoughts.

Jessica skips to my side with Harmony, both with matching French braids parted perfectly in the middle.

'Good morning, girls,' I say, my smile genuine.

'Did you know the police are here?' Jessica asks in a sing-song voice. 'We saw them in the car park.'

'They're going to interview all of us,' Harmony adds.

'Really?' I ask, unsure whether this is imagined, real or somewhere in between.

They both nod before Harmony continues: 'I'm going to tell them about the time Harry stole Archie's apple from his lunch box and used it to play catch.'

'No, no,' Karen says, hurrying up to me and catching our conversation. 'There's nothing to worry about, girls. The police aren't going to be talking to any children. Off you go and play now.'

Jessica and Harmony both pull faces, but they turn away, and, hand in hand, they rush to the corner of the playground where the rest of my class seem to have gathered this morning.

'Yet,' Karen adds under her breath when it's just us.

'Are the police really here?' I ask.

Karen's face is pained. 'Yes. I've had to put them in the staffroom. Steve is already complaining about not getting his cup of tea this morning. I had to tell him that it's hardly a priority whether his routine is messed up, considering poor Cate and Archie are still missing. It's been a week since they were last seen. A week,' she adds for a second time, her voice breathless.

'I really wish they'd waited until after the drop-off to arrive,' she continues. 'I've already had several parents ask me about it this morning. Charlie Bolton's dad has taken him home. He doesn't want Charlie to get worried apparently. I did tell him the police are only here to re-interview the staff. God knows what they're hoping to find this time around,' she says, her eyes straying to Oliver for a moment before turning back to me. 'It's just... it's unimaginable is what it is.'

'I imagine they're just making sure there's nothing they've missed,' I soothe.

Karen gives a long sigh. 'It's all right for you, Lexi. You weren't here when Cate disappeared, so you'll be spared the questioning. Last Friday seems so long ago. I can't remember what I was doing or what I told the police on Monday.'

I give a sympathetic nod, and Karen hurries across the playground to Oliver and Anika. I watch her pass through the parents, stopping to talk to each group. Her frown remains, and it's obvious she cares deeply for the school and all the children and parents. I've no doubt that, behind the scenes, it's Karen who's kept the school running this week.

The bell rings, and my class rush towards me. Jessica and Benjamin jostle to be the first in line, bickering over whose book bag saved their place first. I send them both to the back, and, as Sebastian leads us in, I wonder how long it will be before I'm called to talk to the detectives. Karen is wrong. I am involved in this. The police will want to talk to the person who was threatened.

You'll be next.

My pulse quickens, and even though I should feel safe here, inside the locked school gates with my chattering class, I still find my gaze scanning the windows, lingering on the door, waiting for something or someone. I'm not sure what, just that I can't shake the sickening dread creeping over me again and again.

The routine of the school day helps. I launch us into a lesson on past, present and future verbs, and comprehension sheets on Albert Einstein. Then it's maths – averages and ratios. The break bell rings and the children charge outside. Some to play football and others to the imaginary game they've made up this week – a mix of tag and bulldog and Harry Potter. And still I wait, anxious in the sudden still of a room that should never be this quiet.

I'm sinking into my chair and reaching for my smoothie when there's a light tap on the door frame. I start, and a sound escapes my mouth – a tiny yelp – as my thoughts race straight back to that threat.

'Sorry,' Gemma says with an amused smile, 'I didn't mean to make you jump.'

'You didn't.' I smile, try to relax, although we both know she did. 'Come in.'

Gemma steps into my classroom and perches on Sebastian's desk. She's wearing a tight grey pencil skirt that hugs her curves, a black silk top and kitten heels. Her blonde hair is swept into a neat bun at the nape of her neck, and her make-up is flawless.

I wear foundation and mascara, and sometimes I brush a touch of bronzer on my cheeks, but Gemma is a level above. I know very little about contouring, except that Gemma has done it and the result is stunning.

We're around the same age, I think. She's, perhaps, a year or so older, although I don't feel like the younger one. I've lived two lifetimes compared to her – the one before Brighton and what I did, and the one after. I pull at one of my ringlets and let it spring back into place. There's something about Gemma's cool confidence that puts me on edge. She's barely looked at me this week, and I don't know why she's in my classroom.

'Do the detectives want to talk to me?' I ask, already reaching for my bag, assuming Gemma has come to summon me.

'Why would they want to talk to you? You don't even know Cate.'

She makes that face again. The amused frown. In that moment, I see her nine-year-old self as clear as though she's sat at the desk she's leaning on, hair in braids, legs swinging. The class princess, the one all the other girls aspired to be like. I've seen her type a dozen times and then some. The feigned innocence and casually cruel way they like to play with the friends who surround them. Moths to a flame.

I shrug and give a 'how silly of me' smile. 'I just thought... Never mind. Have they interviewed you?'

She rolls her eyes. 'First thing this morning.'

Her gaze shifts from my face to my desk and the whiteboard beside it. 'What's that?' She raises a finger and points to a line of green writing running down the side of the whiteboard before reading it aloud. 'Frogs' legs, pond slime, bogeys.' She gives a 'ha' of a laugh at the last one.

'It's my smoothie ingredients.' I grin, thinking of the shouts of incredulous glee from the children this morning and yesterday as they called out their guesses. I tap my flask of spinach-and-fruit smoothie sitting on my desk. 'The class are trying to guess the ingredients. I've said there's a prize for anyone who can get them all.'

'It certainly looks... healthy,' she says in a way I'm sure means 'disgusting'. 'It must be hard for you,' she adds.

'Why?' I ask.

'Taking over Cate's class. She's a good teacher. It's a lot to live up to.'

'She is organised,' I say carefully, waving a hand to the neatly labelled binders on a shelf above the desk. Lesson plans and activity sheets already printed out for the rest of term.

'That's an understatement. Has Mrs Kelp warned you about the store cupboard yet?' Gemma nods to the door behind the desk. 'Cate was fanatical about keeping it organised. She wouldn't let anyone else go in there; not even her teaching assistants are allowed in. Mrs Kelp finds it ridiculous. Who doesn't let their TA into their supply cupboard?'

'Every teacher likes to protect their stash of new exercise books, don't they?' I say lightly. 'I'll be careful to keep everything just as it is for when Cate hopefully returns.'

Gemma cocks an eyebrow. 'You think that's going to happen?'

'You don't?' I reply, and I can't help but sit forward as I wonder what, if anything, Gemma knows.

'I've no idea.'

'But what do you think happened to them?'

She shrugs. 'Why do you care so much?'

I think of the note and find myself shaking my head. 'I don't,' I lie. 'Just curious, I guess.'

She waves a hand between us as though shooing the thought away. 'Anyway, I just wanted to say that if any of the class have a wobble about Cate, you can send them across the hall to me. All the kids love me.'

'Thanks. I'll bear it in mind.'

'Karen has set up a kettle in her office for us.' She stands and brushes down her skirt.

'Thanks, but I've got my smoothie,' I reply before realising she didn't actually offer me a drink.

'Rather you than me,' she says before walking out the door.

I sit for a moment trying to wrap my head around the exchange. It feels like Gemma only came in here to tell me how much the children adore her, as though that might bother me. Then again, maybe Gemma is perfectly fine and it's me being weird. Despite what it looks like, and what I'm sure some people think when I flit in and out of schools and lives, I don't dislike people. It's true, children are easier. Nicer. They take things at face value, and for the most part, the games they play are fun and involve charging around a playground together.

I'm happy to stop and chat to anyone, child or adult, and I don't even mind a superficial friendship, a brief chat to pass the time in the staffroom like I have with Karen. I quite like jokes about the weather or the usual moaning about workload – not that I have much to moan about as a substitute. Better pay and less admin.

The problem comes when people try to scrape away the layers of superficial and get to know the real me. When they start asking questions I don't know how to answer. Where are you from? How long are you staying for?

And the question that snags. The one I can't answer. Do you have any family?

How do I explain that I had a sister?

Had.

Not have.

I had a sister but she died, and it was my fault. I couldn't save her.

SEVENTEEN

LEXI

It's a relief when the bell for lunch rings and the children rush into the hall to the fish fingers and chips waiting for them. I'm still agitated. Fidgety.

It's the waiting for the detectives to talk to me. And the phone call, and thinking about Donna too. The skittish fear of that note on my doormat, is still inside me, but I'm torn. I want to talk to the police, to learn what I can about Cate and Archie's disappearance, to tell them about the threat and make sure they take it seriously, but I also want to stay in the shadows. I already have Anika asking about my references. The last thing I need is the police digging into my background. If they start asking questions, it won't take them long to find out what I did and what the staff and parents think of me at Haventhorpe Primary.

I stand up and nudge Benjamin and Harmony's desk back into the straight line with the others on the front row. It will be wonky again by afternoon lessons, pushed forward from Ben's ants-in-his-pants fidgeting.

The urge to do something is a jabbing in the small of my back. But what can I do?

I pull down a ring binder from the shelf above Cate's desk.

It's a project on Henry VIII and the Tudors. The next binder is the Black Death and the Great Fire of London. There's a binder on dividing fractions and another on volcanoes. I'm not sure what I'm looking for, but there's nothing here aside from the printed sheets of a diligent and caring teacher.

I open the drawers and find plastic boxes full of pens – a box for each colour. Green and purple, blue and red. Everything is organised. Nothing out of place, and I don't know what I expect to find that the police missed in their search of the classroom before I arrived in Leedham.

I know I should stop looking, keep my head down and just do my job. The words of the threat cloud my thoughts, and yet I can't stop my gaze travelling around the classroom. Neat lines of tables all facing the front. Coat hooks to one side. Colourfully painted walls with spelling posters and times tables. There's a reading corner with three shelves of books and a few bean bags on the floor.

I turn a full circle until I'm back facing the desk and the wall behind it. And that's when I remember the store cupboard. The door is on the same wall as the whiteboard and the desk, and at some point over the years, the old-style board has been replaced with a bigger electronic whiteboard, so the desk has been nudged further along the wall and half of it now blocks the cupboard door, meaning I need to drag the desk out if I want to access it.

I remember Gemma's warning about how protective Cate is of her cupboard and wonder what she'd say if I looked inside.

'Keep sticking your nose in places and one day it's going to get chopped off.' Donna's voice again. Maybe she's right, but still I find myself nudging the desk away from the wall.

As soon as there's enough space, I open the door and step inside, running my hand across the wall until I find a light switch. A moment later, a single bulb flickers into life, and I find myself in a small space, barely big enough for two people.

There are shelves on every wall, each filled with neatly stacked items. More boxes of pens, more binders. Unused exercise books and stacks of card and coloured paper, organised in rainbow order, with red at the top and blue at the bottom.

On the floor is a box marked 'Archie's toys'. I crouch down and draw the box towards me. It's filled with metal cars, Lego pieces, wooden puzzles and a clear bouncy ball with a plastic dinosaur inside. I imagine Archie kneeling in the reading corner, playing with his toys after the other children had left, waiting for Cate to finish up for the day.

I've seen the photos of Archie standing beside Cate, but my curiosity surrounding their disappearance has been focused on Cate until now. A dull ache spreads across my chest. Archie's just a little boy.

I stand up and stare again at the shelves. There's nothing here, and I feel stupid for thinking I could find something. I'm stepping back, already reaching for the light switch, when something catches my eye. A piece of brown paper among the stack of red card. I've been among Cate's organisation style for long enough to know that, whatever it is, it shouldn't be there, and as I move closer, I see it's the corner of an envelope that's been pushed between the coloured paper.

My breath catches as I pull out the contents. Photos. Grainy from being printed on cheap paper. And yet it's obvious what I'm looking at. The first one is the top of a woman's arm. The photo has been zoomed in, and the focus of the picture is a large, purple bruise. It's circular with blotches and paler at the edges. I imagine knuckles, a fist, slamming into the skin.

The next photo is of another bruise. This one faded to an ugly yellow.

Photo number three is the worst of all of them. It's the side of a body. I can see the ribs pushing at the skin. It's not one bruise this time; it's five. Five small and perfectly round dark purple, almost black, bruises. There's a cruelty to it. This was done to cause pain, to hurt, to humiliate.

Cold rushes over me. The walls close in. I can still hear the shouts of the children rushing out to play, the ticking of the classroom clock with its easy-to-read numbers and big second hand, but it feels muffled, distant, as though I'm underwater. No one deserves this.

And then there's another noise. This one closer. A movement behind me. I spin around and it's as though I've summoned him, because standing in the doorway, blocking my path out of the cupboard, is Oliver.

My gaze moves from him to the sheets of paper in my hand, and I fumble to push them back inside the envelope. They're turned towards me, and I don't think he can see them, but his eyes narrow as he watches me.

'H-Hi,' I say as the final piece slips inside. I want to hug the envelope to my body, keep it safe. I have to show this to the police. Because... if Oliver is the kind of man who can do this to a woman, then maybe he's also the type of man who can kill.

The shock of seeing the photos is still buzzing through me, but I swallow it back. I can't let Oliver get hold of them.

'What are you doing in here?' Oliver shifts position, resting a hand casually against the door frame. Up close, I can see the strain around his eyes, the dull sheen of sweat on his face.

What did you do, Oliver?

'I was just... er... looking for some more erasers.'

'Karen keeps those in the office,' he says. 'So you're settling in OK? Here, and in the village? The pub isn't too noisy, I hope.'

'It's all fine.' I smile and try not to flinch at the mention of where I'm staying. It's not a secret, and I'm sure Paul is the type to talk, but after what happened last night, Oliver's question feels loaded.

He knows where to find me. More than that, he's *telling* me he knows where to find me. My heart starts to pound in my chest. The threat, Oliver's presence, the menacing look I see in his eyes... Is he behind it? Is it because I went to his office last night? He must've known I could have just given the timesheet to Karen.

'What have you got there?' he asks, nodding to the envelope still gripped in my hands.

'Just some extension work to photocopy for a few of the children. I thought it was time I learned how to use the photocopier.'

'Here.' He holds out his hand as though to take the envelope, and I spot the white bandage again. 'I can show you now.'

Instinctively, I move away, my back knocking against a shelf. 'I can't ask you to do that. You're far too busy. I'll ask Karen to show me.' I tighten my grip on the envelope, keeping it close to my side.

A beat passes between us. Neither of us speak. I wait for him to move back, to let me pass, but he doesn't. There's something charged in the air – a tension, a fear. My thoughts zip between last night's threat and the photos in my hand, and then Oliver blocking my path. Heat burns in my face. The feeling from his office returns, and even though I'm sure it's not possible, I can't stop myself wondering if he knows all of my secrets.

I tell myself it's nothing. *Don't overreact.*

'Did you need—?' I start to say as Oliver speaks too.

'It's weird,' he says, tapping a finger to the side of his head as my voice trails off. 'I really feel like I know you, Lexi. Are you sure we haven't met before?'

'I can't think where we would've done,' I reply, trying to ignore the walloping thud of my racing heart.

'Maybe...' he says, almost muttering to himself. He moves further into the cupboard, so close I catch the stale smell of his breath. 'Maybe you just remind me of someone.'

'It's probably that,' I say, keeping my voice light.

'I don't know who though,' he continues. 'It's on the tip of my tongue.' He reaches out, and before I know what's happening, his fingers touch one of my curls.

I want to jerk away, to gut punch him and leave him writhing on the floor, but I'm still frozen. This is not nothing.

'What's your natural colour?' His eyes find mine, staring, probing. The question feels sexual, as though he's imagining me naked.

'Blonde,' I say, and despite the frenzy of fear and my frozen limbs, I keep my head up and stare back.

He huffs a sort of laugh. 'Of course it is.'

I don't know what he means by that, but I don't ask.

'Did you want something?' I ask. 'Otherwise, I really should get on. The bell will be going in a few minutes.'

The question seems to startle Oliver. He steps back, moving out of the cupboard. I follow him and close the door, forcing myself to stay calm. To pretend all is well while inside a voice is screaming at me. *What was that?*

The tension between us lingers as we move into the classroom. As I shut the cupboard, I wonder if he senses it too.

'I've come to tell you that the detectives would like to talk to you,' Oliver says, his tone light. For a moment it feels like the last few minutes didn't happen. 'I told them you only arrived on Tuesday, but they seem to think you might be able to help them with their enquiries.'

He waits for me to explain, but I don't. 'How odd,' I say instead. 'I'd better go then.'

I pick up my bag and walk out of the classroom. In the hall, the kitchen ladies are clearing up the tables and sweeping up escaped peas and stepped-on chips from the floor. Their presence does little to calm my nerves. I force myself not to look back at Oliver, following one step behind me.

From the corner of my eye, I see Gemma standing by the

sinks in the art area. She watches me for a moment, and I smile and lift my hand in a half wave, but she's already turned away.

'Lexi?' His voice is close, and I spin around, jumping as his hand touches my arm.

'The photocopies?' He holds out his hand to take them.

'Oh... I've just remembered – I've got some other sheets I can use. But thanks.'

I turn away and force myself to walk normally. Suddenly the fear of finding the threat on my doorstep is back, but it's not for me this time; it's for Cate and Archie.

What did you do, Oliver?

EIGHTEEN

JEANIE

Jeanie sips from the chilled bottle of Lucozade she keeps in the fridge at the office and looks at the clock for the tenth time that hour – 1 p.m.

Only an hour to go before she can leave. She hopes the bus won't be late. She needs to be home. Her mind jumps as always to the little box room. Anything could happen while she's out. Images press down on her. Fires and burglars, a fallen tree, or even a window cleaner at the wrong address. The possibilities leave her giddy, sick. She takes another sip from the orange bottle to ease her nerves.

All morning her phone has buzzed on the desk beside her mouse. Village gossip. The police have been knocking on doors again, retracing Cate's walk from the school to her house. She wonders if they've knocked on her door again, with a note made to come back, or if she's been forgotten.

The search of the vales is on her mind. Every time she checks the Facebook event page, it seems another dozen people have signed up. She's sure they wouldn't be as keen to volunteer if they knew what was out there waiting to be found. She's going of course. Not to search. That would be stupid. She knows exactly what's out there and where it is, but maybe there will be a discussion, a chance for her to suggest a different route. It seems so futile, but she must try. There's so much riding on this. She doesn't want to spend the rest of her life in prison. And for what? A split-second decision?

A door bangs somewhere nearby. Jeanie puts down her phone and turns back to the screen. It's on days like this, when each minute drags longer than the last, that she tries to remember what it was she wanted to do with her life. Always, she draws a blank. Oh she remembers the childish wants. A ballet dancer and then a singer. And at one point when she'd been given a doctor's kit for Christmas, she'd spent hours pretending to perform surgeries on her teddies. Then her father had told her she was too stupid to be a doctor, and she'd let that dream die too.

At sixteen, she'd messed up her school exams – her father's fault again – and fallen into an administrative role in the bowels of the local hospital. She'd had half a mind to re-sit the exams and look at a nursing course, but she never had.

She's bounced around departments and companies, even had a go at management for a while, but everything changed again in her late twenties – one of her snap decisions pushing her life in a different direction. And now she's here, in a council building, working in the registry office. She likes to think of it as the admin of life. The births, the deaths, the marriages.

It's only part-time. Nine until two, three days a week. The benefit of having no dependants, no life to speak of, is that her outgoings are small. The work is boring, but it serves a purpose. Jeanie isn't unhappy. And all things considered, she feels that is quite enough.

An email arrives. A nonsense energy-efficiency survey from the higher-ups, reminding her to turn off her monitor before she leaves, as though that act alone can halt the melting of the ice caps.

She sighs and takes another sip from the Lucozade bottle, pressing down the edges of the white sticker with her name written across it in black marker pen. She'd spread the word early on that the Lucozade is medicinal and not to be touched. And so far, no one has asked questions. She isn't sure why she does it. She could wait until she's home. The risk is a little thrilling perhaps. The knowing that, at any time, someone could unscrew the lid and take a sip, and instead of a mouthful of fizzing sugary energy drink, they'll taste the cold, crisp tang of Sauvignon Blanc.

It would take all of five minutes for Human Resources to be called and her desk to be cleared. Then where would they be? Without this job, and the access it grants her to databases and personal details, what use is she? Jeanie downs the last of the bottle and decides it's not the thrill of being caught but the courage it gives her to do what she does.

She fills in the survey, then when she's sure her boss is out at lunch, tucking into his mozzarella-and-tomato panini, when there's no one to see her, she slips into his office and closes the door behind her.

NINETEEN

LEXI

I knock twice and step into the staffroom without waiting for a reply. My pulse is still thrumming in my ears from my encounter with Oliver. I'd like a moment to collect my thoughts and process what I've learned, but I can't be in the hall with him for a second more. I can't risk him trying to take the photos again. It could be the only proof Cate has of what kind of man he is.

There are two detectives sitting at the table in the corner by the window. It's a man and a woman sat in the chairs that Mrs Kelp and Robyn – Gemma's TA – like to sit in, drinking their tea and talking quietly among themselves. I'm sure Mrs K, who never likes to be referred to by her first name – Elizabeth – complains about me. She's mentioned more than once that I allow the children too much group time; too much 'uproar' she calls it.

'Hello,' the woman says first, and in that one word I hear the frustration of someone who has a dozen other places to be; a hundred things to do.

'Hi,' I reply. 'I'm Lexi Mills, the substitute teacher.'

'I'm Detective Sergeant Jen Pope, and this is my colleague, Detective Constable Rob Hacker. Have a seat please.'

I like Pope immediately. There's no faff about her. She has the steely gaze of a woman who misses nothing. Hacker, on the other hand, is fidgeting in his seat and looks like he'd rather be stepping in to break up fights and arresting bad guys than interviewing teaching staff.

'I'm sorry it's taken us until now to talk to you, Miss Mills. We got the message about a note put under your door,' Pope says. 'And you think it has something to do with Cate and Archie's disappearance?'

I realise then why it's taken them so long to talk to me. The message I left about the threat has been misunderstood and watered down before reaching Pope and Hacker. I nod, digging out the envelope in its zip-lock food bag and sliding it across the table. My hands shake a little. I don't know if it's for the threat itself or because I'm here, speaking to the detectives.

Hacker picks it up, his eyebrows lifting as he reads the words.

'And this was left for you yesterday?' Pope asks with an inquisitive tone.

I nod. 'It was on my doormat at six p.m.' I carry on talking, telling them about The Old Stable and finding the note. I leave nothing out except the ringing of my phone; that Brighton area code. I bite the inside of my lip and force thoughts of my past away. I can't let them see it on my face. I want to help Cate and Archie, truly I do, and I want to find the person who sent this threat, but I have to protect myself too.

'And have you been asking a lot of questions?' Pope asks when I finish.

I lift my hands in a 'who knows?' kind of gesture. 'Some, I guess. But it's all anyone is talking about in the village.'

'But as far as we know, you're the only one who's been

singled out and received a threat. Why do you think that is?' Pope asks.

'I don't know, but doesn't it show that someone has hurt Cate and Archie? What theories are you working on? Have you had any leads?' I close my mouth, trapping in the next question before it can be asked. Hacker is already raising his eyebrows, and Pope has narrowed her eyes. *Don't draw attention.*

For a split second I'm pulled back to another room, another detective. *'Tell me about your sister?'*

'We are continuing our investigation and following all leads,' Pope says, her words slow, considered, giving nothing away.

There's a pause where I hope she'll say more but doesn't. The silence drags on, and I don't try to fill it.

Hacker clears his throat. 'Do you know Cate? Have you met her before?'

I shake my head. 'I only arrived in Leedham on Tuesday morning after receiving a call from a substitute teaching agency the day before.'

Another pause. Pope's eyes are on me. My face floods with heat. The direction of the questions has jumped from the threat and Cate to me. Any moment now they'll ask about my background.

'There's something else you should see,' I say before we're lost down a rabbit hole of questions I'll stumble and trip over. 'I found it in Cate's stationery cupboard a few minutes ago. I think you'll want to see it.'

I slide the envelope across the desk. Neither of them reach to take it.

'What's inside?' Pope asks me before looking at Hacker. A silent conversation seems to pass between them. Without a word, he pulls out a pair of blue plastic gloves from the inside pocket of his jacket and puts them on.

'Photos,' I say. 'They're of... of bruises. I found them hidden between some pieces of card in the store cupboard in Cate's classroom. She's the only one who goes in there apparently. It's blocked by the desk, so it's not easy to access.'

With the gloves on, Hacker pulls out the sheets of paper, and I watch their thoughts shifting from one scenario to another. An unknown suspect to a known one, just as I did.

'Thank you, Miss Mills,' Pope says. 'Please do not enter or allow anyone else to enter the cupboard you've mentioned. We'll need to arrange for it to be thoroughly searched.'

Another look to Hacker, another silent conversation. I wonder if she's asking him how the photos were missed in their first search on Monday.

'If you could jot your number down here,' she continues a moment later, sliding the open page of a small black notebook towards me, 'then we can be in touch if we have any more questions.'

I'm halfway through writing down my number when the buzz of a phone sounds from somewhere. Hacker reaches into his pocket, looks at the screen and leaves the room.

'What about the threat? Am I... am I in danger?' I ask, when it's just me and Pope, the words coming stilted and then rushed, shoved out at the last minute by the dread still circling. I don't want to go back to the apartment after school. I don't want to be alone there again, but what choice do I have? Maybe I'll ask Paul about the room in the pub he offered me on Tuesday.

'We are taking this seriously,' she says. 'And I suggest you do too. Is there anywhere else you could stay? Or a family member who could come to be with you?'

I flinch at the word family before masking it with another shake of my head. If she notices, Pope doesn't ask.

'We'll ask a patrol car to keep an eye out on their route, and if you have any concerns, please call me or dial nine-nine-nine.' She pushes a business card towards me as Hacker steps back into the room.

He doesn't speak, but something passes between them. The air changes. There's a sudden urgency. For a moment, I worry the phone call was about me, but Pope is already on her feet and moving towards him.

'Thank you, Miss Mills,' she says. 'We'll be in touch if we have any further questions.'

Hacker leans in and whispers something in Pope's ear. I watch her expression change. Her eyes widen. Something in her face lights up. Have they found them?

They move, Hacker first, then Pope, and I want to ask them what's going on, but I know they won't tell me.

'The search,' I blurt out.

They turn back, impatient now. 'What search?' Hacker asks.

'The search of Leedham Vale tomorrow,' I reply. 'Oliver has organised it.' I'm surprised they don't know; there are posters all over the village. 'Should I go?'

'I would suggest staying away from anything related to the investigation,' Hacker says, and with that they're gone.

The bell rings for the end of lunch just as I'm making my way back to the classroom. I have sixty seconds before twenty-four children tumble in. I'm glad it's PE this afternoon and they can charge around the field some more, giving me time to think.

Something has shifted in my mind in the last hour. I might not know what happened to Cate and Archie, but I'm certain I know who's responsible.

Oliver.

But if he is behind the disappearance of his family, then why organise a search of Leedham Vale? The detectives have warned me to leave everything to them, but there's no way I can stay away now.

SATURDAY: EIGHT DAYS MISSING

TWENTY
JEANIE

A jittery, nervous energy races through Jeanie's body as she watches three sets of couples hurry past her house, heading to the cut-through and the park and no doubt the meeting point for the search. It's the kind of energy that snatches sleep and calm and rational thought out from under her and leaves her on edge; breathless.

It's really happening – the search for Cate and Archie. It never entered her mind, not for a single second, that they'd search like this. Organised. En masse. She wonders how long it will take them to find her hiding place. Which group will stumble upon it, dining out on the story for the rest of their small and inconsequential lives. She pictures the parish council chair, Andrea Rowley, hand worrying at the diamond necklace she always wears.

'Did you hear... Yes, it was me... I saw something and screamed... It was so awful.'

Jeanie checks the time again. It's only nine thirty, but there has been a steady flow of people walking past her window for the last hour; voices loud, pace quick, reminding Jeanie in a perverse way of the village bonfire night. That same sense of anticipation and festivity in the air. She half expects to catch the smell of hot dogs and candyfloss. It's as though these people have forgotten the purpose of today – the search for a missing woman and an eight-year-old boy.

So very young.

And such a good boy.

Jeanie remembers his seventh birthday. They bought him a bike. Bright red, with black handlebars and gears. He was allowed to ride from his house on the corner, down one side of the road, past the cut-through to the park and back up the other side of the road. He couldn't go into the park alone, but he was allowed to cross the road by himself and do it all over again.

They watched him at first. Oliver or Cate, standing by the gate, one eye on Archie, one on their phone. The next week they found something to do in the garden – weeding, cleaning the car or that awful camper. But that soon stopped too, and Archie would be all alone on the road. Anything could've happened to him. Anyone could've come along and snatched him. Only Jeanie watched over him.

He'd speed along the pavement for hours at a time. Lips moving, chatting to himself and leaving her to wonder what imaginary world he was in – a fighter pilot, a cowboy, a racing car driver? She could never settle on one.

It was inevitable something would happen. And thank goodness Jeanie was at the window when it did. He was going too fast, sticking to the very edge of the pavement where it sloped towards the kerb. Until his front wheel skidded off the pavement and threw him into the road right outside her house. The poor lamb.

She expected tears when she rushed out to help him. But he didn't cry. She remembers that. As though, even so young, a bloody, grazed knee wasn't something to get upset over. She got him up and out of the road, and he sat on the grass in her front garden with his leg stretched out, more worried about what his dad would say about the scratch on his bike than anything else. She didn't like that.

She got him a cup of squash and a biscuit and a cold flannel to press to his knee.

'Does it hurt?' she asked.

'A bit.' He gritted his teeth, and she felt sure it was more than a bit.

After that, Jeanie would find herself pottering in the front garden when Archie was out on his bike. He'd always stop to say hello, and they'd chat about things. Jeanie learned a lot about the Walker family from those talks. Like how Archie had trouble sleeping at night when his parents were arguing. And how he came out to ride his bike when they were cross with each other because he didn't like it. She'd coaxed it out of him slowly, bit by bit, building a worrying picture of a home life Archie didn't deserve.

Another group pass her window. Four women she recognises from the various village events over the years. One of them has a teenager who works in the supermarket and steals chocolate bars and cans of lager when he thinks no one is watching.

She must get out there too. The need to move is knotting her insides, tugging, pulling. She'd planned to wait until closer to 10 a.m. before leaving the house, but she finds she can't stand it any longer.

The nerves return with a whoosh, like dipping too fast on the rollercoaster at the end of Clacton Pier where her mother had taken her once. Just once. But she'll never forget the feeling, or the sadness that came later when her father had found out where they'd been and what her mother had spent some of the housekeeping money on.

The police were back again yesterday. Parked near Oliver's house and the footpath on the other side of the road that leads out to the vales. She only saw them when she was coming home from work, and it annoys her that she doesn't know how long they were on the street for or what they were doing. She won't miss out again.

She steps away from the window and walks into the hall. She finds her walking boots in the cupboard and thinks about taking a jacket, but the sky is clear, and her fleece will be more than enough.

Just as she opens her front door, she spots Oliver striding down the road. He's wearing indigo-blue jeans and a pale-blue shirt. There's a whistle around his neck and a yellow high-vis jacket in his hand. He's walking with a stoop to his shoulders that Jeanie has never seen before. He looks as though he's carrying the weight of the world.

A flash of red-hot anger pulses through her body. Her hand tightens on the door handle, and she fights the urge to slam it shut.

How dare he?

She pulls back, her breathing fast. She counts to ten and then she leaves, closing the door softly and falling into step five metres behind him.

He must sense her presence because he throws a glance over his shoulder. Their eyes meet, but there's no recognition in his. She's invisible to him. He has no idea that she is his neighbour or how much she knows about his life, his family and lovely little Archie, who deserves a mother and a father who care more about him than themselves.

The anger returns. Hot and bitter.

Her pace quickens until she's three and then two paces behind him. She wants to call out, to ask if the police know yet that, on the Friday Cate and Archie disappeared, Oliver took his campervan out in the evening.

But Jeanie isn't one to show her hand. To him or to the police. Hell will freeze over before she ever speaks to them. Besides, if she says a word, she'll no longer be invisible. And that would be a problem.

TWENTY-ONE

LEXI

Leedham high street is chaos. Haphazard parking and cars driving slowly on both sides of the road, waiting to pounce on a space. There's a sign for a car park fifty metres down the road, but the cars around me seem determined to snatch a coveted space on the high street. I wonder, as I pass a Land Rover blocking a driveway, engine idling, how much of the chaos is because so many have turned out for the search, and how much is a normal sunny weekend in a tourist village.

Most of the shops I pass are closed. Oliver's posters are in the windows, and there's a sign beneath them that reads:

Closed until noon for Cate and Archie search.

I reach the end of the high street and turn right at the war memorial into a large park. There's a line of oak trees down the middle and cherry blossom trees in delicate pink bloom around the edges. Immediately on my left is a playground with a zip line and a curly-whirly slide I remember Benjamin Arnolds telling me about last week.

Despite the gathering crowd, the playground is empty.

There are no children playing today, and it's a stark reminder of why we're all here. A cool breeze rustles through the trees, and I'm glad I threw on a light jacket over my jeans and T-shirt.

I know DS Pope told me not to come, and I know she's right. I'd found Paul behind the bar last night and asked about the room above the pub, but it was fully booked. *'Next week, after the weekend might be better,'* he'd said with an apologetic smile and the offer of a free dinner.

It was another night of broken sleep, thinking I heard footsteps outside my apartment, lying awake with my heart pounding in my chest, breathing too fast. And yet, even though I knew I should, I couldn't stay away. I had to see the search for myself, and after the moment in the cupboard yesterday, I had to see Oliver's reaction; I had to help look for Cate and Archie too.

I weave through the groups, scanning the faces for Oliver or the detectives. I've been checking the news sites hourly, but there's been no update revealing why they rushed from the school yesterday.

There's a mobile coffee van parked in the middle of the playing field and a long queue of men and women waiting for their morning caffeine fix. And moving along the line is a cameraman and reporter with a microphone.

I stop for a moment and pretend to tie my shoelace so I can listen.

'I actually went to school with Cate,' a woman is saying. 'And she taught all three of my children, so of course I was going to come out today and help look for her and Archie... What do I think happened to them? I... I think they went for a walk after school and got in some kind of trouble. I hope they're out there. I hope we can find them today.'

I hope so too, and yet my mind is still fixed on the photos I saw yesterday and the moment in the cupboard with Oliver. The cold darkness in his eyes as he touched my hair. I shiver at the memory and weave among the waiting people, picking up snatches of conversation. Whispers of 'I heard...' and 'Did you know...?' and more and more memories shared about Cate. She really does seem perfect.

'Cate was the first person to come over with a casserole when we had that leak and our kitchen flooded.'

'I heard her family are pretty wealthy and it was Cate behind the anonymous donation to the village hall's roof fund.'

'It's so tragic but they've got to be dead, right? It's been a week.'

'Poor Oliver.'

'A police car has been parked outside his house a lot.'

'You think he...'

I step away. There's nothing new to learn from this gossip, and the more I hear, the more it reminds me of the school playground at Haventhorpe Primary last year, when it was me the parents were talking about.

The school wasn't as fancy as Leedham Primary. There were no designer clothes or nannies in the playground, but it was the same hushed tones, incredulous and yet desperate to dissect every detail.

As I make my way deeper into the crowd, I spot a couple of familiar faces from the playground drop-off, and Paul from the pub. He's in a group wearing white T-shirts with Cate and Archie's faces on them. Gemma is with them, standing beside another woman her age.

I take another step and that's when I feel a set of eyes on me. An innate prickling of hairs on the back of my neck. Slowly, casually, my gaze moves. At first, I see nothing. But then there's something. A man by the oak trees. Him again. The same man I've seen around the village this week.

Our eyes meet, and even though we're standing ten metres apart, and there are hundreds of people around us, a bolt of something shoots through me. Apprehension? Fear even. Is it more than a coincidence that I've seen him so often?

The note under my door flashes in my thoughts, knotting my insides. It was Oliver. I'm sure of it. And yet this man scares me. I've been thinking of what the threat means for Cate and Archie, but maybe I should've been more focused on what it means for me.

Stop asking about the missing teacher... you'll be next.

He starts to move, his eyes still fixed on mine, and I think he's coming for me. I step back on weak legs, but then he turns, changing direction, and despite his height and his build and the fear still coursing in my veins, he disappears.

I spin around, trying to catch him, but he's gone, and as my heart rate starts to slow, I almost laugh at myself. I'm being ridiculous, overthinking a split-second look from a stranger. It's nothing compared to Oliver's behaviour in the cupboard yesterday. If anyone is responsible for the note, it's him. If anyone knows where Cate and Archie are, it's him. He is the only one to fear.

The church bell strikes – ten solemn dongs I'm sure we all count in our heads. A silence ripples over the park. Heads turn towards the treeline. Someone pushes by me, and I turn to see it's Oliver, hurrying through the crowd towards a woman in a yellow vest. She's a petite blonde in her fifties with a clipboard clutched in her hands, and she has the look of someone in complete control.

Oliver, on the other hand, is fiddling with his hair, pushing it away from his face then moving it back again. The woman says something to him as he reaches her, and he smiles – a pitiful smile that I immediately hate.

People are bunching together around me, pushing closer. An elbow knocks into my side, and I fight the urge to shove them back. Oliver steps onto a bench, looking towards the groups of waiting volunteers.

'Thank you all for coming.' He pauses as though trying to keep his emotions in check. He's good. I'll give him that. And before I know what's happening, there's clapping. Actual clapping for this man.

I turn to look at the crowd. Who are these people?

TWENTY-TWO

OLIVER

So many people. All of them looking to him, at him. He didn't think... He didn't expect... His thoughts land half formed. This was the plan, he reminds himself. This is what he wanted – the entire community supporting him. They believe he's innocent.

The church bells strike eight, nine and ten. The crowd seems to move closer, bringing with them a wave of energy that pushes into him. He feels more awake, more alive, than he has in days. With their support, he can almost believe he's innocent too. Almost.

Karen is to one side of him, a hand resting on his arm. Andrea Rowley is on the other. She leans in, and the sharp edge of her clipboard digs into his bicep. 'Will you say something?'

He nods, wishing his legs weren't shaking as he spots the bench behind them and steps onto it. He's good at public speaking; clear, funny. He's always asked to compère at local events – fundraisers and firework night. A month ago, a few weeks ago even, he would've relished this moment; people hanging on his every word.

But the emotion of the day is threatening to take over. His

gaze moves across the waiting crowd, but he no longer sees friends – his community. Just Archie. His little boy is in every face staring back at him.

Tears burn at the back of his eyes. He didn't mean to hurt them. He never wanted it to be this way.

Andrea clears her throat and looks up at him with raised eyebrows. He must get a hold of himself. Everyone is waiting.

'Thank you all for coming.' He pauses and a spattering of applause breaks out, stopping before it really gets going. He forces himself to look up again. One pair of eyes catches his gaze, lighting a fire inside him.

Lexi.

That feeling grabs him again. Why is it that every time their eyes meet, anger seems to burn in the pit of his stomach?

He drags his gaze away and tries to focus on the words he practised in the mirror this morning. Present tense, he reminds himself.

'Most of you know Cate and Archie. Cate is a beautiful person, inside and out. She's the first one to volunteer to man a stall at events, the first one on the dance floor in the evening,' he adds, causing a ripple of laughter among some of the groups. 'She would do anything for anyone, and the number of people here for her now is testament to that.' He pauses, letting his words sink in. There's more he could say about Cate. A side no one else sees, but he keeps it in along with so many other truths.

'And Archie' – his voice cracks for real this time – 'he is...' He takes a shuddering breath and fights the wave of nausea pushing up at the back of his throat. 'I just want him back.'

Andrea stands up beside him on the bench, patting his arm. 'If they're out in the vales, we'll find them. Please, everyone, there are volunteers in yellow vests walking around the park right now. Please go and see them. You'll be given a search area, a whistle and an emergency number to call, should you find anything. Thank you.'

They step down from the bench, and in the silence that follows, another noise fills the park – the loud whine of a police siren. Every head turns as a police car drives into the car park. It's followed by a silver Ford Mondeo that makes Oliver's jaw tighten. Now what?

He watches Pope walk quickly to the boot of the car and pull out a megaphone. Her voice when it comes is loud and echoing. 'Good morning, everyone. I'm DS Jen Pope from Essex police, and I'm the lead detective on the disappearance of Cate and Archie Walker.'

Oliver holds his breath, hoping it isn't a bad thing they're here. Maybe they've come to help.

'I want to thank you all for coming, but I'm asking you all to please return to your homes or go about your days as normal. There will be no search of Leedham Vale today. Thank you.'

Oliver's insides roil – slippery eels. He thinks he might be sick. Why are they doing this? He reaches out a steadying hand, expecting Andrea to support him, but like the restless crowd, her attention is on the police.

'Why not?' a voice yells from somewhere nearby. He recognises it as belonging to one of the dads from the school.

'New evidence has been found in the investigation. I'm unable to go into any details on what that evidence is at this time, but we're asking you all to please go home now.'

The word 'evidence' is a fire alarm in his head – loud and piercing. He tries to swallow, but his mouth is suddenly too dry. What have they found? What do they know?

More questions fire back.

'What new evidence?'

'Where are they then?'

'Have you got any suspects?'

The last question sends a flood of sickening panic sloshing through his veins. Is it just his imagination or have people turned to look at him? *Breathe*, he wills himself. *Don't show the fear*. Oliver rearranges his expression and forces his head up. They're just expecting him to say something, that's all.

He musters an outrage he doesn't feel. 'It's been a week, DS Pope,' he shouts, and all the other voices stop. 'What are you doing to find my wife and child?'

The silence that follows is stony. Tension crackles – an electrical bolt that shoots across the space between his body and Pope's. He catches the narrowing of her eyes as she finds his face in the crowd.

'This is not a press conference,' she replies, her words clipped. 'We are not here to answer questions. Everyone, go home please. And, Mr Walker, we'd like to see you over here by our car. Thank you.'

The atmosphere deflates like one of Archie's footballs left in the garden over winter – saggy and useless. No more questions come. Around him, people move away, some wandering towards the high street, but many stay close, checking phones and talking among themselves, pretending they're not waiting to see what happens between him and the detectives.

Oliver keeps the same pitiful 'look how sad I am; look how I'm trying to cope' half smile, half grimace on his face as he walks towards DS Pope. He looks around for a friendly face, for Karen or Andrea, but they've disappeared.

His heart beats with an uncontrollable speed that causes the cut on his hand to ache. It still isn't healing. He doesn't believe in karma or omens or anything like that, but when he peels back the bandage of his hand each night and sees a red, festering wound, his first thought is always his guilt – an incurable infection burning in the wound.

There's a flash of red from the corner of his eye. He turns his head a fraction, his gaze landing on Lexi again – that bright-red hair that seems to all at once warn him away and draw him in.

He almost calls out to her, barely managing to pin the words in his mouth. Then she's gone, and his feet are still moving forward, his head a jumble of Lexi and Cate and Archie, and this search and these people and all the terrible things he's done.

'DS Pope, DC Hacker, how can I help you?' His voice is too loud, his tone too jovial, but it's out before he can stop it. And although he's sure no one moves, it feels as though the people behind him close in, forming an inescapable wall. There's nowhere to go but forward. Everyone is here. The entire village. He organised this search for appearances. To make it look like he was doing something – a desperate man. But now it's all backfiring. He can feel the shift in energy. Support to suspicion. What the hell have the police found?

'Mr Walker,' Hacker says. 'We have a warrant to search your home, garden and outbuildings in connection with the disappearance of Cate Walker and Archie Walker. We'd like it if you would accompany us now to your home where officers will begin the search.'

'A warrant?' His voice is a whisper, and even though he tells himself that it's OK, that they'll find nothing, fear clenches his gut, and he's sure the colour drains from his face.

The world folds in on itself. DC Hacker hasn't used the megaphone; he hasn't even shouted his request, but he may as well have done. There are enough people close by to hear – and to witness him climbing into the back of the car. It will be on the news too, he realises, as a reporter and cameraman push forward. The reporter is asking something, microphone thrust out in front of him, but Oliver doesn't hear the words.

The hope and energy from minutes ago feels otherworldly to this new reality. In the space of a few minutes, his reputation, his whole life and maybe even his freedom are no longer certainties.

Hacker opens the passenger door of the Mondeo, and as he motions for Oliver to get in, Oliver wonders whether now, today, might be the time to confess.

TWENTY-THREE

LEXI

The crowds disperse as soon as the police leave, Oliver with them. I imagine people returning to their Saturday lives – to chores and children and socialising.

I move with the sea of feet heading in the direction of the high street. The day unfolds before me. Empty. Alone. Once upon a time, on days like today, I would've called a friend, made plans. But now my own company is the only type I crave. I'm too altered by what happened to Donna last year to spend time with those I once held dear. The gap between us is a vast uncrossable canyon, and I don't normally mind, but every muscle in my body feels tense, knotted. I can't relax, and I don't want to be alone. I'm scared, and I hate it.

I need to break out of my spiralling thoughts, and I will. I force myself to make a plan and decide I'll spend the day exploring the village, the streets, the houses, the vales. I'll pull on my boxing gloves and spend an hour pounding the bag, and maybe I'll find a corner of a café and read my book while I people-watch.

I might be alone, but I'm not lonely. I've never been the type. An outsider, Donna called me in her kinder moments.

One of a hundred names. Sometimes, when she was sixteen and I was nine, I'd watch her for hours as she sat at the dressing table in our bedroom, playing with her hair or applying make-up she was too beautiful to need, and she'd scream at me to go away.

'You're a freak.'
'You're a weirdo.'
'Stop watching me.'
'Get a life.'

Then just as quickly she'd flip again, beckoning me over and brushing my cheeks with blush. On the rare evenings she wasn't out, we'd watch *Gilmore Girls* or *Buffy*, and she would put her arm around me and tell me how lucky I was not to crave the attention she did. The attention she always got.

It's hard to remember the times she was nice among all the times she wasn't. I can see now that the age gap was all wrong. Seven years between us. She was a blossoming teen and I was the annoying child our parents made her take with her to places or babysit when she wanted to be out.

Things only got worse as we grew older and I ventured into adulthood. Any kind of sisterly love Donna might once have felt disappeared. It didn't matter what I did, or how hard I tried, she hated me.

Karen appears at my side, a gentle hand on my arm. 'It's all just such a mess, isn't it?' She waves a hand around us, drawing my thoughts back to the present. 'Why call off the search? If for nothing else, it made our little community feel like we were doing something. Even if they're not out there, they could've let us look.'

'Maybe the police don't think they went missing on the walk home from school anymore.'

She thinks about that for a moment. 'That wouldn't surprise me. They're only five minutes from the school.'

'Really?' I ask, curious to know where Oliver lives.

'Yes. They live on Richmond Avenue. Such a lovely house too. Honestly, they were the perfect family. Oh dear, I make it sound like they aren't anymore. But it's hard not to lose hope. You're sweet to have come though,' Karen continues.

'I wanted to help,' I say, but I'm distracted by what Karen has told me. Already I'm changing my plans, adding in a walk to Richmond Avenue. I want to know where Oliver lives. I want to retrace Cate's walk home and see their house.

She gives a dejected sigh. 'We all do. Of course for Archie and Cate, but for Oliver too. Between you and me, he's barely keeping it together. I've no idea what will happen at school next week. I'm covering whatever workload I can for him, but things are still getting missed.'

'He's lucky to have you,' I say.

She nods at this, pleased I've said it. 'But I'm just the secretary. There's only so much I can do. You know, he forgot to sign the forms for the first aid training last week. We've missed out on the slots we needed, and if I can't find someone to come in next week to do a first aid refresher, then we're all going to be out of date on our training. Can you imagine what Ofsted would say to that? The parents would be in uproar if we lose our "Outstanding" rating. Not to mention, Gemma and Robyn need training on injecting insulin. We all need to know how to do it in case Sebastian needs it, but they missed out on the last training because it clashed with a class trip.

'But I can't bring it up with Oliver. One day last week, he was getting milk out of the fridge and took out Sebastian's insulin pouch instead. He just left it on the side and wandered off. It's lucky I was there to put it back.'

We slow down as we near the playground – boxed in and jostled by too many people going the same way. Karen is drawn into a conversation with a man in a high-vis vest a step ahead of us. There's a bottleneck as the path to the high street narrows, and no one seems in any kind of hurry to get away. Someone's shoe scuffs my heel and I throw a glance over my shoulder, a 'don't worry about it' smile to the apology they give.

It's as I'm turning that I catch the rustle of something in the pocket of my jacket. I reach for it without thinking, expecting a forgotten receipt, but the paper is too sturdy. I pull it out and straight away the scrawled words leap from the card, grabbing at me – the thickest of brambles that won't let go.

STAY AWAY FROM THE POLICE OR YOU'LL DIE JUST LIKE THEY DID.

The air that hits my lungs feels stifled, not enough. This note wasn't in my pocket when I left the house. I'm sure of it.

I'm suddenly aware of the noise and bustle, voices coming from every direction. There are people all around, and yet someone still got to me, stood close enough to slip this threat into my pocket as easily as the note beneath my door.

When did it happen?

Are they still near me?

My gaze darts left and right. No one is looking my way. But when I throw a glance behind me, I see the man again. He's four or so people behind but a head taller than everyone else and easy to spot. Up close, I notice his clothes – dark-blue overalls over a white shirt and black tie. It's an odd outfit, as though he's part-mechanic, part-office worker. And on a Saturday too.

I look up at his face. He is clean-shaven and has a forehead lined in a permanent frown. Our eyes meet again, and he stares right back at me. There's no expression, no registering of emotion in the pools of his dark eyes. A bolt of terror hits my chest.

You'll die.

I want to run, but I'm boxed in. All I can do is keep shuffling forward at the same pace as everyone else.

Who is this man?

As soon as I reach the end and I'm on the high street, I hurry away in the direction of the pub and The Old Stable. I'm desperate to get away, to lock myself somewhere safe, or even better, to jump in my car and drive and drive.

Except that's not what I do. Instead, I double back, walking a full circle around the vast stone war memorial, until I'm back where I started. I return to the groups of people still exiting the park. Someone knocks my shoulder, but this time I'm too focused to look around. The man is now six or so people ahead of me and I follow as he walks in the opposite direction of the pub and the church.

Fear is still pulsing through my veins, but with it is a need to take control. I don't know what's happened to Cate and Archie. I don't know if my gut feeling that Oliver is responsible is right or not. I don't know who's behind these threats, why I'm being targeted or how much danger I'm in, but it can't be a coincidence that I've seen this man so many times this week. There's something dark in his eyes that I can't ignore, and so I tune out the pounding of my heart in my ears and keep putting one foot in front of the other and follow him.

The man pushes his hands into his pockets, walking with purpose past the supermarket and the pink café on the corner. The high street is still busy, and I get caught behind a dog walker; their chocolate-brown Labrador jumping around the pavement, desperate to greet everyone that passes.

I step into the road, and when I look up again, the man is gone. I stop dead, my eyes searching for him. The shops have petered out, replaced with houses and the occasional office front. It's quieter on this stretch of road and there's nowhere he could've gone except inside one of the buildings. I keep walking, slower now, searching for any sign of movement at doors and windows.

Nothing.

And then something.

In a window of a shopfront, I see a movement. It's brief. A flash of navy in the corner of my eye. I carry on walking for another twenty metres before crossing the road and walking back on myself. From this distance, I see the name in swirling silver lettering that sits above the door.

J. Simpson Funeral Director.

There's no more movement inside, so I carry on to The Old Stable, my thoughts erratic. Bouncing between the threat and Oliver, the man and the investigation. This new threat is warning me to stay away from the police. Why? What does someone think I know that could change anything? And should I listen or give the note to Pope and Hacker?

I look down to my hands, surprised to find them empty. I pat my pockets, reality dawning. My eyes dart to the ground around me, but there's nothing there. I must have dropped the note when someone knocked into me. It's gone.

As I unlock my apartment and catch the smell of the familiar damp, the final words come back to me. *You'll die just like they did.*

Icy knowing hits me – hard, chilling.

Cate and Archie are dead.

TWENTY-FOUR

OLIVER

Oliver perches on the edge of the sofa in his living room. He tries to be still, calm, but he can't stop his leg from its frenzy of jiggling. What evidence have they found? What are they looking for?

There's movement in the doorway. He looks up as the family liaison officer appears in the doorway, carrying two mugs of tea.

'Nice socks,' Denise says, placing his mug on the coffee table in front of him.

'Thanks,' he mumbles, nodding to the mug. He doesn't want a damn tea. He doesn't want to sit here with this woman breathing down his neck. He does not need a babysitter.

He wants his house back to himself. He wants this all to be over.

'I loved *Road Runner* as a kid,' Denise says, and he knows exactly what she's doing. She's trying to engage him. To build a faux rapport she can use against him when the time comes. No way is he falling for it. But he has to be careful. He can't close up. That would make him look guilty. He has to tread a middle ground, give a little.

'Me too,' he says before glancing down at his socks. He doesn't remember consciously choosing them this morning, but he must have done because on his feet are the navy socks with the Road Runner character on the side. His favourite cartoon as a kid – and Archie's too. In the Easter holidays, when Archie had turned three, he'd caught chicken pox. They'd had to cancel their holiday to Bali with Wally and Lisa, Cate's parents. Cate had been gutted, but the only emotion he'd felt was relief. No matter how many years they've been married, no matter what he does, her parents will never think he's good enough for their precious daughter. He never used to let it get to him. Not until Cate started thinking it too.

Thoughts of his in-laws cause a dropping sensation in his gut. They've been texting every few hours for updates. But it was the last message that really worried him.

We've booked flights home. We will be there on Friday.

Six days to get out of this mess before Wally and Lisa arrive on his doorstep and start telling Pope and Hacker and anyone who'll listen that he's responsible for their daughter's disappearance.

His thoughts return to Archie. That Easter he'd spent hours with him on the sofa, snacking on toast cut into the shape of stars, and watching episode after episode of the cartoon. For months afterwards, Archie would race around the house pretending to be the little bird.

Meep-meep.

The socks were a gift from Archie last year. The first present he'd chosen all by himself instead of the usual aftershave or beer selection box with Archie's name stuck on it. He remembers Archie's glee, the infectious childish delight.

'I love them,' Oliver had said, pulling Archie into a hug. 'Finally at the age of forty-three, I own a pair of *Road Runner* socks.' If he really concentrates, really clears his mind, he can almost hear Archie's laughter.

The memory stings like a deep paper cut across his heart. Tears build in his eyes. He's messed everything up.

There's a noise – the unmistakable bang of the door that leads to the garage. He tries not to wince at the sound and the knowledge of where the search is taking the officers in his home.

There's nothing to find in the campervan, he tells himself. He's cleaned and scrubbed it. And yet he can't shake the fear of DNA and fibres and things he knows nothing about except from the handful of crime shows he's caught over the years.

'How long will this take?' Oliver asks.

'I'm not sure,' Denise replies. 'These things can take a few hours. The officers like to be thorough.'

DS Pope appears in the doorway. She's alone this time. Oliver wonders where she's left her sidekick.

'Found anything?' Oliver asks. The regret is instant.

'Should we have?' she asks.

He shakes his head. 'No, of course not. I meant, anything that might tell you where Cate and Archie have gone or were going on Friday.'

'Nothing yet.' She says *yet*, like it's only a matter of time. His pulse starts to race again. 'But several pieces of new evidence have come to light in the last twenty-four hours which I'd like to discuss with you.'

Pope crosses the room and sits down opposite him. In the pause that follows, it feels like his airway is closing. He can't breathe. Have they found them? Have they found out what he did?

'I need to tell you, Oliver, that we are now treating Cate and Archie's disappearance as a murder investigation.'

The words are a sledgehammer to the last remnants of his calm. A noise escapes his throat, a 'ha' of disbelief that sounds almost like a laugh. He coughs, trying to mask the sound. 'What? You think they're dead?' They can't be serious.

'Yesterday a witness came forward who saw a woman and child matching Cate and Archie's descriptions on the evening of their disappearance.'

'How are they only telling you this now?'

'It was a dog walker who's been away on business and only got back yesterday. Last Friday, at around six p.m., she was walking her dog along the river, halfway between Leedham and Barton St Martin. She believes she saw a woman and a boy running across the field on the opposite side of the river. She showed us exactly where she saw them. Would you be surprised to learn that it was only a few hundred metres from your house?'

'Where exactly?' he asks, avoiding her question.

'There's a lane just across the main road. You can see it from your kitchen window, I believe. If you walk down that lane, you come to a sheep field and a path that takes you along the river.'

'I know it.'

'The dog walker saw someone else too. She saw a man with dark hair running a little way behind them. She didn't think anything of it at the time. She thought he was running to catch up, but now she believes he may have been chasing them.'

'What?' Oliver shakes his head, fighting the desire to leap up and pace the room. 'Someone was chasing Cate and Archie? Is that what you're telling me? Why aren't we all out there? Why call off the search?' Another question races through his thoughts – one he can't voice. What the hell is going on?

Pope continues, ignoring his outburst. 'When officers searched around the path early this morning, they found some items.' She unlocks her phone and turns the screen towards him. 'I'm sorry if this may be distressing for you, but I need to ask – do you recognise this shoe?'

A pressure builds in Oliver's skull as he looks at the screen.

It's a white trainer lying discarded on the ground. There's a strip of leopard-print fabric across the side. Her pumps, Cate called them. A lump forms in his throat. A jagged, unmoveable rock. How did he miss this?

'Oliver?'

He nods. 'It's Cate's.'

'And this—' Pope swipes to a second photo, tapping the screen to zoom in to a pearl stud earring. Bile burns the back of his throat. He nods again.

'Both the shoe and the earring were found less than a few hundred metres from your front door, and strongly point to Cate being involved in a struggle.'

'I... I... It doesn't make sense.' It really doesn't. A wave of guilt hits – acid in his veins. The desire to confess, to spill his guts and all the sordid, horrific details rises inside him. But his mind is spinning. He needs time to think.

'When did you last see your wife and son, Oliver?' Pope asks, slipping her phone into her pocket.

He replies, the same answer he's always given. 'Lunchtime at the school.' But the questions about that Friday keep coming until he's exhausted, spent. Tears threaten at the backs of his eyes. He wants to tell her to leave so he can think, but he can't do that.

'I'm going to show you some other photos now, Oliver, and I'd like you to tell me if you recognise them.'

There's a folder in Pope's hands that Oliver didn't register before. He's losing his grasp on the conversation; on his life, it feels like.

'These are copies of photographs found in Cate's classroom. We believe from the location of the photos that Cate would've been the only person to have put them there.'

Pope takes her time opening the folder. She selects a single piece of paper and holds it out for him to take.

The moment it's in his hands, his eyes fixed on the image,

the world around him collapses, folding inwards. 'What are these?' he asks, hoping the faltering in his voice doesn't give him away. He knows these bruises. Of course he does. But what he doesn't know is how there are photos of them. And more than that, how they found their way into Pope's hands.

He tries to think. Tries to connect the bruises, the photos, Cate. Her shoe discarded on a footpath. It's like the logic puzzles they give to the Year Six children to prepare them for their SATs, except without the logic.

It's not possible. It can't be. Unless... No. He won't go there.

Something clicks – a small piece of the puzzle. Pope's words circle in his mind. *'We believe from the location of the photos that Cate would've been the only person to have put them there.'*

The cupboard in Cate's class. Yesterday, Lexi was in there.

That bitch. She must have found them. She could've shown him. She could've allowed him to explain. Although, even now, he's not sure how he would've done that. One thing is for sure – he won't let her get away with this. Lexi needs to learn to keep her nose out of other people's business.

'There are more,' Pope says. She holds out another sheet of paper. This one has the bruises on the ribcage. The circular indents of knuckles. Not a punch but a press. A hard, long press. The nausea returns.

'Do you recognise these bruises?' she asks, and he feels the intensity of her gaze.

Oliver forces himself to shake his head but can't bring himself to speak the lie.

'You can't think... You're not really suggesting I was hitting her? That's madness. I'm the head teacher at a primary school. Look around you. We're not those people. I am not that person.'

'How would you explain these photos if you were us?' Pope asks.

'I don't know. Maybe... Cate, she was always helping people. Maybe she was looking after these photos. Maybe they're of a friend or someone she knew.' He's clutching at straws, but what choice does he have? He passes the paper back to Pope, averting his eyes from the purple splodges, that pale skin and the wisp of blonde hair that's been caught in the frame.

'I had a very interesting phone call with your in-laws last night, Oliver. They're understandably worried.'

'They hate me. Don't listen—'

'To a word they say?' Pope cuts in. 'Funny, that's exactly what they said about you. They also said that you and Cate had been arguing a lot and that you briefly separated at Christmas.'

'That's a lie.' The words blurt out, angry, too loud.

A silence falls. He waits for Pope to fill it with another question, but she doesn't. The anger dissolves, leaving only the guilt behind. It's fierce – a medieval torture rack, tightening and tightening until he wants to cry out. The lies he's told this week close in. Hot and smothering.

He takes a shuddering breath and lets the tears build in his eyes. 'Please,' he says, forcing himself to look Pope dead in the eyes. 'You have to find them.'

He covers his face then, lets himself fall apart. He's running out of time. He will have to tell them everything and soon. But he needs to be sure first.

They think his wife and son are dead. Murdered. They think he did it. But how much can they actually prove?

TWENTY-FIVE

It's late. The sky above me is dark, suiting my mood. The air is close. A storm is coming. I like it like this. No stars. No moon. No light. No one to see me.

The faint mooing calls of the cattle in the vales carry on the wind. It's the only sound, aside from the occasional car passing through the village.

I look down at the pile of your things on the ground, a riot of colour against the scorched firepit.

It shouldn't be so easy to erase a life, but a good scrub and a careful eye, fire and ash, and it is.

I must admit, I was worried when the posters for the search went up. Not for you, but there are other things out there, bad things. It would be hard for me if they were found. But they called it off at the last minute. Can you believe that?

It's happening already. People are forgetting about you and your boy. The police are clueless, and already the papers are moving on to other news stories – a fire in Manchester, a footballer accused of having an affair. Everyone will forget soon, just like they always do.

The matchbox is nearly empty. I shake it in my hands,

hearing the rattle. It's an old habit. Something my mother would do when she lit the gas hob for dinner, before she bought a clicker lighter, before we moved to the house with the electric one. I used to like watching her cook dinner. Sitting at the table with a colouring book and then homework. Mash and sausages were my favourite. And now her habit of shaking the matches is my habit too; passed on from one generation to the next, reminding me of my mother and a childhood best forgotten.

The match catches first strike, the flame bursting into life. I drop it to the pile in front of me. Nothing happens. For a second, it seems like the match died too soon. I shake the box again, ready to repeat the process, but then the little flame catches, dancing across the clothes and the papers and the handbag. Everything apart from one of your shoes and the earring I threw to the side of the path by your house, waiting to be found.

The air carries the unmistakable fumes of lighter fluid, and soon the fire is hot and menacing, the flames darting out, searching for more things to burn. But there is nothing more here. This space is empty. A paved courtyard with a firepit in the centre, hidden behind high walls. No one knows about this place. It's just for me. For this. I wonder how many times I've stood in the darkness, the heat of the fire hot on my face, and watched another life be erased.

It's hot now, but I don't step back. Despite all I've achieved, I still remember the days of cowering and fear.

A distant rumble sounds from the sky. The storm is coming. I hope the rain won't reach me yet. Whatever happens, I'll stand here until every last scrap before me is black, charred and unrecognisable.

It takes an hour for the fire to burn out. Nothing left to feed it. Lightning strikes above me, but no rain yet. The thunder when it comes is loud, angry. I kick at the pile of ash, checking, always checking. But the fire has done its job, like it always does, and what little there is to find, I'll dispose of carefully.

I collect my rain jacket and pull up my hood before walking into the quiet night. I take the same route that finds me back in the car park of the pub. I don't like the teacher's arrival. An outsider observing things. Disrupting. I'll do something about it soon. Whatever it takes to keep my secrets.

Some would call me cruel. Unfeeling. But they wouldn't understand. These lives I take, they're not random. These people I erase, they deserve it. You deserved it. Just like all the others that came before you. Just like all that will come next.

SUNDAY: NINE DAYS MISSING

TWENTY-SIX

LEXI

I wake with a start and a gasp.

It's dark in the room. Pitch-black. Donna's name is on my lips, and I almost cry out for my big sister as though this is my childhood bedroom and she's sleeping in the bed next to mine.

Was I dreaming of her again?

Reality tiptoes slowly into my body, my mind. This isn't my old room, and Donna will never again huff a sigh of annoyance, throw off her covers, and step across our bedroom to shush me and tell me there's nothing to fear.

I swallow, mouth dry, and reach for the glass of water I left on the nightstand, gulping down one, two, three mouthfuls until it's gone and the liquid sloshes in my empty stomach. I rest my head back on the pillow, but something doesn't feel right. Fear is snapping at the edges of my thoughts. I can't grab hold of it. It feels like I've woken from a nightmare I don't remember. The words of the threats whisper in my ears, slow and menacing.

The room is warm. Stuffy. My body is clammy with sweat. Outside, thunder booms – a deep, crashing sound. Moments pass, then another flash of lightning at the edges of the blinds. One, two seconds before a boom of thunder.

I shake off the last of the sleep and blink in the darkness. I tell myself it's the storm that woke me. And yet the feeling of needing to move – throwing myself forward, fighting, screaming – lingers in my body. My fingers find their way to the jagged scar on my forearm, and I trace the bumps. Was I dreaming of that ten-year-old girl again and the night my life and Donna's changed forever? When I close my eyes, I can still feel the iron vice of the hands gripping my arms, holding me back.

When the next streak of white comes, it lights my bedroom and the apartment beyond the open bedroom door with the same intensity as turning on a floodlight. And that's when I see it.

There, in my living room, barely three metres from my bed, is a shadow... a figure all in black... a man.

A man in my apartment.

A shout catches in my throat – a strangled gasp. Before I can move or react, I'm plunged back into darkness. I hold my breath and listen, but there's only silence. The logical part of my mind is explaining the figure away as a trick of the light, the remnants of the nightmare, but the more primal part of me believes what I saw, that through the open door of the bedroom, standing in the space between the living room and the kitchen, was a man dressed in black.

My body is frozen, but my mind is charging full speed towards panic. My hand darts out to the bedside light, but I'm rushing and clumsy, and I knock it from the table. It clatters to the floor, the sound lost to the next rumble of thunder.

I force myself to move, scrambling from the bed and standing in the middle of the room. Feet parted, fighting stance. My breath comes in short heaving gasps as I wait for hands to grab me in the black. In the seconds that pass, I'm aware of how little I'm wearing – knickers and a crop top. My fists tighten; my guard is up. The fear has morphed into a hot anger I haven't felt since Donna and all that happened between us sixteen years ago; one year ago. That same anger.

Time passes. Seconds, then minutes. I stand waiting. Ready. I don't shout out. I don't want to give my position away. Another strike of lightning comes, the flash of white across the small apartment.

I expect to see the figure looming, rushing at me. I squat down, ready to knock them off balance, but the figure is no longer there. The place is empty.

I take a step forward and turn on the bedroom light. No one steps out of the darkness. It's the same in the living room.

I move from space to space. I open every cupboard, search every possible hiding place like a twisted game of hide-and-seek.

Come out, come out, wherever you are.

'Hello?' I call out. My voice is weak, scared. I feel stupid, unnerved too, but I say it again with more strength. 'Is someone here?'

I hold my breath and listen to the silence until my lungs feel like they'll burst. Was I really expecting someone to answer? A cheery 'hi' from whoever is here. Was. They're gone now.

Doubt creeps over me. In my half-awake state, with thoughts of Donna in my head, and the remnants of a nightmare clinging on, could I have imagined the figure?

The answer is obvious. Yes.

In the kitchen, I pour myself a glass of water and try to calm my breathing and the adrenaline raging through me. I want to laugh. I want to shake off the moment and tell myself I imagined it. I almost convince myself too. But then as I'm heading back to the bedroom, I see something.

A feeling creeps up my spine, like two fingers gently tracing each vertebrae. There's another white envelope. Not on the doormat, not pushed under the gap beneath the door, but sitting on the table.

I didn't put it there.

But someone did.

Someone was in this apartment. I didn't imagine it. The realisation makes my skin prickle and my pulse pound in my head.

I snatch up the envelope and rip it open. It's another thick piece of white card. The words swim across my vision.

YOU'RE NEXT!

I drop the card onto the table, realising too late that I shouldn't have touched it. There could be fingerprints or DNA, something to tell the police who did this.

Who came into my apartment while I slept? Were they planning to do something else? Did I wake and scare them away before they could hurt me?

I spin towards the front door. It's the only way in and out. I didn't hear them leave, but with the crash of the lamp, the roaring thunder, it would have been easy to sneak out. But how did they unlock the door? I reach out, my hand clasping the door handle, jerking it up then down, expecting to hear the rattle of the bolt, but instead the door flies open in my hand, letting in a gust of muggy night air.

I gasp, slamming it shut. I reach for the key sitting where I left it on the kitchen counter and lock the door, leaving the key in this time, half turned, unmoveable. How was the door unlocked?

I retrace yesterday's movements in my head. The called-off search, following the man from the funeral director's. After that I walked the vales and read a book in one of the cafés until closing time, I picked up a couple of beers from the corner shop and fish and chips from a van parked in the high street on the way back from the walk. My hands were full, and my phone was ringing in my hand. That Brighton number again, sending my thoughts spiralling. I was distracted; scared, staring at the screen until my phone fell silent, before sinking onto the sofa and crying deep wrenching sobs for all that happened a year ago, for all that I'm being dragged into now. But I'm sure I locked the door.

I wiggle the handle again, and this time the deadbolt rattles in its place. The sound gives me little relief, so I drag my punch bag back across the floor and lay it against the door. Someone could still push it open, but it will be a lot harder. And I doubt I'm going to sleep for the rest of the night anyway.

I'm right.

But still I climb into bed and use the time to think. About Oliver and the photos I found in Cate's cupboard, and the threats I've had since arriving in Leedham. Three of them now. I still don't understand why I'm being targeted.

I shiver, more from fear than cold, as I think about my walk today. Up and down Richmond Avenue half a dozen times. It was obvious from Karen's description which house belonged to Oliver and Cate. I couldn't stop myself from gazing at the windows as I passed. Did Oliver see me?

He had time after our chat in his office to post the first note. He was at the park yesterday of course. The shove of people, it would have been easy to get to me before he addressed the crowd. And now this. He must know about the photos I found in Cate's cupboard by now. The detectives will have talked to him about them. He'll know it was me that found them.

What did he do to Cate and Archie? What does he think I'll uncover?

On and on my mind races. I think about Cate and Archie who I've been told are dead. And I think about Donna and the past I'm running from, until I'm exhausted and wired at the same time, and the past and the present feel knotted together like the fairy lights Donna and I would spend a whole afternoon untangling, while singing Christmas songs and eating all the good Quality Street chocolates from the tin.

I've been warned to stay away from the police. If I tell them about these new threats, am I putting myself in more danger? And yet, a man was in my apartment tonight. The note says I'm next. I don't how much more danger I could be in.

Still, it's not a simple decision to make. There's Haventhorpe Primary to consider and my trouble with the police in Brighton. If I talk to the detectives again, they might start digging. I don't want that, but I have to do the right thing, even if it means risking everything all over again.

TWENTY-SEVEN

OLIVER

The police station is new – a large, three-storey glass building on the outskirts of a nearby town, and the result of a merger of a dozen village constabularies with the town. The size, along with the fleet of police cars and vans parked in neat rows outside, is imposing.

Oliver can still taste the lingering burn of whisky in his mouth and hopes he won't throw up as he stops by an oak tree on the opposite side of the road. One glass to take the edge off and clear his thoughts after the hoard of officers had packed up and left his house yesterday. Then a second because fuzzy felt so good. He's not sure how many times he topped his glass up, or where the rest of the evening went, only that the hangover is the kind that can't be fixed with painkillers and a pint of water.

A sheen of sweat coats his face despite the cool wind on his skin. He's pretty sure he smells as bad as he feels. Beneath the bandage on his hand, his cut itches with a fury that threatens to drive him to insanity. All he wants to do is crawl under the covers and sleep until the nightmare is over. But somewhere between whisky shots three and four, he thought about Cate's lost shoe and that one earring, and he started to worry. Really worry. He couldn't figure it out. No matter how many times he spun it, the shoe was a problem.

He was still worrying when he woke up with the hangover roaring in his temples. And he found he couldn't stand the quiet of his house, the guilt eating him up, and so he'd come to the police station with half a mind to confess.

Except now that he's here, standing across the road and staring up at the building with all its glass, he's not so sure, and he doesn't like that. He tries to grab hold of the certainty he felt picking up the phone and calling the police on that first Saturday. He'd seen exactly what he had to do, exactly how it would pan out – the rallying of village support, the clueless police investigation – and how he would survive it all. Except Pope and Hacker haven't been clueless. They've found things. The shoe, the earring, the photos he didn't know existed.

And after the failed search yesterday, the only thing he's now certain of is that the police and the majority of Leedham think he killed his family. He should've known they'd all pine after Cate. All her perfect little ways, all the things she did for people. They have no idea. Cate was the most selfish person he'd ever met. She didn't lift a finger for anyone but herself. Of course he can't say that, not to those who knew her. They'd never believe him. And not to Pope and Hacker either. If they knew the truth about their marriage, it would only be another step towards charging him with whatever it is they think he's done.

Oliver rubs at his face and wishes he could run away. He pictures a beach somewhere, sand and cocktails. But then he imagines Archie splashing in the sea, and the thought almost breaks him. He misses his boy with a visceral longing.

'We're now treating Cate and Archie's disappearance as a murder investigation.'

Murder. They can't really think...

His stomach rumbles in that empty, sickening kind of way,

and he thinks of finding a café somewhere. Not the sourdough-and-smashed-avocado kind of place he and Cate would go to with Archie after a walk sometimes, the kind of place filled with middle-class families ticking off quality time from their to-do list on a Sunday morning so they can spend the rest of the day ignoring their kids. No, he means the greasy spoons frequented by delivery drivers and truckers and men accused of murdering their wives and children.

He starts to walk back to his car, parked out of sight around the corner. And with every step, he feels better about the decision to leave. He's almost giddy with the freedom of it, the knowledge that he could be stuck in a police cell right now and isn't. He just needs to really think it through. Every option. Every way it could go right or wrong.

He's nearing his car when a woman catches his eye on the opposite side of the road, striding in the direction of the police station. Long legs, athletic build and bright-red curls that bounce with every step. Lexi.

His thoughts return to the cupboard and how nervous she seemed, hiding those photos from him. Anger rises up inside him.

'Lexi,' he calls, and she turns. Her eyes widen for a split second before she paints on a smile he's sure is fake. *Bitch.*

He jogs across the road to meet her, ignoring the pounding of his headache. Suddenly, everything has gone wrong – the called-off search, the spotlight of suspicion on him – and it's Lexi's fault. There's nothing he can do to bring back his family, but the woman standing before him, that he can deal with. 'What are you doing here?' The words land sharp, accusing.

She takes a step back. 'I'm going to the police station.'

'Why?'

There's a pause, a fraction of a second where all she does is stare, and he gets that sickening déjà vu feeling again that he knows Lexi from somewhere. God, his head hurts.

'Oliver, are you OK? You don't look well. Do you need me to call someone for you?'

He shakes his head. There's no one to call, but her sympathy, even if it's fake, unnerves him. A lump forms in his throat. He swallows it down. 'I was just dropping off some more photos of Cate and Archie to the police station,' he lies, sounding smooth now. 'I'm surprised to see you here, that's all.'

'Sure. Of course. Don't worry about it. I'll see you tomorrow.' She takes a step to the side, and it's then that he realises she hasn't answered his question. Before he can stop himself, he moves into her path. If she's about to give the police something else that's going to screw him over, then he needs to know.

'Tell me,' he says, 'why is a substitute teacher who's been in Leedham less than a week needing to talk to the police? Oh don't bother answering,' he continues. 'I know all about your little search of Cate's cupboard and what you found. You have no idea what's going on here, Lexi, and you're making everything worse. Stay in your lane.'

'For whom?'

'What?'

'Who am I making this worse for, Oliver? You?'

'I...' A heat fizzes beneath the surface of his skin, fiery and hot. 'Just stay out of this, OK? You're not helping anyone. So either turn around and go home, or don't bother coming into school on Monday.'

Her mouth drops open. 'You're going to fire me?'

At last he's rattled her, and that feels pretty good.

'You're a substitute, Lexi. It will take one phone call and I won't even have to give a reason.'

His words hang between them. The more the thought settles, the more certain he is that the school will be better off with a teacher down and Mrs Woodcock teaching the Year Three and Four classes together than having an outsider among them digging around.

'You're the one threatening me.' Lexi moves away from him, changing her position as though she's about to make a run for it.

'It's not a threat. In fact, I've decided. Don't bother coming into school tomorrow. Is that clear? You're fired.'

He waits for her reaction, and when it comes, it's not what he expects. She smiles. A tight, knowing kind of smile he instantly hates. 'You can't do that.'

'I'm the head teacher. I can do what I like.' It's not technically true, but he'll find a way to spin it with Anika.

'I was hired by Anika. If she wants to fire me tomorrow morning when I get to school, she can; otherwise maybe it's you that needs to stay in your lane.' She walks away then, moving fast towards the police station.

He turns back to his car, his pulse thumping in his temples. Once inside, he starts the engine and watches Lexi up ahead. She's crossing the road, and just for a split second, he thinks about throwing the car into gear and mowing her down right outside the police station. A stupid move, and he's too late anyway, because he'd never reach her in time.

Oliver waits until she's disappeared into the building before driving away in the direction of home. He can no longer face the thought of sitting in a café and decides on beans on toast once he gets back.

It's only as he's driving away that he thinks about the evidence again. Not the shoe or the earring. But the photos of the bruises that Lexi found. How the hell did Cate get those images? And what's he going to tell Pope and Hacker when they ask him about them again? Because he knows they will.

Neither option looks good. If he tells them he's never seen them before, they'll guess he's lying and assume he was hitting his wife. It's hardly a hop, skip and jump from wife-beater to wife-killer.

But if he tells the truth about those bruises, he'll open a whole other can of worms that could destroy him just as easily as a murder charge. Because the truth is, he knows those bruises. He watched them transform from their first red welt, to the dark blue, the deep purple and then the ugly yellow, fading to nothing then reappearing somewhere else on her body. He also knows that the pearly-white skin of the woman in the photo isn't Cate.

TWENTY-EIGHT

LEXI

My heart races as I shove open the heavy door of the police station and step inside. I wait for the calm safety of the waiting room to take hold, but my fear has chased me inside. Oliver's face jeers in my thoughts. He didn't even look surprised when I asked if he was the one threatening me. I tried to stay calm and not show the terror thrumming in my veins, but he saw it anyway; I'm sure of it.

Oliver's face is replaced with the shadowy figure in my apartment last night. So it was Oliver. And now he's tried to fire me.

'I was hired by Anika. If she wants to fire me tomorrow morning when I get to school, she can.'

I sounded so confident, but I have no idea if what I said is true or if when I arrive at school tomorrow, I'll even have a job to go to. The thought of leaving Leedham now, even with the threats from Oliver hanging over me, leaves me feeling sick. I have nowhere to go, but how can I stay?

The desk sergeant clears her throat, and I shake the thoughts away and explain why I'm here, pulling out another clear plastic food bag, another threat. She picks up the phone and nods to the chairs by the wall.

It's nearly an hour before DC Hacker appears from a white door leading further into the station.

'Miss Mills, come this way.' He walks fast down a corridor into a small room with two sofas and a low coffee table in the middle. I sense the urgency to him, an impatience. I'm pulling him away from more important things.

'I got another threat last night.' I place the bag on the table, and Hacker tilts his head, reading the message without reaching to touch it. 'Someone broke into my apartment last night and left it on the table.'

That gets his attention. 'A break-in?'

I nod and launch into everything that happened, starting with the storm and then tracking back to the park and the note in my pocket.

'And where is this other note?'

'I... I think I dropped it in the crowd.' I have a sudden desire to mention the man from the funeral director's, but what do I really have except a suspicion? And it's Oliver who's been threatening me. I'm sure of it now.

There's a pause. Hacker takes his time noting down what I've said. In the harsh light of the small room, he looks washed out. I wonder how close they are to finding Cate and Archie, and what it means for my time in Leedham.

'It was Oliver,' I say then, blurting out the accusation.

'You saw Oliver Walker in your apartment?'

'No... I mean, it could've been him. I don't know, but I just saw him outside the police station, and he practically admitted he'd been threatening me.'

We go back and forth for a while, questions and answers, and then Hacker sighs and closes his notebook. 'Miss Mills, we ran a fingerprint analysis on the note and envelope you gave us yesterday and found only one set. I'd like you to give us your prints as a comparison, but assuming you touched the note, I'm confident the prints are yours.'

'There weren't any others? Are you sure?' I ask.

He nods. 'Yes. Now, this is obviously a difficult time for many people in the community.' His tone has changed. It's gone from all business to sympathy. 'Everyone is worried about Cate and Archie, and we're doing everything we can to find them. We have to talk to a lot of people and among them, sometimes, we find individuals who are so desperate to help us, and to perhaps be involved in some way, that they give us wrong information—'

'You think I'm making this up?'

He doesn't answer for a moment. He doesn't have to. The sentiment is clear. Then he says, 'I think you're someone who wants to help. And I think we're very close to answers that will finish this investigation, and these notes don't tie into anything else we've found.'

My cheeks blaze with heat. Anger and humiliation battle for space in my head. I stand up, searching for a throwaway comment and finding none. 'I want to leave now.'

Hacker leads the way back to the waiting area. 'Miss Mills,' he says at the door, 'please understand we are taking all enquiries seriously. I would urge you to think long and hard about your involvement in this investigation and suggest you give it a wide berth.'

I don't bother to remind him that it was me that found the photos of Cate hidden in her cupboard, something the police should've found a week ago. If I hadn't stuck my nose in, they might never have known what kind of person Oliver is. I leave without a word, longing for the cold air of the morning to cool my face.

I put everything on the line to come here, and it's all been thrown back at me. If the police don't want to believe me, then I'll handle this myself. The thought is a boost that carries me home, but when I'm back in the gloom of my apartment, the fear of last night returns, shrinking the walls and pushing at my body.

The threat is no longer unknown. It's Oliver – a man who's capable of hurting a woman and God knows what else. He's told me to my face to get out of Leedham, to stay in my lane. If I don't listen, what will he do to me? One thing is for sure: I can't continue like this – scared, alone, panic jumping through my veins. For the first time, I wonder if sleeping in my car isn't the worst thing that could happen to me.

TWENTY-NINE

Sundays are my favourite. A day that's just for me. No work, no jobs. Alone with my thoughts. At peace.

I've never been like you. Always with your need to socialise, to gather people. Barbeques and picnics, or drinks in the pub on Sunday afternoons. You seemed to come alive around others, like you sucked their energy from them, or perhaps they gave it willingly to be in your company, just as I did.

There's no energy now. Just as there's no peace for me.

I drive through the winding lanes and back roads. The landscape has changed in the last few weeks. The fields are gold with barley and the hedgerows a vast green and growing over into the road, narrowing the lanes.

The turning for the cottage has almost disappeared in the foliage of the trees, hidden from all except those who know to look for it. I like that. It's safer. Less chance of anyone finding my secrets.

It's rather funny when I think about it. You aren't that far away at all. Although it might as well be a thousand miles for how close the police are to finding you.

I ease the car down the steep single-track driveway until the dirty white walls of the cottage appear in my windscreen. It's an old holiday let, sitting alone and forgotten. The elderly owner let it fall into disrepair. I heard about the place at his funeral when the family were despairing over what to do with it. I offered to take it off their hands for a good price.

I've done some odd jobs and maintenance. Fresh paint and whatnot. And I always keep the curtains drawn just in case a passer-by should look in. I can't let anyone see what's inside. You tried to hide your disdain when I first opened the front door into a narrow hall. It surprised me, that look. That even when terrified, clutching at your child, you could take a moment to be disappointed.

I cut the engine and step out into the warmth of the late morning. The air smells of pine cones and dewy grass, and I take a moment to breathe it in. I heard an interview about mindfulness on the radio once. It sounded like a load of crap to me, but maybe this is it. Taking a moment from my day to appreciate something in the world.

I open the front door, and the smell hits me. It's a problem. Stale. Festering. A sign I'm dragging my heels on the next part. I bought a plug-in air freshener once, but it only made it worse – the chemical sickly-sweet smell took nothing away, only mixed with the smell of you and the ones before.

I sigh. The calm I felt outside is long gone. There's no fun for me in the cleaning up. I always delay this part, but it must be done and soon.

MONDAY: TEN DAYS MISSING

THIRTY

LEXI

I wake on Monday morning from another restless night certain of three things: firstly, that I locked the door to The Old Stable on Saturday. I can remember dumping my fish and chips on the table and turning to lock the door. The second thing I'm certain of is that Oliver is behind it all – the threats and Cate and Archie's deaths. Which makes the third a given – I have to take Oliver's warning seriously and get out of Leedham. Today. I'll speak to Anika this morning and tell her I'm leaving at the end of the day.

I'm used to running away. I've been doing it since Donna's death almost exactly a year ago, but this doesn't feel right. I hate leaving my new class in the lurch, all those children who are so worried about their teacher and their friend. And I hate leaving without knowing what's happened in this village, and how a woman and child could disappear without a trace.

There's no time to dig around, and I don't know where I'd start to look, but there is one thing I can do – I can find out how Oliver broke into my apartment. And so as soon as I'm dressed in a simple navy skirt and a white top with gypsy sleeves that cuff at the wrists, I make my way across the car park to the pub.

The storm from Saturday has broken the hot weather, and I'm glad for the cardigan tucked in my bag.

'Morning, Lexi,' Paul calls as I step through the doors and into the restaurant area. He steps out of the swinging door to the kitchen. His smile is broad as he wipes his hands on a tea towel slung over one shoulder. 'Finally tempting you with breakfast, are we? I do a mean bacon bap to go.'

'Thank you, but I'm all set.' I tap the smoothie cup in my hand. 'But I wanted to ask a quick question if that's OK?'

'Fire away. But if you're still looking to move into one of the rooms in the pub, I'm afraid I'm now fully booked this week.'

'No.' I shake my head. 'Nothing like that. The Old Stable is fine.'

Paul pulls a face – half grimace, half smile. 'Are you sure? I'm really sorry, but a couple have extended their stay unexpectedly.'

I wave my hand in a don't-worry-about-it gesture. As soon as I've told Anika I'm leaving, I'll only be coming back to pack my bags anyway.

He waits for me to continue, but I hesitate. Thoughts of the break-in, the man in my apartment, the note in my pocket – they race through my mind, squeezing the air from my lungs. If I tell Paul, it will upset him, and I don't want to do that, especially as I'm leaving. DC Hacker's pitying expression floats across my mind. If he didn't believe me, Paul might not either.

'I… thought I'd lost my key yesterday,' I say, landing on a lie that sounds plausible. 'I had a bit of panic and thought I'd never be able to get back in.' I fake a light-hearted 'silly me' laugh. 'Luckily I found it, but I just wanted to check if you have a spare key, just in case?'

He chuckles too. 'Of course. You wouldn't believe the number of times guests check out and leave without giving their key back. It costs me a fortune every year at the key cutters. So don't worry. If you lose your keys, pop into the pub and tell me or whoever is behind the bar. We keep all the spares hanging up on the corkboard.' He points to a board behind the bar. 'Three sets for each room. One for the guest, one for the cleaners and one spare.'

There are a dozen or so hooks screwed into the cork, and hanging from them are keys. Some hooks have three sets, some two. I look for the label of The Old Stable. Two keys hang on the hook.

I start to doubt myself again. Does that mean I left the door unlocked after all? Or that someone took the key and put it back?

'They're pretty visible there,' I say carefully, when I mean *accessible*. Anyone could step around the bar and take a key. It would only take a quiet moment, a few seconds.

'The keys?' Paul tilts his head to one side, looking from me to the corkboard. 'Sure, but this is Leedham. Nobody is going to steal them, if that's what you're asking. We're good people here.'

I smile. 'Of course. Well, I'd better be going.'

We say our goodbyes, and I leave Paul to cook his breakfasts without asking the question humming in my thoughts: if Leedham is so safe, then why did a woman and child go missing?

By the time I've written the thinking starter anagram on the board and stepped into the playground, it's buzzing with hissed voices. There's something in the air among the parents, just like at the police station yesterday with Hacker. Something has changed. It's zigzagging across the playground like a game of shared whispers.

I search the playground for Anika and wonder if Oliver has followed through on his threat outside the police station. Should I even be here? Before I have time to question it, Anika finds me, stepping away from a group of three other mums, all in maxi dresses with blonde bobs.

'Miss Mills, good morning.' Anika smiles. 'How was your weekend?'

'It was fine, thank you,' I lie, not wanting to tell her the truth. 'Actually, I'm glad I've caught you.'

'Oh?' She tilts her head a fraction to the side. 'What can I do for you? I hope it's not an issue with Sebastian. I know he gets frustrated with the speed the other children learn at, but the extension sheets should be helping.'

'No, it's nothing like that.' And then I pull off the Band-Aid and say the words I've been practising in my head all morning. 'I'm sorry, but I don't feel I'm quite the right fit for Leedham Primary. I think it would be best if I leave at the end of the day.' It's a relief when they're out. Oliver has won, the fear has won, but right now I don't care. I just need to leave this place and feel safe again.

'No,' she says as though I've asked her; as if I'm a child who needs to be scolded. She glances behind her at her friends before stepping closer. 'You can't leave. This school is barely keeping it together. If you desert me now, it will crumble. I won't allow that to happen.'

'I'm sorry, but—'

'I'll end you,' she cuts in, the words landing like a slap. 'I'll call every substitute teaching agency in the country and make sure you never get another job.' The noise of the playground – the children playing, the parents talking – disappears, and I have no doubt Anika means what she says.

'I know last week was hard for everyone,' she continues. 'I'm going to make sure this week is better.' A beat passes between us, and then something relaxes in her face and she uncrosses her arms. 'So you'll stay?'

I nod, unsure what else I can say. I thought staying in my car wasn't the worst thing, but I assumed I'd still be able to work. I have to be able to work, and teaching is all I know how to do. I have no one I can turn to. My parents are a no-go for obvious reasons. They blame me for what happened to Donna. Not as much as I blame myself, but they're still hard to be around.

My pulse races, an out-of-control rollercoaster. I'm scared, not sleeping, unable to shake the threats from my mind, and yet there's nothing I can do about it. I'm here. I have to find a way to live with it.

'Wonderful. I'm so pleased,' she says, her tone sugary-sweet once more. 'Now, there are a few things to say with my mummy hat on. Firstly, Sebastian had a stomach bug on Saturday.' She turns the corner of her mouth down and frowns.

'I'm sorry to hear that.'

'Thank you. I wouldn't mention it, but his diabetes means that even a little bug can cause us such problems. We've been extra vigilant, and he does seem fine right now, but would you mind keeping an extra careful eye on him this morning?'

'Of course. No problem.'

She beams at me. 'Thank you. I'll be checking the app on my phone that tells me his glucose levels, and I'll be around the school for a lot of the day anyway.'

I smile back and wait for the second thing. I expect it to be about setting extra work again, but I'm wrong.

'And the other thing. It's Tuesday tomorrow. Obviously last week you were just getting to know the school that day; now we're in a new week, and you're settled in, I'm letting you know that Cate always invited parents into the classroom on Tuesday afternoons to share in the learning.'

'I see,' I reply carefully. I really hate having parents join the class. It's always disruptive, and there are always children who are left disappointed when their loved ones can't make it. There's a time and a place for parents to take part in their children's education, but a weekly trip into the classroom feels edged with competitiveness in that passive-toxic way mums can be with each other.

She nods as though I've agreed. 'Wonderful. I'll put something on the class WhatsApp, and we'll see you at two tomorrow. Last term we all did a project on family trees, which was such fun.' She claps her hands again, three little clap-clap-claps.

'I've never known parents to be as dedicated,' I say. Interfering is the word I mean but don't say. This school takes helicopter parenting to a whole new level. I wonder why they don't just home school their precious darlings if they want to be so involved.

'You've no idea. We'd do anything to protect our children and the school's reputation, lols.'

There it is again. That added lols. It's a softener, I realise. A way to make her comment land better than the words suggest. I don't have time to dwell before Anika is moving on.

'And I'm still waiting on details for that other reference. If you could let me know the name of the school, I'll—'

'I've called them already,' I jump in with the lie, hoping it will squash Anika's question on the name of the school and her threat to end my career. I can't have her contacting Haventhorpe Primary. 'I spoke directly to the head teacher, and she assured me she'd put a reference in writing in the post. So I'm sure it will be with Karen today or tomorrow.'

'Well, I look forward to receiving it, and...' She trails off, distracted by a movement at the gates. I follow her gaze and see Oliver. He's walking down the path and appears to be heading straight for the playground. A bolt of terror races through my body as though I'm back in my apartment in the pitch-black, waiting to be attacked. After my chat with Anika, it seems my job is safe... for now. But am I?

Anika's lips purse, and she hisses a swear word under her breath before hurrying across the playground to greet him, leaving me to collect my thoughts.

I've just promised Anika a reference will arrive in the next few days. It won't. I could fake something of course, but after the week I've been here, I can say with certainty that the moment a letter arrives, Anika will be picking up the phone, dialling that Brighton number and double-checking. But now, if I don't supply it, it won't just be the end of this placement, it will be the end of my teaching career.

Like DC Hacker's impatient energy on Sunday, and the groups of parents around me, I sense time is running out, but it's not for Oliver, or even for Cate and Archie. It's for me.

I need to focus. I can't let Oliver and the threats distract me any longer. I can't let my own fears control me. I take a breath, trying to ignore the glass shards of terror rubbing against my insides. I won't run. I can't even if I want to.

For the last week, I've been telling myself that I'm here because I need this job, but in truth, that's not the only reason I'm in Leedham.

It's time to remember that.

THIRTY-ONE

OLIVER

Oliver's alarm beeps for a second time. A persistent, brain-piercing noise he didn't realise until that very second he hated. He reaches for his phone, squinting at the screen and swiping twice before the alarm stops and the silence resumes.

He flops back onto the pillow and thinks of all the times he's lain in this bed listening to the soft thud of Archie's footsteps in the hall outside and how he and Cate had kept their eyes closed and wished for just five more minutes of peace. What he wouldn't give to hear those footsteps now.

The sob when it comes is guttural and shuddering, taking him by surprise. He never claimed to be perfect. He knows that's what everyone always thought. The perfect family, the perfect life, the perfect man. But he's human. He's made mistakes like everyone else, but he's always tried. One little slip and this is his punishment.

He shifts in the bed, catching the stale smell of the bedclothes that need changing. Except Cate normally does that. He isn't sure he knows where the clean sets are kept. The stink turns his stomach, reminding him of the whisky bottle he'd gone back to last night.

Yesterday, it was easy to focus on his anger. Anger at Lexi for showing the photos to the police and interfering in whatever else she was doing yesterday. He'd driven home, knowing really that his anger was at Cate and what she'd driven him to.

But in his first waking moments, it's impossible not to let his feelings for Archie rip him in two. Tears stream down his face. A screamed 'sorry' lodges in his throat. He didn't mean to hurt them.

Memories of Christmas flood his thoughts. Christmas Day at Cate's parents' house, smiling at everyone, pretending they hadn't been arguing non-stop for the last week, putting on a show and talking to everyone but each other.

Then Boxing Day when he'd woken up to an empty house. He'd freaked out that time. He'd called everyone he could think of. Her parents and all her friends. Disturbing people's Christmas celebrations and making a fool of himself, just like she'd wanted. No one had seen them. He'd called her hundreds of times. She hadn't answered. In the early evening, when he'd been unable to think of anything else he could do, he'd texted her, telling her he'd be calling the police in an hour, begging her to come back.

Fifty-five minutes later she'd returned, self-righteousness, smug. Archie had been giddy on the high of Grandma and Grandad's sweets and attention, oblivious to the game his mother was playing. Oliver had spoken to Wally that morning, plucking up the courage to ask if Cate was there, and the man had lied through his teeth.

That Boxing Day night she'd told him she'd found the receipt for the hotel. His stay with another woman. A stupid mistake. Meaningless, he'd told her, grovelling and pleading for another chance. She'd lorded it over him, enjoying the power, but she'd allowed him to stay, and he'd sworn it was over. And then he'd made a second promise to himself that he'd never let Cate take Archie and leave him like that again.

Oliver forces himself up to take a shower, careful to keep the bandage of his right hand away from the water.

The house feels alien to him. As though the presence of the officers on Saturday has stamped out whatever essence of his wife and son had been clinging to the air to make it a home. The silence throbs in his head. He has to get out, to find some fragment of normal among the shards of his life now lying shattered around him.

He thinks of his office at school, the welcoming smiles of the children who will look at him today with the same wide-eyed adoration they always do. And Karen. Her unwavering support. That's what he needs.

The whisky bottle is still on the side by the kettle, and he thinks about taking a nip, just to chase away the dregs of the night before, but however low things are right now, he's not sure they'll ever be whisky-in-the-morning low.

He chooses coffee instead, and by the time he reaches the school, the caffeine is trembling in his hands, jittering right into his bones. He heads towards the front doors, wanting to avoid the playground and parents, but when he taps his pocket for his school keys, they're not there.

'Stupid,' he hisses under his breath. He's left them at home along with his wallet. Staring first at the gates and then at the playground, he wonders if he should go home and get them? No. He'll be late then and that won't look good. There's only one thing for it. He holds his head high and walks with a confidence he doesn't feel towards the playground.

He's always loved how approachable he is for parents and children, but today he feels like he's walking into a viper's nest. He remembers the looks on the staring faces as Hacker and Pope had driven him out of the park on Saturday. But maybe today won't be so bad. The children still adore him.

The thought lands just as Anika comes into view, hurrying towards him.

He rearranges his face into a smile. 'Good morning, Anika. Did you—'

'Oliver,' Anika cuts him off, 'can we talk privately in your office?'

'Of course. I have a meeting first thing. Would this afternoon work?' It's a lie, but he doesn't want her to think he's free all day, that despite coming into school for the past week, he has done no work. The backlog has stacked up fast, and there's no way to keep on top of it now. He already knows he'll spend another day hiding and scrolling through photos. 'I'd also like a quick word actually, about the substitute teacher – Miss Mills. Shall we say two p.m.?' he adds, remembering the decision he came to yesterday to get rid of Lexi.

She frowns. 'Now would be better.'

Unease coils tight around him, but he keeps it hidden along with everything else. 'Lead the way,' he says, not wanting to tell her he's forgotten his keys.

Neither of them speak as he steps into the quiet cool of the school. The scents of cleaning products linger in the air. Oliver prefers the smell of poster paint and books, and even school dinners.

He opens his office door and motions to the seat beside his desk. He clears his throat and steps over to the window to open the blinds a fraction. 'What can I do for you?'

'Well, first of all, how are you coping?' she asks. Her tone is caring, but the look pulling at her features isn't concern or even pity. It's suspicion. An old anger flashes through him – a rage he hasn't felt for years but which has been bubbling up more and more recently. He can't stop his left hand from closing into a fist.

'I'm fine,' he says in a way that suggests the opposite. He tries again. 'It's obviously very difficult. I'm very worried about Archie and Cate, but I'm committed to keeping the school running to its usual standard.'

'Of course. Sit down please, Oliver,' Anika says then, and even though he wants to refuse, that would be churlish, and he is many things but not that.

He sits at his desk and taps the keyboard. The screen jumps into life, and he makes a show of checking his emails. 'Just a moment please. I need to deal with this.' He pretends to type a reply, making her wait. Maybe he is churlish after all.

'Oliver,' Anika snaps, and he forces himself to look up, 'this isn't easy for anyone, but you need to go home.'

He gives a loud sigh, wishing everyone would stop telling him what he needs. 'I'm fine.'

She shakes her head. 'No, you're not. You look terrible. Are you even sleeping? And' – she narrows her eyes – 'have you been drinking?' Anika spits out the question, no longer masking the disdain in her tone.

'Of course not,' he says. 'Don't be ridiculous.'

'I can smell whisky,' she says, not backing down.

'I have not been drinking.' His voice is louder than he intends, and it's an effort not to leap up again and pace the room. 'So if there's nothing else, I have a lot to be getting on with—'

'You're not listening to me. We – the governors and I – need you to go home,' she continues. 'You may be fine, and I really hope you are, but this is bigger than you. We must consider the reputation of the school. The safety of the children and staff must be our first priority.'

'How are they not safe with me here? Don't be ridiculous.'

'No one is being ridiculous.'

Oliver huffs, his temper fraying a little more. 'I appreciate your concern, but I'm staying.'

'Oliver, I'm not asking you to go home. I'm telling you. The governors held an emergency meeting last night, and we voted unanimously that you should take a leave of absence while the police investigation into Cate and Archie's disappearance is ongoing.'

The words smack him in the face. Finally he gets it. 'What? You can't be serious.' He didn't see this coming. Stupid now it's in front of him. Everything he did was to protect himself and his place in Leedham. It was all for nothing.

'We are,' Anika replies. 'I'm sorry, Oliver, but we need to think about what's best for the school here.'

'You can't think I had anything to do with Cate and Archie...' He can't finish the sentence. His throat closes in until his breath is a ragged wheeze. He sinks into his chair once more. It's all slipping away. Family. Career. His whole life. 'Has Lexi been speaking to you?'

'No. Why? What would she say if she had?'

'Nothing,' he says quickly. 'I just... I didn't hurt my wife and son. I didn't do anything.'

'No one thinks you did,' Anika soothes. 'But we have to consider what it looks like. Members of the press have been reporting outside the school gates since Cate... and, well, when you walk in, it looks... it looks odd, to be honest. You should be at home.

'We've had a lot of emails and calls from concerned parents. A lot of questions we can't answer. The police calling off your search on Saturday didn't look good, Oliver. You must see that.'

He opens his mouth to reply, but no words come out. Anika reaches a hand towards him as though she might pat him but quickly withdraws. He follows her gaze to the bandage.

'Cut it on a bread knife.' He mumbles the lie.

She nods and looks away. 'The leave doesn't have to be permanent. As soon as... we know more, we can readdress the situation. In the meantime, Steve is going to take over as temporary head.'

'Steve Bishop? He'll be terrible at it. And he's got the Year Six SATs to think about too.'

'He's deputy head. We'll give him lots of support.'

Oliver takes a deep breath in and releases it. 'I'll create a handover today for him and leave at the end of the day.'

Anika shakes her head. 'Please go home now. We can sort everything.'

'You're not even giving me a day?' The indignant anger he felt pulsing beneath the surface earlier rises again, a hot blaze that feels like it might blind him. He stands, looming over this pathetic, power-hungry housewife.

Who does she think she is? His hands ball into two tight fists. The pain of the cut adds fuel to his anger.

'I'm not going anywhere,' he half shouts. He grits his teeth, desperate to lash out at something. Someone.

He watches her cower in her chair. Her fear is both thrilling and horrifying.

'Sorry,' he splutters. 'I... I'm upset. Of course I'll go.' He grabs his phone from the desk and leaves without another word.

He will get her for this. He will make her pay. And that bitch Lexi too. They all deserve what's coming for them, but there'll be time for that. He relishes the energy the anger brings. For the first time in days, he feels in control again. As soon as he gets home, he's going to find a solicitor and get Pope and Hacker off his back. He tries to remember the name of the man who helped him out all those years ago with the other bother, but it's a blank. It doesn't matter. He'll find—

The thought dies in his mind as he rounds the corner and sees six police vans parked on the road. Not outside his house this time. But opposite. Next to the path that leads to the sheep field that Archie used to love running through.

It's the path to the field where the dog walker saw his wife and child running on Friday. Being chased by a man. And the place they found Cate's shoe and earring.

'We're now treating Cate and Archie's disappearance as a murder investigation.'

He realises then what's going on and a new fear thumps through his body. The vans, the officers – they're not looking for evidence anymore; they're looking for bodies.

THIRTY-TWO

GEMMA

Gemma steps into the staffroom on Monday's lunch break and allows the first sob to shudder through her body. Thanks to the Year Five and Six school trip to the zoo, and the other class teachers on duty in the playground, the staffroom is blissfully empty. She shuts the door as the first tears spill onto her cheeks. Her make-up will be ruined, she's sure, but it's too late to do anything about it, and right now she doesn't care.

The same question snags in her mind. Why her? Why does this stuff always happen to her? So many of her Instagram friends are getting engaged or married. But she's prettier than all of them and more fun too. And yet all she gets is a pile of steaming manure for a life. It's not fair.

She's been holding it together for days and days, lying through her teeth to everyone – to the police. She's committed a crime. And the whole time she's been blindly hoping it'll be worth it, but will it? It feels like everything is going wrong.

The panic inside her is a swarm of hornets, buzzing and stinging her insides. All that's left to do is cry, so she sinks onto the sofa and buries her head in her hands.

Except she can't even get a minute to herself. Just her luck for Karen to bustle in.

'Oh my dear. What's all this?' Karen says in the same voice she uses to soothe the children when they cry.

'It's nothing. Sorry,' she adds, because sorry is what she always says. The result of living with a mother that makes her feel a constant need to apologise for not being good enough.

'A good cry is what we all need sometimes. I'll put the kettle on.'

A minute later, Karen is by her side, a cup of tea in one hand and a box of tissues in the other. 'Take this.' She holds out the yellow spotty mug for Gemma to take. It's Karen's favourite mug, and it's sweet of her to make Gemma a cup of tea in it, because it shouldn't matter what mug you drink from, but somehow, it does. Maybe Karen and her motherly ways and silly voices aren't so bad after all.

'Thank you.' She sniffs and takes a sip of hot sweet tea.

'I've felt a bit tearful myself today. I couldn't believe it when I heard,' Karen says.

'Heard what?' The panic prickles again. Gemma sits forward too fast, causing drops of hot tea to spill onto her skirt.

'Oh my, I thought that's why you were upset. It was on the village WhatsApp group. The police are searching the vales today. There are vans and officers all over the place.' Karen rattles on, naming roads and telling Gemma who said what, but she's barely listening.

They're searching the vales. For what? And more importantly, what does this mean for her?

She takes a sip of tea. The sweet warmth slips down her throat, but there's no comfort in it now.

'And of course,' Karen continues, 'Oliver has been put on leave. I'm sure that's upsetting too.'

She nods, not bothering to correct Karen's assumption for why she's upset. Because despite how desperate she feels, how certain she suddenly is that there's no coming back from this, the desire to protect herself and what she's done is still strong. She's under no illusion that if she turned to Karen right now and blurted out her part in Cate and Archie's disappearance, there would be no sympathy. Only shock and anger and a hurried phone call to the police.

'These things shouldn't happen in a place like Leedham,' Karen continues, putting an arm around her shoulder.

The door to the staffroom opens again, and of course it's Lexi, breezing in, wearing a pink cardigan that clashes with her hair. How many hideous outfits can one person own?

'Hi,' Lexi says, giving them both that sweet smile that everyone seems to be falling for. 'Sorry, am I interrupting something? I can come back.'

Gemma's about to tell her that yes, she is interrupting something, and yes, she can sod off, but Karen's already waving her in.

'No, come in,' Karen says. 'We're both just having a moment. I'm sure you've heard about Oliver being put on leave by the governors, and now it's all over the village that the police are back. They've come to search the vales.'

Gemma closes her eyes and lets the final tears fall – angry and stinging this time. She can't fall apart like this.

'I don't understand it,' Karen continues, looking from her to Lexi. 'Why call off the search on Saturday if they're just going to do it themselves? Another forty-eight hours have gone by. Anything could've happened in that time.'

'Maybe it makes sense,' Lexi says as she heads for the kettle. She waves it in the air at them in an 'anyone for a drink?' gesture, and they shake their heads.

'How?' Karen asks.

'I was just thinking about what DS Pope said on Saturday when she called off the search. She said there might be evidence in the vales and they don't want everyone stomping through it.'

'So you don't think they're looking for them?' Hope carries in Karen's voice.

'That would be my guess. And maybe...' Lexi's voice trails off.

'And what?' Karen pulls her arm away and sits forward.

Lexi makes her pained face. 'It's been ten days. Maybe they're looking for evidence and... bodies.'

Karen gasps, a hand flying to her throat. 'You think they might be dead?'

'I don't know,' Lexi is quick to say. 'I was just wondering if the police might be looking to rule it out at least.'

'Oh my God,' Karen says. 'Do you think someone killed them on Friday? I haven't wanted to think about it, but could they have been dead all this time? Who would do that?'

Lexi shrugs. 'I don't know.'

Annoyance burns through Gemma. 'She doesn't even know Cate and Archie.' The words are out before she can stop them. 'She can't think anything.' The harsh snap of her voice hangs in the silence that follows, but she doesn't care.

'I didn't mean to upset you,' Lexi replies carefully before turning her back to make her coffee.

'Of course you didn't,' Karen says. She stands up and wipes some crumbs from the worktop, positioning herself halfway between Gemma and Lexi. 'Do you think...?' she starts to say. She pauses, shakes her head, then looks between them. 'You don't think Oliver could have... Sorry, of course he didn't. I don't know what I was thinking. It's just...'

'The police do seem pretty interested in him,' Lexi says.

'We don't know anything,' Gemma snaps again before turning to Karen. 'Thank you for the tea,' she says before walking from the room without a backwards glance. Why is Lexi even here? The school could've managed. They didn't need to get a substitute. Especially one like her. For a moment, Gemma imagines the new term. Cate not back, and Lexi still teaching her class, and Gemma still stuck with the snotty Reception kids.

A bitterness burns in her chest. She knows it well. It's the same feeling she'd get with Cate. A slow fury. A 'why her and not me?' question with no answer. Why does her life get to be perfect? Why does she get everything and Gemma gets nothing?

The jealousy isn't pretty, and she loathes herself for it, but she's always been this way. One of her earliest memories is from a playgroup at the cricket pavilion in the park. Gemma pushing over a boy who wanted to play with her friend. She sees the same thing in the children in her class sometimes too – those who haven't learned to share.

Gemma walks quickly to her classroom, digs out the small make-up bag she carries with her everywhere and reapplies her foundation. The guilt hits her again – sharp. For a second, she wonders if she's gone too far.

She didn't mean for anyone to get hurt. Except that's another lie. Because she did, didn't she? She wanted to hurt Cate.

Lexi's comment rings in her thoughts. *'Maybe they're looking for evidence and... bodies.'*

When Gemma's face is perfect and the only sign of her tears is the tint of red at the edges of her eyes, she opens a new message on her phone and begins to type.

We need to talk!

THIRTY-THREE

Jeanie knew. She knew, the second she looked out of the window this morning to watch the bin men do their Monday recycling collection and instead saw the police vans parked at the end of the road, that they would find her secret. That they would find the body she'd dragged across the bumpy ground on that dark night and tipped into the well.

And she was right.

Her phone lights up again with the chat of the neighbourhood watch group. She grips the phone tighter in her hand, fighting the urge to throw it against the wall.

Did you hear? The police have closed Oak Lane.

The replies come fast. Ping, ping, ping. She can almost hear their voices, their excitement.

Which one is that?

The road that leads down to that old farm building you can see from the top of Sully's hill.

The abandoned one?

Yes!!!

Have they found something?

????

Looks like it!

Jeanie knows Oak Lane. She knows the old farm that used to belong to Mr Fairfield. In the summer, she'd pick apples from the orchard and old man Fairfield would give her 20p for a full bucket. Sometimes she'd use the money to buy sweets, but often it was something for her mum. A loaf of bread or a pint of milk.

But then Mr Fairfield had died suddenly of a heart attack, and with no immediate family, he'd left the farm and land to a small animal charity. Jeanie remembers his kind eyes, and she's sure his vision was for a community farm, a place of refuge for neglected farm animals. But it never happened. At first, the will was contested by two distant cousins. The court case went on for years. But then the cousins ran out of money to fight, and the charity closed, and no one knew what to do after that. And so the farm fell into disrepair. It's sat empty and forgotten for over thirty years.

Almost forgotten.

Jeanie will always remember it of course. She used to think it was the most perfect place on earth with its orchard and its fields. But as it fell into disrepair, it became perfect for something else – the perfect place to hide a body. Or so she'd thought.

She shuffles closer to her bedroom window, the binoculars gripped in her hands. Her back aches, her head throbs, her bladder pushes painfully against her insides, but she doesn't move.

The vans arrived first thing – four of them and more police officers than she could easily count from her position in the living room. She moved upstairs then, arriving at the window in time to see Oliver stalk home, head down, door slamming. She wonders if he's at his own window, watching too. Did he see them walk off in their groups of fours and fives, holding long sticks to push at the undergrowth.

Maybe if that had been it, she might have told herself it was OK. The police missed things all the time – always messing up, that lot. But then the dog unit had arrived. Four German shepherds, barking and straining at their leads. Jeanie wasn't naïve enough to think that the dogs would miss it.

The morning came and went and then lunchtime. The officers returned in groups to have a break, a sit-down – tea from a flask, a packet sandwich – before getting up and going out again.

At one point after lunch, when it was just the coordinator down by the vans, a map in one hand and a radio in the other, she'd thought about leaving her spot at the window and walking to the end of the road to talk to him. A friendly chit-chat, a nosey neighbour offering more tea, all the while asking how the search was going and, more importantly, where. But she couldn't risk it. He might remember her prying later, or he might ask if he could use her facilities. And she couldn't have that. She couldn't let them in her house. Too many secrets. The thought makes her turn to the bed and the pile of clean clothes that needs to be folded. Brightly coloured T-shirts in blue and green. Shorts and joggers and a set of green PJs with some character on she's never heard of.

She has a sudden desire to scoop up the clothes and hide them somewhere, but she still can't move from the window. The officers start to return. Not weary from a day of fruitless searching but buoyed by a find. They jump into their vans and drive away, and Jeanie knows the WhatsApp messages are right. They've reached the farm. They've found it. They found the life she stole in a single flash of rage.

She'd known this day would come, but she'd hoped for more time.

Her phone lights up from the window ledge. Not a message this time but a call. She tries to remember the last time he called. It's usually her that calls and him that reassures.

'They've found the body,' he says.

She tries to find the words to reply but can't.

'Jeanie?'

'What do you want to do?' she asks.

'Nothing. That's why I'm calling – to tell you to do nothing. The police are bumbling everything up. They'll never connect it to you.'

'And if they do?'

'They won't. Hold firm, Jeanette.' The use of her full name jolts her. Only her father called her that. Her mother always preferred Jeanie, and that's what stuck.

There are questions, what-ifs, but she knows better than to ask. He's said his piece and hangs up.

She moves through the house to the kitchen and opens the fridge. The wine bottle is out before she even registers it.

They've found the body.

They'll know what she did.

The police are bumbling idiots, but even idiots stumble across the truth sometimes.

TUESDAY: ELEVEN DAYS MISSING

THIRTY-FOUR

LEXI

I cast my eyes around the classroom and resist the urge to pull the fabric of my top away from my body where it's sticking to my back. It's hot, despite the open windows, and it's bursting at the seams with my class plus a dozen mums, two dads and one grandmother.

I catch the whispers of three mums at the table in front of me, oblivious to their listening children.

'Did you see the news this morning? They're saying the body is someone else. It's not Cate or Archie.'

'I know. And more police vans in the village this morning too. I can't believe—'

'Thank you all for coming,' I say in a loud voice before the mums can continue. I'm sure most of the children know about the body found yesterday. Skeletal remains, according to the news this morning, so not Cate or Archie, thank God, but it's still very upsetting to a small community. I can sense a difference in the mood of my class. More outbursts, more tears, or maybe they don't want to do a parent-sharing session any more than I do.

Everyone's attention turns towards me. I feel Anika's gaze

more than the others. No reference arrived in the post this morning. I'll have to say the letter got lost. How much longer can I drag this out before she asks me point-blank for the name of my old school?

Despite my attempts to take control of my fear, I'm on edge. I can't stop the threats spinning in my head. The notes, Oliver, Anika.

You're next.

Stay in your lane.

I'll end you.

You'll die just like they did.

I force myself to smile anyway and try to focus. 'As you can see, we've moved the classroom around a little bit so each table can work in groups rather than just parents with their children.'

I catch a look passing between Anika and another mum. It's a 'this isn't what Cate would do' look, but I plough ahead anyway. I know already that Benjamin's parents are both working today and little Sol's mum was in tears in the playground this morning, explaining how she had to take her mum to her next chemotherapy session and couldn't attend. There's no way I'm going to have children feeling left out or parents feeling like they've failed.

'I thought it would be fun,' I continue, reaching for one of the school ukuleles, 'if we wrote a song.'

There are grins from the children, and I smile at their delight.

I find the string positions and strum a few notes of George Ezra's 'Shotgun'. 'Don't get too excited – this is the only song I play. Each table has been given a different verse to write, and the theme is friendship and kindness. Any questions?'

Anika's hand shoots up. 'Miss Mills, this is... a lovely thing to do,' she says in a way that suggests she thinks the opposite, 'but will there also be time for the children to show us their workbooks?'

This isn't the question she's really asking. What she means is: will there be a chance for me to show off my son's work to the other parents?

I keep my smile fixed and nod. 'Of course. The workbooks are in the children's trays. After we've written the song and had a few practices, they can get their books out to show you if they'd like to. But' – I grin at the children – 'we're performing this song in assembly on Friday, so we're going to need lots of practice time.'

My comment elicits the appropriate gasps of excitement from the children, and I know already that none of them will want to stop the practice to get out their books, but Anika seems satisfied, so I let them get on with the task and wonder what Friday will look like. It's only three days away, yet I don't know if I'll still be here or if more threats will come – or worse, if Oliver will follow through on his threats.

Pencils are picked up and scribbles begin. I drift from one table to another, suggesting rhyming words and strum out the melody when I'm asked to. It's only when Karen appears in the class doorway that I leave the children and parents to their work.

Her cheeks are flushed, and she fans her face as I approach. 'Sorry, Lexi,' she says quietly. 'Would you be able to make sure these leaflets get put in the children's book bags before home time?'

'Sure,' I say, taking the stack of paper. 'Is everything all right?'

Before she can reply, Anika is out of her seat and by my side. 'Are they the flyers for tomorrow's meeting?' she asks.

'Yes. It's all sorted, and I've shared it on the village Facebook group too.'

'Thanks, Karen,' she replies before turning to me. 'I trust we can count on your support, Lexi.'

'Of course. But what for?'

'I've been fielding constant questions and concerns about the school this week, especially after the police found a body yesterday. There are a lot of upset parents here. We felt it was important to call a meeting so we can address everyone's worries in one go. It's open to the whole village, and I've asked DS Pope and DC Hacker if they can attend as well.'

'Did you hear' – Karen begins, dropping her voice another notch – 'they think the body has been in that well for over two decades. And George from the post office heard one of the officers say that a knife was found with the body. They're out again today, still looking for poor—'

'Mum?' Sebastian calls out. I look up to see him waving the paper in his hands. 'You've got the pencil.'

'I'll be one moment, darling,' Anika replies before turning back to us. 'Karen, while you're here, has Lexi's reference arrived in the post yet?'

I fix my face in expectant hope and look to Karen, despite knowing the answer.

Karen shakes her head. 'Nothing yet, although you know what it's like in Leedham. Our post always seems a few days behind the rest of the world.

Anika turns back to Sebastian, and I take the flyers to the desk and catch the hum of my phone. I forgot to tuck it in my bag after lunch break, and it's sitting out beside my day planner. The same Brighton area code rolls across the screen.

The colourful wall displays, the chatter and voices of the children and parents, the soft hum as they sing their lyrics to the 'Shotgun' tune – it's all sucked away at the sight of the number on my phone.

Why are they trying to contact me? Has something changed? Have they found out something new? I should just answer. They won't give up. And yet, something always stops me.

'Is that a Brighton number?' Anika says from beside me.

I jump, lurching forward and snatching up my phone before shoving it into my bag.

'I don't know,' I say, the words too loud, too quick. A dad in the corner looks my way. I force myself to smile.

Anika leans over the bin by my desk with the pencil and sharpener. 'I recognise the area code because my sister lives there. It was Brighton you said you'd moved from, wasn't it?'

'I don't think I ever said that.'

She tilts her head and looks at me. 'Oh I'm sure you did.'

I'm sure I didn't, but I say nothing.

'Which school was it you taught at?'

Here it is – the question I can't avoid. I flounder. 'Oh... I... It was—'

It's Benjamin that saves me – jumping up and down in his seat, hand waving in the air. 'Miss Mills? Miss Mills? We're finished. Can we sing it now?'

I grab the ukulele and step forward. 'Of course. Let's give it a go.'

We launch into a wobbly version of 'Shotgun', with each table singing their verses. All the while I imagine my phone still ringing in my bag.

With everything that's been happening here, I've almost forgotten that it's nearly a year to the day since Donna died. No matter what all those parents at Haventhorpe Primary thought, and the police as well, and even though Donna hated me in the end, I really did try everything to save her.

THIRTY-FIVE

OLIVER

'What's happening? What's going on?' The questions fire out the moment Pope and Hacker appear in the doorway. He's been stuck in this grey windowless room with his solicitor for an hour, and no one is telling him anything. The frustration is a noose around his neck that tightens with every passing minute he waits. His solicitor – a bushy-moustached man in a grey suit by the name of Philip Dunstable, whom Oliver found by a Google search – has been no help so far. Philip has the personality of a potato, as Cate liked to say, and is being infuriatingly calm and possibly not even listening.

Pope gives him a tight smile. 'Sorry for the delay, Oliver. As you can imagine, the discovery of human remains in our search of Leedham Vale has thrown up a lot more questions than answers. As you know, we've continued the search today for the bodies of Cate and Archie.'

The words sink into his mind, and he feels sick, but as the silence draws out, there's anger there too. The desire to scream at the detectives to just get on with it yanks and pushes at him – a playground bully. He fights it with every ounce of the control he's built over the past fourteen years. He's not the fly-off-the-handle man he once was.

'There have been some developments since we last spoke,' Pope continues at last. 'Which we'd like to discuss with you. Before we begin, we'd like to record this interview.'

The attempt at calm slips away. His pulse quickens. He wants to object, he wants Philip to object, but the man – and his stupid bushy moustache – is already nodding, so there's nothing Oliver can do but agree.

The detectives settle into their seats, and a red file is placed on the table. It's closed with no way to know what's inside, but it causes a sick feeling to roil in his stomach. He thinks of the photographs of the bruises. Then of Cate's shoe. What else have they found?

Hacker runs through the formalities of the recording, and Oliver tries to keep his voice steady as he gives his name and address. Sweat is pooling under his armpits, and there's a tang of stink to the room that he thinks is coming from him. The cut on his hand starts to itch. The damn thing is refusing to heal. A heat has started to smoulder beneath the bandage, which he's pretty sure isn't good. He really needs to do something about it, but the thought of seeing a doctor, answering more questions, is too much to think about.

There's a pause and Oliver looks to Pope, but it's Hacker that starts.

'Thank you for coming in today, Oliver. We appreciate that this is a difficult time for you, and we'll try to make it as quick and as simple as we can.'

'Thank you.' The sentiment of Hacker's words does nothing to appease him, but he takes a deep breath and pretends.

'The reason we'd like to talk to you today is because we found something during the search of your property that we believe may be connected to our investigation into the whereabouts of your wife and child.'

In the pause that follows, Oliver closes his eyes, picturing DNA and blood and fingerprints and all the things he can't explain.

'The item in question,' Hacker continues, 'is a VW campervan stored in your garage.'

They know! The thought explodes in his mind as Hacker continues. 'Whose campervan is it, Oliver?'

'Mine,' Oliver says, his voice strangled. 'Ours, I mean. We use it for holidays every year.' When Cate's parents aren't paying for them to fly off somewhere exotic that is. Cate never took to the camper, but they always had a good time in it, just the three of them. Until Cate decided to ruin everything.

'It's not registered to your name or property, which is why we had no idea about its existence until the search.'

There's an accusation to his tone that makes Oliver's insides squirm.

'Is there a question here, DC Hacker?' Philip asks, and Oliver shoots him a grateful look. Maybe he has been listening after all.

Hacker gives the briefest of nods. 'Why didn't you disclose the vehicle to us, Oliver?'

He does his best floundered face and raises his hands in an 'I don't know' gesture. 'You didn't ask, and I didn't think to mention it. It belongs to Cate's dad. He gave it to us as a wedding present. He didn't want the hassle of changing over the paperwork, so it's still registered to him.'

'And you have access to the campervan? You drive it?'

'Yes,' he says, glancing to Philip, willing him to step in again. He doesn't.

'Once we became aware of the campervan, we began searching traffic cameras in the area around the time we believe Cate and Archie went missing. Would you be surprised to learn that we found something?'

His head starts to spin. There's no way out of this. He gives a strangled, 'No.'

'I didn't think so.' Hacker opens the folder, but it's Pope that takes out the first sheet.

'This is an image of your campervan from a CCTV camera by the supermarket on Leedham high street at seven p.m. on Friday,' she says.

For the briefest moment, he considers lying. What's one more to add to the pile of bull he's been spewing this week. The orange-and-white van in the photograph is clearly his, but the driver isn't visible. Could he say it was Cate? But even as the thought lands, Pope is reaching for the next image.

It's from the dual carriageway half a mile from the village and shows the camper's windscreen and the unmistakable image of him at the wheel.

'You previously told us that you returned from school at soon after five p.m. on Friday and spent the evening home alone. Would you like to revise this statement?'

He nods and clears his throat. 'I'm sorry I lied. I went out driving. I didn't say anything because I thought it made me look guilty.'

A silence draws out. An unspoken agreement that yes, it does make him look guilty.

'Where did you go?' Hacker asks.

'I drove to Barton Woods. There's a car park that looks over the vales. It's quiet on Friday evenings, and I wanted to be alone.'

'Why did you take the campervan?' Hacker asks.

'Excuse me?' Oliver realises exactly what Hacker is asking, but he needs to buy himself some time to formulate an answer.

'Your car was parked on the drive. It would've been a lot easier to take that, but instead you took the campervan out. I was wondering why?'

'I...' A reason. There has to be a logical reason that isn't because he needed the space in the back. *Think, think, think.* 'The engine,' Oliver says at last. 'The battery. It goes flat if it doesn't get used regularly. I often take it out at the weekend.'

'What did you do in the woods?' Pope this time.

Images press down on him. The shadows of the trees. The dirt beneath his fingernails. What was he thinking? He swallows and tries to focus on the interview.

'Nothing. I just thought. Things with Cate... they hadn't been great for a while. I wanted time to think about what to do.'

'Are you now telling us that you and Cate were having marital problems?'

'Yes.'

'What kind of problems?'

'I don't know. The usual kind. We argued about stupid stuff. Holidays and what we spent our money on. What clubs Archie should be doing. And...' He pauses, steadying himself for the next confession. 'You were right, DS Pope. Cate did leave me at Christmas, but only for a day.' He thinks again of her little game and waking up to an empty house on Boxing Day.

'And what did you decide about your marriage that night?'

'I decided I wanted to make it work.' It's the truth, but it feels like the biggest lie he's told so far.

He and Cate haven't been happy for a long time, but he doesn't want a divorce. The lifestyle they have – the four-bed corner house in a coveted position in Leedham, the car, the decent clothes – it isn't because of his salary or even his and Cate's combined, although Leedham Primary pays better than most. It's all because of Cate's family.

The youngest of three children, Cate is the only girl, to wealthy parents with careers in private medicine, and Oliver suspects an inheritance in their past. They dote on Cate. They want her to have everything. Nothing is too much. Nothing is good enough for their little girl, including him. They paid the deposit on their house and contribute to the eye-watering monthly mortgage. And on top of that, they're always giving generous cash gifts to her and Archie on birthdays and Christmas and any time they feel like it.

It was a source of fights between he and Cate in the early years of their marriage.

'I'm the man of the house. It's belittling that they keep trying to support us.'

'Don't be so old-fashioned, Ol. They don't see it that way. They want to give it to us – why shouldn't we enjoy it?'

Eventually he'd caved. And for the most part, the lifestyle he got to lead was more important than his feelings of inadequacy.

So if his marriage ends, if they divorced, the money and all that it brings disappears too. And with it, his standing in the community, not to mention his job. He was under no illusion that his position as head teacher at a school in Leedham was part of the package deal. He and Cate were the perfect couple. The perfect family with Archie too; the three of them arm in arm and grinning on the front page of the school website.

So it isn't a lie that he wants to stay married to Cate, but his reason has nothing to do with love or even obligation.

'That's convenient,' Hacker replies.

Oliver rubs at his temples. Tiredness is making him zone out, and he has to concentrate. They're peeling back the layers of his lies and he can't afford to trip up. 'What is?'

'It's convenient that you went for a drive alone to a secluded woodland area at the exact time your wife and child went missing. You were having marital problems. Your wife had already left you once, but at this point you decided you still loved her. Can I tell you what I think?' Hacker continues.

Oliver doesn't reply. It's not really a question.

'I think Cate had enough of your physical abuse towards her and on Friday evening she planned to leave you for good this time. You argued, and she and Archie got away, running towards the river. But you caught up with them and, somehow, you convinced Cate to return home. Perhaps you picked Archie up, and Cate had no choice but to follow. Then, as soon as you were home, you killed Cate and then Archie.'

'No,' he cries out. 'None of this is true. I'd never hurt Archie. I'd never do anything to hurt my boy.'

'I believe you, Oliver,' Pope says, and for a second, he thinks it's going to be OK, but then she continues. 'I don't think you would do anything to intentionally hurt Archie. But if he got in the way, if he tried to help his mother, then in a moment of rage... an accident could've easily occurred.'

'No. This is madness,' he says, but there's a lump lodged in his throat, and the words are barely a whisper.

'We'll now search Barton Woods. What will we find there, Oliver?'

Hot tears pool in his eyes. 'Nothing. That's not what happened. I would never—' His voice cracks, the tears falling.

'We have something else we'd like to show you, Oliver,' Pope says, not giving him a second to breathe or think. He feels himself breaking; splintering. There can't be more.

Pope slides another piece of paper across the table. He expects another photo, but it's not. 'These are emails sent to Cate that we recovered from her cloud storage. She'd deleted them from her phone, which is why it took us some time to find them.'

He scans the page, words jumping out at him.

Do you know what kind of man your husband is?

You're in danger, Cate.

Don't stand in my way...

'What... who sent these?'

'That's what we'd like to know,' Pope replies. 'The email is registered to a fake name, and the IP address has been hidden by a virtual private network. There may have been more, but the deleted folder only holds emails for thirty days. Do you know why anyone would be warning Cate about you?'

'No,' he lies. There's only one person, but it's not possible. There's no way. His mind races back to his past. 'You see what this is?' He taps the page. 'Someone is saying they'll hurt Cate.'

'That's one possibility we're considering. However, it seems more likely, given the other evidence, that whoever sent these emails could have been trying to protect Cate. From you.'

Oliver swallows down the panic. He feels sick. This can't be happening. They were never supposed to think he was involved.

'Are you charging my client with murder?' Philip asks, his tone so casual in the crackling tension, it's as though he's asking if anyone wants a cup of tea.

'Not at this time,' Pope says. 'You're free to go now, Oliver, but we are asking you not to leave the area. We'll need you to return for further questioning.'

Oliver drops his head into his hands. He needs to confess, to tell them everything about the photos and what he did on that Friday night, but the room is spinning. There's so much to take in. He just needs a little more time. One more day.

He thought he could outrun the lies and stop his life from exploding, but the pin has already been pulled from the grenade. It's too late.

WEDNESDAY: TWELVE DAYS MISSING

THIRTY-SIX

GEMMA

They've set up the hall like it's the Christmas nativity, and now Gemma is stuck sitting on the raised stage, feeling as ridiculous and useless as a papier-mâché prop.

'We need a show of unity,' Anika had said earlier, striding into the staffroom like she owned the place and roping them all in after school to help with the set-up. 'We must show we're still a family in this difficult time.'

A family? Ha! Oliver has been banished, Cate's missing and not even the police seem to know where she is. Archie too, a voice whispers in Gemma's head. She tries not to think about Archie. The one truly innocent victim in this. Cate might be a victim, but she's hardly innocent. She got what was coming to her. But Archie, when she thinks of him, she hates what's happened, and more than that, she hates herself. A deep, knotty loathing that makes her wish the earth would open and swallow her up.

Gemma grits her teeth and stifles the yawn that keeps threating in the stuffy heat of the hall. She would rather have hidden in the back row of the green plastic chairs that face the stage. She's hot. And tired. And hungry. And more than anything, she's fed up with everything being about Cate's disappearance.

The hall is filling fast with people; the air already too hot in that muggy kind of way that makes it feel more like July than May. Her thighs are sticking together, rubbing and uncomfortable. The first burn of a sore is forming, and she's desperate to peel off her clothes and stand in a cold shower.

The last few hours have been spent fuming as she's watched Lexi smile and chat and take her position beside Karen like she's one of them. The jealousy that's been murmuring beneath the surface since Lexi's arrival, which reared up on Monday in the staffroom, has yet to cool.

If Gemma thinks about it, she knows her fixation with the pretty substitute teacher is a distraction, a way to focus her mind on something that isn't the mess she's made of her own life. But she's not thinking about that. She's thinking about how everyone is falling for Lexi's perky look-how-perfect-I-am act. And Gemma is sure it's an act. She pretends to care, pretends to worry about Cate like everyone else, but she doesn't even know her.

Where has this woman come from?

Gemma glances discreetly at her watch. There's still ten minutes before the meeting is due to start, but Anika is already stepping to the front of the stage wearing a white power suit; dressed for a board room she's never been in as far as Gemma knows. She's sure Anika used to work in a high-end curtain store before her reign as head governor and chair of the PTA.

'Take a seat anywhere.' Anika waves to a group entering the hall. She's had her hair done since this morning. The black, gleaming bob sits perfectly in line with her jaw.

It's the same mix of parents and grandparents that turn up to all the school events, plus a few faces Gemma recognises from the village. She catches sight of her own parents, stepping over legs and feet towards two chairs in the fourth row. She hides a smile at the pursed-lipped annoyance of her mother, who clearly feels the chair and vice-chair of Leedham Parish Council deserve a seat on the stage, or, at the very least, in the front row. Gemma lifts her shoulders back, sitting a little straighter, enjoying a rare moment of getting one up on her mother.

The feeling lasts as long as it takes them to sit down. Then it disappears in a puff of reality. Her parents want to talk later.

'We're worried about your future,' her dad had said this morning as he'd poured granola into a bowl. His so-called worry is code for 'we're concerned about our future'.

Not for the first time, Gemma wonders why they bothered to have her. But then deep down she knows the answer. She is, and has always been, a prop. The country cottage, the flash car, the careers and the child. She's just another prize to show off to friends. Except she's let them down. Chosen a career they don't approve of, one with little in the way of prospects. Maybe it would've been fine if she'd found a husband they could brag about instead, as if her life was something from a Jane Austen novel, but she hadn't even got that right.

Tonight, they will pat the middle cushion on the sofa, deliver a well-choreographed speech and ask her again when she's planning to move out. She wants to tell them she's been working on it. That the mess she's in, the very reason half the village are cramming into this hall right now, is because she's been working on it.

Her parents can share in the blame, she thinks with a stab of bitterness. If they hadn't always made her feel so inadequate, if they'd put her first just once, maybe they wouldn't have driven her to trying a shortcut to getting her life together – a home, money. Even a husband. It had all been going so well until Friday last week.

Emotions clog her throat. She might be a prop to them, but they're still her parents. If she tells them what she's done, they'll help her. It doesn't matter that they'll be doing it for themselves rather than her. The important thing is they'll help. She just has to find the words and the courage to explain everything.

The seats fill quickly, but still people push in, standing at the back. A hum of chatter picks up. Anika seems determined to wait until the strike of six to start, despite the restless energy. Gemma catches snatches of conversations from the first few rows.

'Has anyone considered if the body they found might be connected to Cate and Archie? It could be a serial killer.'

'Oliver grew up two villages from here, you know.'

'Will he be here?'

'... probably killed them.'

Anika must hear the whispers too and the growing levels of speculation, because she claps her hands and a hush falls across the hall. 'Thank you all for coming,' she says in a clear voice. 'We're going to keep this as brief as possible. I know it's hot in here and we'd all rather be somewhere else.

'I've got DC Rob Hacker joining us,' she continues, pointing a hand to the back of the hall where the detective has just entered. He's wearing the same yellow tie from that first interview, but he looks nothing like the fresh-faced man who'd spoken to Gemma over a week ago.

'He'll be able to give us an update on the investigation. I will also be talking about a few changes currently happening in the school. And I've also got Dr Rosie Matthews with us, who I'm sure many of you recognise. Dr Matthews is a parent to one of our Year Six children, and she's also a clinical psychologist. She's going to give us some tips for how we can keep talking openly with our children without causing them alarm during this very difficult time.

'Before we hear from DC Hacker, I want to reassure you all that every staff member at Leedham Primary School is pulling together. We've always prided ourselves on being a family, and nothing has changed there. And we're very grateful to our deputy head, Mr Bishop, for stepping in as temporary head teacher.'

From the other side of the stage, Steve Bishop begins to stand, but Anika waves him back down, and he sits, an obedient puppy.

Gemma likes Steve. He's a good teacher. He's strict and gets the children ready for life beyond the colourfully painted fences of the school. But he's not a leader. He has none of Oliver's charisma, and the man is completely out of his depth.

A hand rises in the audience. It's one of the dads with a boy in Year Six. 'What about teaching?' he calls out. 'How's Mr Bishop doing both? Our kids have exams in a few weeks.'

'If we could save questions until the end,' Anika replies, 'that will keep us from running over. I will say that I'm in school every day, giving Mr Bishop all the support he needs. We are all rallying. It's very much business as usual.'

It really isn't. Gemma heard Karen tell Lexi earlier that they've still not organised the first aid training, and yesterday, Anika realised Sebastian's insulin pouch was missing from the fridge. She was furious, and for good reason.

Karen had to tell her one of the cleaners must have thrown it away over the weekend by mistake, but no one remembers the last time they saw it. There have been other things too. The food delivery for the lunches didn't arrive, and the cook had to improvise with turkey dinosaurs and chips instead of the sausages that were on the menu. Anika can say what she likes but, beneath the surface, chaos is reigning.

'DC Hacker,' Anika says then, 'would you like to join us now?'

She takes a step back, and as Hacker approaches the stage, Gemma feels her phone vibrate from the pocket of her skirt. She pulls it out and glances discreetly at the screen.

Meet me tonight. The usual place.

The words swim across her mind. They haven't seen each other since that Friday night and swore they wouldn't, but the police investigation, the reporters at the school gates, an actual body, the days that have passed – it was never supposed to go this far. But now that it has, now that they're meeting, Gemma wonders if it's safe. She thought they needed each other to keep their secrets, but is she needed at all? Is she a loose end – a piece of evidence to tidy up, get rid of?

She shivers in the heat. It's a risk, but she can't exactly ask someone to come with her. She'll have to go alone. Whatever happens, this could be her final chance to salvage her future. The plan is dead. She can see that now. But there's more at stake. She has to fix this before the detectives discover she's been lying about her whereabouts on the Friday Cate and Archie never made it home.

THIRTY-SEVEN

JEANIE

'As many of you know already, I'm DC Hacker.' The man on the stage is one of those overly groomed types that Jeanie sees on the TV so much now. Since when did beards become such a fashion statement? He's just like the rest of them. Caring more about themselves than any kind of proper police work. A burst of anger – sharp and stinging – hits her. She hates them. She hates them all.

Scum.

The thought drags her into the dark pit she's been dwelling in too often lately. Imagined scenarios that feel almost as real as the life outside her window. Jeanie nods to herself, almost missing the detective's next words.

'I'm here to give a brief update on the remains found on the Fairfield Farm property to the west of Leedham on Monday, and we ask for anyone with information on the details I'm about to cover to please come forward.'

Jeanie sits straighter in her chair. Alert now.

'Is it Cate?' someone shouts from one of the front rows.

Fool.

'It's too old, right?' another voice shouts. 'How long have they been dead for?'

Something shifts in the set of DC Hacker's jaw. He raises a hand – the gesture enough to quiet the idiots.

'As reported in the news, the body found is not that of Cate or Archie Walker. We do not believe the discovery is linked to the disappearance of the mother and son. The remains were discovered at the bottom of a derelict well at the edge of an unused farm. No wallet or identification were found on the body, but certain items, including a train ticket in a pocket, lead us to believe that the death took place in August twenty years ago. The deceased is male and estimated to be between the age of forty and sixty-five. We are treating the death as a murder investigation and have evidence to believe the man was stabbed in the chest and abdomen.'

Jeanie takes a sharp inhale of breath. They're bones. Decayed and forgotten for twenty years. How can the police know so much? How did they miss the train ticket when they searched his body?

The hall is suddenly a furnace. Her face dampens with sweat. Beads trickle from her neck down her back. She's on fire from the inside out and it's impossible to concentrate on anything but the heat.

She closes her eyes and feels herself back in that kitchen. Twenty years have passed but it feels like none at all. That snap decision, that rage. The grip of the knife in her hand, the thrust as it slipped through the skin and the layers of muscle and fat so very easily. The blood splatting to the floor, the horror in the eyes draining of life. She's thought of that moment every day for twenty years, and in all that time, she never felt a single moment of regret. But then, she never thought they'd catch her either.

'We expect to have more details in the coming weeks. For those residents who were living in the area twenty years ago, we're asking you to think back to this time and to anyone you can remember who may have disappeared. We believe that identifying this person will lead us to the assailant. Thank you.'

'What about Cate and Archie?' a voice calls out.

'The investigation is ongoing. Once again, we urge anyone who was in the village on Friday between the hours of four and eight p.m. to come forward. Please check all dashcam and doorbell footage and any CCTV security you may have.'

'Have you arrested Oliver Walker yet? We all know he killed them.'

'My neighbour is missing too. I heard there's a serial killer in the village?'

'Your neighbour is Sally Thwaite, and she's on holiday in France, visiting her mother, Stan,' someone else replies.

'Well, no one told me that.'

Anika Jones steps forward, hands raised, asking for quiet as though she's addressing a hall full of children, then raises her voice to be heard over the chatter. 'Thank you, DC Hacker. I'm now going to ask Dr Matthews to join us and talk through how we can approach these difficult and tragic topics with our children.'

A murmur of disquiet wends across the hall. Jeanie guesses she isn't the only one who came here for the police update and not a batty psychologist who looks as pleased to have been roped into this as the audience. Jeanie's eyes travel across the fidgeting groups to the back of the hall, and that's when she sees him.

He's by the doorway, and she wonders how long he's been there for, how much he's heard. Their eyes meet, and he raises his eyebrows in a silent question. He's asking her if she's ready to go. She nods, glad to be escaping the hall.

The air outside feels no cooler on her skin, but the smell is better. Cut grass and the bloom of a lilac by the path.

'Are you all right?' James asks, scanning her face as they walk towards his car.

'Hot flush,' she says, like it's nothing, before changing the subject. 'What are you doing here?'

'The same as you,' he replies.

'Did you hear what he said? They even know the month.'

He nods, looking at her for a long moment. His face, like hers, has aged, but it's happened slowly; she still sees the big brother he once was. Always kind. Always willing to help. But is he still that person?

Unease trickles down her back – a bead of sweat rolling down her spine. What he's doing, what she's helping him do... it... it isn't right, no matter how she tries to reckon with it in those restless hours of the night when she wakes in a tangle of covers, drenched in sweat, a hangover pressing behind her eyes.

'I think we should stop,' she says.

'No,' is all he replies.

She grits her teeth, keeping back the scream fighting to be set free. There's nothing more to say. She's a coward. She let herself be this person. Twenty years ago, he witnessed what she did, he helped her cover it up and now she's trapped helping him.

THIRTY-EIGHT

LEXI

The woman on the stage is talking in a soft, calming voice about all the ways parents can protect their children from the news and gossip. I zone out and look out across the hall. The air is hot and thick like soup, and suddenly it feels like every face is staring at me, like they know what I did. I tell myself I'm being ridiculous. That the dozen calls I've had from Brighton in the last few days have got under my skin. But it doesn't help. The need to run itches beneath my skin.

They know what I did.

I shift in my chair, aware of the sudden racing of my heart, a pain snaking across my chest.

'You OK?' Karen asks, her voice a whisper in my ear.

I shake my head. 'I've come over feeling unwell. I need to go.' The walls tilt around me, and I fix my eyes on the exit at the back of the room and try to breathe. 'Tell Anika I'm sorry.'

I don't wait for a reply as I slip out of my seat and keep my head down as I hurry out of the hall. There will be blow-back. I told Anika today that I've asked my old school to resend the reference.

'By email this time,' she'd replied, and I'd nodded, knowing I was out of time.

The evening air is still warm, the sun still bright, as though it's refusing to set. But it feels fresh compared to the hall. I'm not the only one to leave. There are a few other people walking towards the gates. I stop by the car park, slowing my breathing until the panic subsides.

It's then that I catch the murmur of voices and a single word carrying on the breeze.

'No.' The tone is sharp, the voice male and raspy.

I step closer and see the man from the funeral home. The height of him is unmistakable; those dark eyes that make my skin crawl, a thousand insects scurrying over my body. In the last few days, I've started to convince myself that I'd imagined the darkness in him – that all the times I've seen him have been a coincidence. Those thoughts evaporate in a split second of watching him.

The terror I've been barely containing this week explodes inside me. I want to move away, to hide, but my legs feel weak; I'm rooted to the ground.

He's talking to a short woman of a similar age, and there's something menacing in his stance.

I crouch down, hiding myself behind the car next to them.

'You're planning to take another one, aren't you?' the woman says after a long pause, and I'm sure I catch a tremor in her words. I feel her fear – a fluttering baby bird in my chest.

Another what?

'I'll let you know when I need your help,' he replies. And then, 'We need to go.'

'Where?' she asks him.

'St John's.'

'I thought you were going to cancel.'

'Why would I do that? Get in.'

I stay in my crouch until car doors bang and an engine

starts, the hum of it disappearing. My heart is still racing, a thudding drum. But I'm no longer paralysed with fear. Adrenaline is shooting through my body, and even though the fear is still whispering in my thoughts, I leap up and start to run, sprinting out of the school gates as one question thuds in pace with my racing heart. This is something I can do. A focus, a start. Of what, I'm not sure, but I can't be frozen by fear any longer. I have to find out what happened to Cate and Archie.

'You're planning to take another one, aren't you?'

Another what?

The question turns over in my thoughts, and by the time I reach the village high street, my phone is in my hand and I'm tapping St John's into Google Maps. I dodge lampposts and dog walkers as I scroll through colleges and car parks and playgrounds.

It could be anything. Planning to take another one – another holiday, another pill? The possibilities are endless, and yet, the fear in that woman's voice; the way he looks at me, the darkness I sense in him...

I think of the first threat. That thick white card pushed beneath my door.

Stop asking about the missing teacher... you'll be next!

I thought it was Oliver. The photos of the bruises, that way he spoke to me in the cupboard and then outside the police station. But what if I'm wrong? What if the photos I gave the police have led them to focus on Oliver and stop considering other options? Other suspects. What if this man has taken Cate and Archie and is planning to take someone else next?

Theories and questions and a hundred unknowns stumble through my head. By the time I reach my car, I'm breathing hard and pulling out my keys. I've found a St John's Church and hall five miles away. I don't know if it's the right location, but it's the only St John's nearby, and I don't stop to think as I tap into the directions and drive out of Leedham.

. . .

Ten minutes later, fields are replaced with houses and the outskirts of a town. I slow down as I turn onto a long high street and catch a glimpse of a steeple up ahead. St John's Church would once have been an imposing structure. A tall tower at the front in dark-grey brick, surrounded by a graveyard and a stone wall. But the town has expanded and swallowed it up, and it seems almost hidden beside a row of shops on one side and a street of houses on the other. There's a sign for the hall and a car park on the next road. As soon as I turn in, I see the same red estate car from the school. There are six other cars in the car park, and I tuck my Citroën in the corner.

My confidence at what I'm doing starts to waver as I step towards the hall. What am I walking into?

There's a woman standing outside the doors, smoking a cigarette. She's stick thin and pale and has the haunted look of someone who wants to be alone. She jumps at my approach, throwing her cigarette on the ground and stepping back inside the hall.

I give her a moment before following her through a set of double doors covered in posters for baby-and-toddler groups and Zumba, a bible study for teens and a poster for addiction support. I scan the times and dates, but there's nothing here for a Wednesday evening. But then I notice a sign further in. It's one of those plastic standing ones that someone has placed in the middle of the doorway. There's a printed A4 sheet stuck on the sign with Sellotape yellowing at the edges.

Weight Loss for Beginners
Private Group
Wednesday, 7.30–8.30 p.m.

I step around the sign and into an airy hall that looks like it's seen better days. The curtains are green-and-pink zigzags, the floor dusty and scuffed. There's a faint smell of cat piss that makes The Old Stable seem almost pleasant.

In the centre is a small circle of a dozen chairs, all filled with women. They're a mix of ages; one looks only a year or so older than me, another is in her sixties, another has a young baby sleeping in a sling on her body.

To one side is a table set up with jugs of squash and a plate of sugary donuts. My gaze falls to the man. He's sat behind the table, away from the others, and drinking from a steaming mug. He looks up as I enter, and I see the first flicker of emotion on his face. Alarm. It's gone in an instant, replaced with indifference once more.

The group of women fall silent as I approach, trainers squeaking on the wood floor. All eyes are on me. I wave my hand in a half greeting, half apology. 'Sorry I'm late,' I try, wondering whether I've got this all wrong and will be spending the next hour hearing about a diet I don't need or want.

The man starts to stand, but it's the woman from the school car park who reaches me first, waving at him to stay where he is. 'I'll be right back,' she calls to the group before grabbing my arm and yanking me towards the doors I've just stepped through.

Her grip is tight. Painful. She's squeezing hard, nails digging into my skin. Up close, she's younger than I thought. It's her haircut and clothes that make her look older. The skin on her face is puffy, her eyes bloodshot and fierce, but she can't be older than early fifties.

'Hey,' I say, but I don't pull away. Curiosity outweighs the pain, so I let her drag me out of the doors and into the car park, where the sun is now dipping towards the horizon.

'What are you doing here?' she hisses. 'Have you followed us?'

The question surprises me. She's talking like we've met before, but I'm sure we haven't.

'Hi.' I try my sweetest smile and ignore her questions. 'I was just driving by and saw the sign about a weight-loss class.'

'You did, did you? You?' Her top lip curls into a sneer as she looks me up and down. 'The sign that's inside the hall. Don't bother trying it on with me. I've seen you snooping around Leedham. I know exactly who you are. And whatever you're doing here, you need to leave. This doesn't concern you.' The accusation in her tone startles me.

'I'm staying in the village right now. I've been out walking, that's all. I wasn't—'

'Save it.' She cuts me off. 'How do you know them?'

'Who?' I ask.

'The Walker family. You must know them or why take such an interest?'

'I don't. Honestly. I'm just worried about Cate and Archie.'

She purses her lips, unconvinced. 'And yet you're the only one who's been snooping around by their house.'

'What?' How does she know that?

'I've seen you walking up and down their road, always glancing at the house. Don't bother trying to deny it.'

I shift back a little, surprised. Has she been following me? I try again to explain. 'A woman and child disappeared in broad daylight. I think it's understandable that people are concerned and curious. Did you know them well?'

'People need to mind their own business,' she says, and by *people*, it's clear she means me.

I shrug and nod back to the hall. 'Can I join your meeting?'

'It's a private group and new members have to apply. We're very selective.'

'For a beginners weight-loss group?' It's my turn to sound unconvinced.

'Yes. Now please leave.'

I'm about to say something about the women in the hall. They don't look like a weight-loss group. The one smoking her cigarette when I arrived was so slim. Frail, even. And why is the man there too? But there's a movement in the doorway, and as though my question has summoned him, he appears, arms folded across his chest.

'Jeanie?' he calls out.

'It's fine, James,' she replies before turning back to me. 'Please leave.'

It's not venom I hear in her voice anymore. It's fear. Who is she scared for? Herself or me?

'Sure,' I reply. 'Sorry to have bothered you.' I walk away with my pulse racing through my body. I start my car and drive out of the car park. A minute later, there's a red traffic light and I'm grateful for the moment to collect myself.

'You're planning to take another one, aren't you?'

I don't know what's going on inside that hall, but weight-loss groups don't have plates of donuts on offer.

Could Cate have been a member of this group? Does that man run this group to find his victims? But what about Archie? Why take him too?

I want to drive straight to the police station and tell the detectives what I've found. Except... what is that? A man I don't like the look of. A rude woman who won't let me join her weight-loss group.

Hacker's response to the threats runs through my mind.

'... sometimes, we find individuals who are so desperate to help us, and to perhaps be involved in some way, that they give us wrong information.'

He didn't believe me when I had physical proof; he's hardly going to believe me now. And if I go back, there will be more questions about me and my past and why I'm in Leedham. They're questions I'm no longer prepared to answer.

I think about what other options I have. What else I know, what I can do. There isn't much.

An idea starts to worm its way into my thoughts as the light changes from amber to green. All I know about this man – James – is that he runs a funeral home in Leedham. There could be evidence there, but the only way to be sure is to go and look.

I press my foot to the accelerator, a plan forming. I know James is at the church hall, which means the funeral home might be empty. It's the perfect moment to snoop around.

THIRTY-NINE

OLIVER

Oliver keeps his head down as he walks through the village. He made sure to leave it until after the meeting had long finished. His world is in ruins and yet it still grates that they held that meeting without him. It's his school. His wife and son who are missing.

Worse still, Anika messaged him earlier, begging him not to attend. He thought about ignoring her and walking in with his head held high, showing them all that he has nothing to hide. But it would only have damaged whatever tatters of his reputation he has left and pissed Anika off.

He reaches the footpath that leads across the fields and climbs the stile before turning left and out towards the edge of the village. He keeps close to the fence and the shadows until he finds the place. Then he waits. It's only a few minutes before he hears her call his name.

'In here,' he says, stepping out from behind a hay bale.

She turns to the sound of his voice, and despite the crushing reality of his situation and the trouble he's in, he still feels that spark of desire. The need to pull her body to him pulses through him. They haven't spoken properly since that Friday, and he realises he's missed her. He opens his arms and steps forward, but she doesn't rush into them.

They've been sleeping together for almost a year. He knows how to touch her body to make her cry out just as she knows his body, and yet it's more than sex. They've talked and laughed and made silly plans. There were times when he even wondered if he loved her, but all he sees in the beautiful eyes staring at him now from the light of her torch is a weary resolve.

'Gemma,' he whispers. 'It's me. Come on. It's OK.'

'What are we going to do?' she asks. She places the torch facing up on the ground of the stable before hugging her arms to her body.

'Hi to you too,' he says in the teasing voice he always uses with her. 'Come here,' he says, smiling, trying again to coax her to him.

'Oliver, don't be ridiculous,' she says, sounding just like Cate. 'Everything has changed... You can't expect...' Her sentence trails off and she steps back, realising, just as he does, that yes, he had expected.

It wouldn't be the first time or the tenth. He can't count how many times they've met in the stable; him telling Cate he's training for a half-marathon and buying himself hours of free time; sneaking across the fields and climbing the fence. They've peeled off each other's clothes, kissed every inch of each other's bodies in this very stable. He'd even had the best blowjob of his life sitting on a hay bale with his trousers around his ankles, the hay scratching his bare arse.

'We have to talk,' she says.

He sighs. Another part of his life over then. He thought he'd at least have Gemma's support. She's kept her word this week and told no one of their affair. 'Let's talk then.'

'What's going on? Where are Cate and Archie? You said they'd be back by now.'

'I don't know,' he replies, the truth grabbing him by the throat again.

He'd thought she'd run off. Who could blame him? After the hotel incident and her little game with him on Boxing Day when he'd promised to be faithful and meant it too. Except, he was weak and stupid, and it's never the last time, is it?

That Friday night, after he'd returned from the woods to an empty house, he'd known straight away that she was playing with him again. But this time she'd gone too far. Disappearing on the way home from school. Ditching the pool party Archie had been so excited about. Staying out all night with his son. His boy. Turning off her phone.

He'd waited her out at first. He'd even driven over to her parents' house, but they were on their cruise, the house loaned out to a friend.

By Saturday lunchtime, Oliver was ready to play his own game – the worried husband. He'd called the police. Upped the stakes. He'd made it about more than them. He'd made sure she wouldn't be able to just slink home now with all of her smugness. It was on the news. There was an investigation. She'd have to explain herself.

But she still hadn't returned. Not even when he'd planned the search. He'd been sure that would do it. That the thought of her whole community, all her friends, searching for them would drive her home.

'Oliver!' Gemma says.

'I don't,' he says. 'Honestly. I thought she'd found out about us again, and—'

'What do you mean, "again"?'

'Relax. She didn't know it was you. She found a receipt for our night at The Argyll Hotel. The champagne and the two breakfasts. I told her it was a one-night stand with a stranger after a training course. She wasn't happy, but she never suspected it was you.'

'But now?'

He rubs a hand through his hair. 'The police have gone crazy, Gemma. They think I killed them. They're saying it's a murder investigation. I'm going to have to tell them about us. You're my alibi for that night.'

'No,' she says, the surprise in her voice making it sound a little like she's laughing. He doesn't like that. He doesn't like being turned down and then laughed at. Who does she think she is? He catches himself. He can't risk pissing Gemma off by lashing out. He needs her.

'I can't tell the police I was with you,' she continues. 'I've already lied to them. You asked me to, remember? You came here on that Saturday morning, and you told me Cate had taken Archie and was playing a game. You told me to stay quiet and let it blow over. And we promised each other that, no matter what happened, we would tell no one about us. If I backtrack now, I'll be in serious trouble. Not to mention what this will do for both of us if it gets around the village – which, if you'll remember, is the reason we lied in the first place. Your job. My job. My parents. All the school parents. Everyone will turn against us. You know that, and I know you know that because we've discussed it many times.'

She's right. The thought makes him feel slightly sick. The affair is bad enough. The end of a marriage terrible, but it's nothing compared to the fact that Gemma is the one he's been sleeping with. Nearly twenty years his junior, and him her boss. On top of the community going crazy, he'd never get another job.

And yet, he has to tell the police now. For one thing, they're wasting their time searching Barton Woods.

'No one else has to know. Just the detectives,' he says.

'Don't be naïve. It will get out.'

'So it gets out,' he replies, voice rising again. 'You see how much trouble I'm in? My solicitor thinks they're going to charge me with murder by the end of the week.'

She turns away, fiddling with a rein hanging on the wall so he can't see her face. 'Were you ever going to leave her?'

'Yes,' he lies, resisting the urge to groan. He's been such a fool. 'I was just waiting for the right time – you know that. We had to be smart about it. We had to do it in stages. I was ending my marriage. Cate and I were talking about separating.' Another lie.

'Is something going on with you and Lexi?' she asks.

'What? Of course not.' He exhales and shakes his head. His thoughts snag on the substitute teacher. He pictures her red curls and that smile she always has. It keeps happening. No matter where his mind is at, it always seems to find its way to Lexi.

'You think with everything else going on this week, I've been making a move on someone else?' he asks.

'She's been asking a lot of questions about Cate.'

'Has she?'

Gemma nods. 'And I've seen you looking at her.'

'Not because of that.'

'Then why?' she asks.

'Lexi reminds me of someone, that's all. I've been trying to figure it out.'

Gemma has always been jealous. Of Cate and their marriage, or any time a mum chatted to him, she'd ask about it. It was kind of sweet. He liked that she needed him to reassure her, but now it's exhausting him.

She's quiet for a moment before she turns back to him. 'I need money.'

'What do you mean?' For a horrible moment he thinks... 'You're not—'

'Pregnant? No,' she says, and even though he's relieved, it annoys him that she could say it with such scorn. She's just like

Cate. How has he fallen for a woman just like his wife? Blonde, beautiful and a spoiled bitch. Christ, he's got a type all right. He's spent his whole life with the same kind of woman and only one of them he truly loved, and look what happened there.

'My parents are kicking me out,' Gemma says. 'They want me to find my own place. I need some cash to get me started.'

'What makes you think I have any money I can give you?'

'Of course you do. Look at where you live. Look at your life. You said—'

'Do you have any idea how much a criminal solicitor costs?'

'So?'

'So I don't have any spare cash.'

Gemma narrows her eyes and tilts her head a fraction as she looks at him. 'But if I tell the police I was with you on Friday night, they won't charge you, and you can give the money to me.'

Her eyes are on him, determined and pleading all at once. The affair is over. That much is clear, and yet it still hurts a little to tell her the truth.

'It wasn't my money,' he says, dropping his gaze to his shoes and a scuff of mud at one edge. 'The hotels, the gifts – it's all because of Cate. Her family is loaded. That's where the money comes from. I can't get my hands on more than a few hundred pounds right now.'

'What? You're joking.' Tears well in her eyes, but all he sees in her face is anger. 'You lied to me! What about the house we saw that you promised you'd buy for me? And the livery for Ginger? All the clothes you promised. The Caribbean cruise at Christmas...' She trails off, and he watches the realisation dawn. She closes her eyes. 'It was all lies.'

It's not a question, but he nods anyway. 'I'm sorry. What you and I had—'

'Was nothing,' she hisses. 'I thought you were rich. You told me you had money. I'm such an idiot. I wanted a different life-style, and I thought you could give it to me.'

Her words slice through him. He senses a pulsing anger throbbing at the edges of his mind, but it's buried beneath a hundred other things – bigger, more important things than this woman and what she thinks of him.

He was with Gemma for the thrill and the sex at first, and was surprised when it became more. Love even. Though he's not sure now. But he was never going to leave Cate. And thank God he didn't, seeing as Gemma was using him too. Did she really think he could've given her the life she wanted? Either way, they're both screwed now.

'I should go in,' she says. 'I need to talk to my parents.'

'Gemma,' he says, 'I'm going to tell the detectives tomorrow that I was with you on Friday night. I know it's going to be bad for both of us, but I don't have any other choice.'

'So I lied for nothing?'

What can he say to that? He shrugs. A headache starts to push down on the top of his head. 'I didn't think it would be for nothing.'

'And if I carry on lying?'

He's consumed with a sudden desperation. 'I've got our messages. I can show them.' It's another lie. He always deleted their messages straight away so Cate would never find them. She knows that.

Gemma gives him a final look. She's hurt and angry and maybe she doesn't believe him. He waits for her to agree, reluctant and furious, but still willing to help. Instead, she walks away without a second glance, and he has no idea what she'll do.

He drags himself home, weary, hungry but too tired to eat. His thoughts turn over everything that's happened these past weeks. He was so sure Cate was playing him when he woke up on that Saturday morning and decided to call the police. He was so sure she'd come home when the news broke, but it's been nearly two weeks without a word.

Anger burns through him. Cate had better hope the police find her first, because he'll kill her for taking his boy from him.

Then another thought lands so fast it almost knocks him off his feet. He can't believe he hasn't thought of it until now. He rushes through the front door and up the stairs two at a time, flying into Archie's bedroom.

The sight that greets him is a gut punch. He stumbles to the edge of the bed and drops to his knees. His hands reach out for Dog Dog – the tatty, grey cuddly toy that Archie's had since he was a baby and sleeps with every night, tucked in the crook of his arm. Then he remembers the camping trip to the coast they went on two summers ago, when they forgot to take Dog Dog. Archie was so upset that they ended up packing up and driving home in the middle of the night.

Cate would never have left Dog Dog behind.

What if... what if he's been wrong all this time? What if this isn't one of Cate's games? What if something really has happened to them? A rush of emotion hits him square on – a wrecking ball.

Oliver collapses to the floor as all the worry and fear that he's been pretending to feel floods through him.

FORTY

LEXI

The sun has disappeared by the time I return to the village. The cafés and houses I pass are cloaked in darkness. My determination to find answers falters as thoughts of the threat and the figure in my apartment start up once more. I'm even less certain now that it was Oliver.

I pull into the pub car park and manoeuvre into my usual spot outside the apartment.

My fear reminds me of being a child. Five years old and convinced a monster lived under my bed. I could picture it. Long, hairy arms and sharp claws desperate to reach out and grab me and suck me under. Every evening, I would take a running jump onto my bed, certain it was the only way to avoid capture. Sometimes, I swear the tips of its claw scraped my foot as I flew through the air.

That fear was as real as anything that followed into adulthood. It's the same fear that urges me to run into The Old Stable now, lock the door and hide.

But there's something very wrong going on in this village, and it's bigger than me and my emotions and my past. So I ignore the voice in my head questioning what I'm doing and stride in the direction of the village, away from the safety of the pub – the lights and the noise. The beer garden is full. Loud voices carry in the evening air. The trellis surrounding the tables is decked in fairy lights; their soft glow enough to light the faces of the drinkers. I recognise many of them from the school earlier.

I keep to the shadows, invisible in the darkness, and make my way onto the main road.

My run-in with Jeanie plays on my mind, pushing me onwards. Who is she? How is she involved in whatever is going on?

I reach the shopfront of J. Simpson Funeral Director. It's closed and locked, the lights out inside, but there's an arched driveway beside the building I didn't notice the last time I walked this way.

It must have a back entrance for hearses and funeral cars. I throw a glance over my shoulder. The only light is from the glow of streetlights and the supermarket on the corner. In the distance, a woman in PJs hurries out of the shop with a carton of milk in her hands. She doesn't see me. No one does, and I'm not sure, as I turn on the torch on my phone and step between the buildings, if that's a good thing or not. No one knows I'm here.

I check the time. It's already gone eight. I don't have long before the weight-loss meeting finishes.

The driveway leads to a small gravel area that I guess is used as a car park. On my left are two large, black wooden gates.

Another burst of adrenaline. Another stream of 'what am I doing?' thoughts, then I'm hoisting myself up and over the other side in seconds. The movement reminds me of teenage years spent climbing the fence at school to ditch classes and escape. I was never the good child. That was Donna. I couldn't compete with her perfection. And then one night, when she was seventeen and I was ten, she changed everything, stealing the final scraps of attention my parents gave me, keeping it all for herself. It's easy to see why I rebelled as soon as I could.

My feet land with a thud that echoes too loudly around a stone courtyard. My pulse starts to race. There might be other employees. I'm trespassing. If I get caught...

I pause, holding my breath. Listening; taking in my surroundings. The property is bigger than it looks from the high street. Beyond the shopfront is a long, attached building, and across the courtyard I'm standing in is a workshop or garage.

I try the back door of the shop. It's locked. The warehouse doors are the same, and I'm halfway to thinking how stupid I was to think I could do this – I have no idea how to break into a locked building – when I spot an open window to the side of the warehouse. It's small. One of those old-fashioned top panes, held open by a metal lever. It's only open a fraction, but when I climb onto the ledge, it's enough for me to push my hand inside and open it wider. Wide enough to reach down and pull the lever at the side of the larger window beneath it.

The pane swings out, almost knocking me off the ledge. I yelp, freezing again at the noise and digging my fingertips into the wooden frame to steady myself. I pause, listening beyond the thudding of my heart in my ears. Then I step carefully through the open window and drop down into a small toilet room. I shine my torch around the room. There's a toilet, a sink and a pile of cleaning products beside a mop and bucket.

The room leads into an open space with a cement floor and a line of three black cars parked beside an older blue van I recognise from the high street and the pub car park.

Beside the toilet room is another self-contained unit, and I open the door and find myself in a small cubicle space with a table in the centre and two chairs beside it. Peach-coloured silk fabric hangs from the walls, reminding me of the inside of a coffin. I spot a box of tissues and realise this must be a place the grieving relatives come to say their goodbyes.

A shiver races down my spine. Images of Donna intrude into my thoughts, and I force them away, hurriedly closing the door and opening the next one. It's an office with an old wooden desk and a set of drawers, and lever files on shelves. I step inside and close the door behind me. There's no window to this room, so I shut the door and turn on the light. I don't know what I'm looking for, but if there's anything to find in this warehouse, it'll be in here.

There are invoices and receipts and bills, and a stack of order-of-service booklets. Nothing out of the ordinary. I open the top drawer of the desk and find only pens and paperclips and a diary filled with funeral dates. I tuck it back into place and flinch as I catch sight of the clock on the wall. I'm being too slow, too cautious. Time is on fast forward. The weight-loss meeting will have finished by now. James could be back any minute, and I'm no closer to answers.

The second drawer down is stiff and doesn't open. It moves a fraction but not enough, so I yank it hard. Something gives in the wood, and the drawer flies out, hitting the end of the runner with a bang that sounds deafening in the silence.

I swear under my breath and listen as the silence rings in my ears. Was that an engine?

I'm out of time.

My hands start to tremble as I try to push the drawer shut. It won't budge. As hard as it was to open, now it won't close. There's something caught on the runners. I crouch down and run my hand around the drawer. It's just notebooks and A4 diary planners. Why isn't it shutting?

The sound of the engine comes again. Nearer now.

Suddenly I find something. There's a hidden compartment beneath the drawer. It must have sprung open when it hit the runners. I prise my fingers into the hidden box until it's all the way up and I can see inside to the pile of glossy photographs.

A gasp leaves my mouth. The photographs are of women.

At least a dozen different women, with four or five photographs each. They're smiling at the camera – some in gardens, some on sofas, some beside tourist attractions. Snapshots of lives that people used to stick in albums and now post on social media.

There's nothing obvious that connects these women. Some are old, some are young, some thin, some larger. Blonde, brunette, redhead. Nothing is the same. I skip through them until I come to a face I recognise. Two faces actually. The same two faces that have been splashed across news sites for nearly two weeks. Cate and Archie.

A knot of dread tangles in my stomach.

I drop the rest of the photos in the drawer and put Cate's on the desk. I can't stop staring at it. I can't connect it. I can't believe it. This man with his dark eyes and soulless expression has a photo of Cate and Archie in a hidden drawer in his office. Other women too.

A bang startles me out of my thoughts. A car door shutting. Then the hum of an engine again and a bang of wood so close that it can only be the courtyard gates. He's back. And I'm still here.

I slam down the hidden compartment and shove the drawer shut before leaping up and turning off the light, throwing myself into a wall of complete black. My phone is gripped in my hand, but I daren't use the torch now as I rush through the warehouse. Heart thundering, barely breathing.

Footsteps crunch outside the warehouse. A key scrapes in the lock. He's here. He's inside the building, and there's nowhere to run.

FORTY-ONE

LEXI

Adrenaline charges – a stallion – through my body. I want to drop to the floor and close my eyes; I want to grab a weapon and rush at the man when he enters. I want to run as fast as I've ever run in my life and never look back.

I do none of these things.

Quickly, on feet as light as I can make them, I dart back to the toilet room and the window – my escape. The warehouse door opens. There's a rush of cool air. He's here. He's in the building. I step through the doorway just as the lights flicker and turn on. My heart feels like it will explode from a chest too tight to contain it.

I move silently behind the door and listen to the man move into the warehouse. Footsteps draw nearer. He coughs, and it sounds like he's right outside the door. I hold my breath, certain he'll hear each shallow inhale. There's nowhere to hide. If he steps into the toilet room, he'll see me. I cast my gaze around for a weapon but find only the mop.

Another cough. This one further away. I hear the flick of a light switch and guess he's in his office. Indecision rips through me. The warehouse doors are open. I could make a run for them, but he'd be sure to hear my footsteps on the concrete.

I peer through the crack in the door frame and watch him step into the middle of the warehouse. He seems suddenly so much bigger, threatening.

The photos replay in my head.

Does he run a weight-loss class to find these women? Preying on those who are insecure and vulnerable? Does he wait for the right moment before snatching them from the street? Then what? I know nothing about the role of a funeral director, but if they have access to coffins and cremations, could they dispose of extra bodies? My head starts to pound. The questions, the fear and the rapid firing of my pulse.

In the middle of the warehouse, the man remains as still as I am. Why is he just standing there?

A gut-wrenching weight drops in the pit of my stomach. Realisation dawns with horrifying clarity. The photo of Cate and Archie. I put it on the desk, but in my haste to get out, I don't know if I dropped it back in with the others before closing the drawer. And the more I think about it, the more certain I am that I didn't.

Does he know I'm here?

The desire to run is spikey and innate. A plan starts to form. My gaze moves to the door. There's a lock, but it's flimsy. It will only buy me a few minutes. If he turns, if he makes any move towards me, I'll slam the door, lock it and make a dive for the window.

I wait and wait. And then suddenly he's moving. Long, fast strides, but not towards me. Instead, he's heading to the doors. A moment later, the door clangs shut, and the warehouse is thrown into darkness once more. I listen to his footsteps as he walks across the courtyard before another door shuts with a thud.

Then there's only silence. I watch the minutes pass on my

phone, my heart rate refusing to slow. Only when five minutes have passed do I risk moving to the window. Slowly, carefully, I push open the glass and glance towards the main building. There's a light on upstairs. He must have a flat above the shop. I watch for any movement from the window, and only when I'm sure it's clear do I move, climbing back to the courtyard and shutting the window.

In the open, I'm exposed, and I dart to the shadows of the gate before climbing over. My leg catches on the metal screw of a hinge, and I feel the sharp sting of a cut as I drop to the ground.

The alley between the buildings is in darkness, but there's the glow of streetlights ahead, so I don't use my phone as I hurry out of the driveway and onto the high street. There's no one around, but I catch my breath, feeling almost safe as I force myself to walk normally in the direction of The Old Stable.

I'm not sure what makes me glance back, but when I do, my gaze is drawn to a light in the first-floor window above the funeral home. I gasp, the cool air hitting my lungs. There, standing in the window, is the tall, shadowed figure of the man – James. I can't see his face, but I sense him watching me. I whirl around, striding, hurrying, all but running, and don't stop until I'm pushing through the door of The Old Stable. For the first time, the smell of damp is a welcome relief.

My hands shake as I push the key into the lock on the inside, checking and double-checking the bolt is in place before moving my punch bag alongside it.

I make myself drink a cup of tea. My pulse slows, but the jittering fear remains. Did he see me leave the alley? Does he know I was in the warehouse? Will he come after me next, like the threatening note promised?

FORTY-TWO

The fun is in the planning. I like to imagine and prepare; to savour. But there's no fun right now. Not with the discovery of a body and the police in the village so much.

Every day, I've expected them to come. The waiting is as bad. My thoughts run away with me. What will I say to them? I flip wildly between declaring my guilt – 'they deserved everything they got' – to denial.

All these years, I've taken what isn't mine. Stolen beautiful treasures like the magpies.

I remember Bella Godwin. My first.

She was thirty but looked a decade younger. Dark-blonde hair and pale-green eyes, always pleading with me. The need I felt to take her was a physical thing – a fever that wouldn't break. How many years ago was that? Ten? No, eleven.

I've lost count of how many women have come since Bella. That makes it sound like I don't care, but it isn't true. Each was special. Each deserved my attention, just like you.

Perhaps I got a little too... not complacent – never that – but confident. Who could blame me? So many of the women I've taken haven't even been reported as missing. And those that were, well, the interest waned fast. People move on. They tell themselves they care, but they turn a blind eye when it threatens to destroy their rose-tinted view of the world. I've seen it happen enough times, and the truth is, they can't wait to relegate the messy and painful to the backs of their minds, to twist it into a story of something that could never have happened to them. They'll tell themselves they're too careful, too nice. Then they'll pat themselves on the back and wash their cars and go to their barbeques and do their DIY and pretend their mundane existences matter. The same will happen to you.

I'll admit it's been harder this time and not as fun. The police presence in the village and the interest in you has added pressure I haven't enjoyed. It makes me wonder if maybe I'll stop. A stupid thought. Like an alcoholic waking with a hangover, promising themselves they'll never drink again.

I will never stop. Already, I have another woman in mind. She's not like you, Cate. She won't put up such a fight. Sadly, it means it's the end of our time together. I must clean up the cottage and prepare it for the next guest. You understand, don't you? There's always another one to take.

THURSDAY: THIRTEEN DAYS MISSING

FORTY-THREE

OLIVER

Oliver's headache has morphed into something more. It feels like his skull has cracked right down the middle and his brain is being prised apart.

He's taken triple the recommended dose of painkillers, but nothing is getting through. The cut on his hand hurts more than ever too. It's infected. Badly. He saw the nurse first thing and even though she looked at him like he was a goddamn murderer, she'd still winced when she'd peeled off the bandage.

'How long has it been like this?' she'd asked.

'I thought it was healing,' he'd replied, not wanting to explain that it had happened the same night his wife and child had disappeared, cut on a sharp piece of metal in the door frame of the van while he and Gemma had frantic sex on the bare ground beside the camper.

'It's trying to heal, but you're going to need some antibiotics. You're lucky. Infections should never be ignored. You could've lost your hand. Keep it clean and dry, and if it gets even a little bit worse tomorrow or the next day, go straight to hospital.'

She'd wrapped a clean bandage over the festering hot wound and printed a prescription he'll have to drive out to the nearby supermarket to collect. The shop that houses Leedham's pharmacy and post office is the hub of the village, and there's no way he can stand all those buzzing bees, humming with gossip about him.

They've turned on him. His own community – the people whose children he taught and supported. After all the charity work he's done; all the events he's helped at. Years and years of doing his bit, and it's all been forgotten. Erased. Now they think he's a murderer capable of killing his wife and his little boy.

God, he misses Archie.

Sudden tears threaten. He's losing his grasp on his life, his emotions, his actual mind. He thinks of his boy, who loves football and strawberry ice cream, who used to beg him to take him on bike rides or camping or boating on the river. But there was always something. A job around the house, a secret visit to Gemma or, and he's ashamed to admit this now, but sometimes he just couldn't be bothered.

'Next weekend, Arch. Let's make a plan for next weekend.'

They never did. He's been a crap husband, a mediocre dad, but he would never, never, *never* hurt his boy. He has to tell the police everything. He sees that now.

He'll still be in trouble. He'll have to explain why he hid not just his affair and alibi from them but that he reported Cate and Archie missing when he didn't actually think they were. He'd thought Cate was playing a game and so he'd reported her missing to call her bluff, but now he thinks his family really are in some kind of trouble, and he has to make the police see this; has to get them help.

It won't be easy. They think he's guilty of murder. The village does too. He saw it in Anika's eyes, and in the look from the receptionist at the doctors' surgery, and the nurse too. So much for pity and support. Was it really only Saturday they'd come out to help him?

When had it changed? When had the kindness splintered into suspicion and hate?

The search, he decides. The crowds gathered. They'd all been supporting him then. Right up until the police arrived and told everyone to go home. They'd searched the house that day and shown him the photos.

The pivotal moment in his downfall. Those awful photos that Lexi had found and given straight to the police.

Lexi. Again. She's like a parasite burrowed into his mind. He rakes over his memories and his past – the places he's been, the life he's had. It's hardly much. Education, teaching, marriage, promotions. Nothing stands out, no occasion where their paths would've crossed. She's so much younger than him. And yet, he's certain they've met before. He sees her face in his mind again. The rosebud lips, the big eyes. She's beautiful, but that doesn't explain why he's drawn to her, why every time he sees her, an anger fires through him and he has the desire to punch something.

Maybe he's thinking about this all wrong. Maybe there's another way Lexi is connected to this.

He stops suddenly in the middle of the pavement. He hasn't paid much attention to his wife lately, but he remembers now a blue car dropping her home one evening last month. A new yoga class, she'd told him. But... he searches his memories. She wasn't wearing her yoga kit. That's it. And if he thinks about it, wasn't it a woman driving the car – a blonde? Was it Lexi? Does she know Cate? And more than that, does she know where Cate is? Are they working together to bring him down?

Oliver checks the time. It's early. He can catch Lexi before school if he's quick.

He spins on his heels, turning in the other direction, away from his house and towards the pub. Footsteps pound the pavement. A runner tuts at his change of direction, leaping into the road to avoid a collision. Oliver doesn't bother to look up or offer the friendly apology he'd have given a week ago. Instead, he mutters an expletive under his breath and carries on in the direction of the pub, reaching the car park just as Lexi steps out of an apartment at the end of the block.

For the first time, it occurs to him how strange her situation is. Most substitute teachers bounce around the local area, filling in for a day or two whenever needed. Lexi has come from... He realises he doesn't know. Did she say London? And staying in the village too. He knows what the rent on these places is, and he knows what she earns. It's ludicrous. Unless there's another reason for her to be here.

The bright red of her curls bounce with every step as she makes her way towards the high street. He stops and waits. She's digging in her bag for something and hasn't seen him.

A pressure builds in his chest. All the things he doesn't know twist in his gut. He side-steps, putting himself in her path, and waits until she's almost upon him. 'Why are you so obsessed with my wife?'

The question lands with the desired effect. Lexi's eyes widen with alarm.

'What are you doing here?' she asks.

No peppy smile this time, he notices.

'I want to know why you're here – in Leedham. And why you're interested in Cate. I saw you walk by my house, and I know you've been asking questions about them.' And even though he doesn't mean to do it, he finds his finger jabs out, pointing at her.

'The substitute agency called me. I think I was the only one available who could cover for an extended period of time. And I guess taking over Cate's class meant it all got under my skin a bit this week, and—'

'And what?'

'Someone's been threatening me.' She chooses her words

carefully, head tilting a fraction to one side, watching his reaction. Another person thinking he's done something he hasn't.

'What kind of threats?' he asks.

'Threatening notes telling me to leave Leedham or I'll be next.'

'What?' He runs a hand through his hair. His head continues to pound. 'Have you told the police?'

She nods. 'But they don't believe me.'

'That makes two of us.' He pauses. Thinks. He remembers what Lexi said outside the police station. 'You thought it was me?'

'Yes.'

'Well, it's not.'

'I know.'

'Good. And what else do you know?'

She bites her lip before shaking her head. 'Nothing.'

'I don't believe you.' There's a desperation in his voice he hates. 'You're out to get me. You gave the police those photos.'

'Of course I did. I found them in Cate's cupboard. Anyone in my situation would've done the same.'

'But they think I killed them because of that. The detectives called me last night. I've got to go back to the police station today. They're going to charge me with murder. Everyone thinks Cate is this amazing woman, but she was a manipulative, controlling bitch, and no one believes me. They all think my perfect family are dead and I killed them.

'I know you didn't kill them.'

He takes a step back, surprised. It's the last thing he expected her to say. 'How?'

'It's... I found something. But I can't explain it now. I need more time.'

Her gaze roams their surroundings again. Who is she scared of? Him or someone else?

'I don't have more time. If you know something, you have to

tell me.' Again with the jabbing finger. Why is he being like this with her? She steps back.

His phone buzzes from his pocket. He pulls it out and winces at the sight of DS Pope's number. 'See? They're calling me now.' He rubs a hand over his face. The world is closing in again.

'Did Cate ever go out on a Wednesday evening?'

Lexi's question takes him by surprise.

He starts to shake his head but then remembers the car dropping her home and the excuse of the yoga class. Was that a Wednesday night? It might have been. 'Once, I think. A few weeks before she went missing. Why? Do you know where they are? Are you and Cate in this together?'

'No. I've never met Cate. I'm sorry. I need to check on some things. I'll come to your house tonight once I have more.'

She moves, stepping around him. And even though he doesn't mean to, and he can't explain it, his hand reaches out, grabbing at her arm through the sleeve of her top.

'I might be locked in a prison cell by tonight.' His voice breaks. 'Please help me. You're the only one who thinks I didn't do this.'

She nods, but she's squirming away from him, trying to pull out of his grasp. He's scaring her. Her sleeve moves up, and his fingertips brush over the bumps of a scar on her forearm. His grip tightens. He steps closer and stares at the puckered skin, pink and white. It's a cut that runs from the top of her wrist all the way in a diagonal line to her elbow.

A sickening déjà vu floods his body. He knows this scar from somewhere.

'Where did you get this?' He splutters out the words, his gaze moving from the scar to her face and then back to the scar. A memory starts to prod at the back of his mind. The crunching metal. The explosion of glass. The metallic taste of blood in his mouth. His hand drops away. It can't be connected to his past.

'It's nothing,' she says, pushing her sleeve down. 'I cut it as a child.'

His phone rings again. The moment of distraction is enough. She steps around him, and this time he lets her go; his mind is reeling.

He looks down at his phone. Pope again. The memories disappear before he can grab hold of them and what they mean. He swipes his phone and swallows back a mounting fear as he says a hesitant, 'Hello?'

FORTY-FOUR

LEXI

The school day drags more than it should as we practise for tomorrow's assembly. I love teaching. I love the all-consuming distraction and the fun of it, the sense of achievement when you see the answers click in a child's face.

But today, I can't concentrate. There's too much fighting for space in my thoughts.

James Simpson. The secret compartment of photos. All those women. Cate and Archie among them. The figure at the window watching me leave. The threats. The sense that more is to come and I'm running out of time.

Then there's Oliver. If James is responsible for Cate's disappearance, then Oliver is innocent. And yet there are still the bruises I can't shake from my thoughts. That anger I see in him. I know he can't be trusted.

Questions and suspicions build and build until my head feels like it'll explode. I'm desperate to tell someone. To let everything that's happening spill out in a frenzy of words and have someone tell me it'll be OK, someone to help me. But there's no one. No real friends anymore. And certainly not my parents after how we left things. I've shut myself off from the world because I thought I was protecting myself, but all it's done is left me alone, exposed.

I think of DC Hacker and DS Pope, and what they'd say if I told them all I know. But then I remember the disbelief on Hacker's face, that pity and exasperation. They didn't believe me before. What will they say when I try to explain that a serial killer has been operating in Leedham for at least a decade. They'll laugh in my face.

The children sense my preoccupation. They're chatty and restless, until I can't stand it anymore and give them an extra play in the field in the afternoon.

I use the time to google missing women in the area. There are more than I would've imagined. I find missing-person posters of runaway teens and social-media appeals. I find an entire Facebook group dedicated to a woman called Bella Godwin. Hundreds of posts, photos, fundraising and pleas.

It takes five minutes of scrolling for me to feel as though I know this woman's life inside and out. She was married for a year before, one day, she didn't come home. She'd been to the doctor with depression. The police believe she killed herself, but the husband and family are still holding out hope she's alive.

I didn't spend enough time looking at the photos in the secret drawer to be sure, but one of the images of Bella on a beach with her arms outstretched looks familiar, and I think it was in the drawer too.

There's only one way to be sure. I must go back.

The timer buzzes on my phone. The children's extra play-time is over, and I call them in before unboxing the art supplies. They spend the afternoon painting self-portraits instead of studying the Romans, and I sit at my desk, screen-shotting the photos of more missing women. I find six that span the last seven years and wonder how many more are out there.

By the time the school bell rings to mark the end of the day, the paints are packed away and the portraits are pegged out to dry on a string that runs the length of the classroom.

One painting stands out, and I look on the back and see Sebastian's neatly written name. Yet the boy in the picture is blond.

'Sebastian,' I call to him as he loops his book bag over one shoulder. 'Your painting is very good. You have a lovely talent here.'

His cheeks colour and he smiles. 'I like painting.'

'Why did you do yourself with different-coloured hair?'

He fidgets and looks at his shoes. 'It's not me. It's Archie. I didn't want anyone to forget about him.' The sadness in his voice makes me want to hug him, but he's already moving, following the other children into the playground.

I wave them off to their parents, nannies and grandparents. I watch Sebastian talk to Anika, and I imagine him telling her about the afternoon of play and painting. She looks up at me, her expression fierce. She shakes her head a little before pulling out her phone.

Another nail in my coffin. She called the substitute teaching agency this morning. There were two missed calls on my phone and a voicemail asking me to get in touch when I checked at lunchtime. The Brighton number has called again too. I can't avoid it forever. The need to hide, to run, is battling with the need to know what they want from me.

I'm waiting for Anika to talk to me again, give me another warning about my career. But then again, she's made it clear that the school needs me. Either way, right now she's the least of my worries.

The sense of time running out is building up and up. I'm hurtling towards something.

When Oliver grabbed my arm this morning, when he saw

the scar, I thought it was all over. I could almost see something dawning on his face. If he hasn't realised our connection now, then he will do soon, and then maybe he'll connect the dots and realise that I'm the reason Cate and Archie are missing. It's why I must find them.

FORTY-FIVE

OLIVER

Oliver gulps back the last mouthful of water from the plastic cup in front of him and waits for Pope or Hacker to say something. The water is warm and does little to quench the dryness of his throat.

From beside him, Philip clears his throat and shuffles the notes he'd made from their talk earlier. Oliver has just told the detectives everything. A long, garbled statement about being with Gemma on that Friday night, the affair, and how he'd thought until yesterday that Cate and Archie were fine.

'So you believe Cate left and took your son and told no one, not even her parents, that she was going, allowed everyone to worry, became a national news story, all to punish you?' Pope asks with an incredulous tone.

'Yes. I mean... no. I did think that, but now I think something has happened to them.'

Pope and Hacker share a look – a secret message passing between them – before all eyes fall on Oliver.

'Why was Miss Rowley not captured on the traffic cameras in your campervan?' Hacker asks.

'I drove to Glebe Lane to collect her. It's quiet there. She hid in the back of the van to avoid being seen by any villagers. We drove to the car park in Barton Woods, where we' – he clears his throat – 'had sex and then talked. We spent around two hours together before I drove us back to Leedham. I arrived home at around nine thirty to an empty house. I didn't see Cate or Archie at all that evening.

'I see,' Pope begins. 'And this affair with Miss Rowley. Did Cate know about it?'

'I... I don't know. I didn't think so, but when she didn't come home on Friday, I thought... I wondered if she'd guessed and that's when I thought she'd left me.'

'Why have you waited until now to tell us all of this, Oliver? You realise that you've wasted valuable police time and if, as you now believe, your wife and son are in trouble, this delay may have dashed any chance of us finding them.'

'I know. It was wrong, I'm sorry. I... I just needed you to think it was real so it would become a news story. I didn't think it would get this big. And I couldn't tell you about the affair with Gemma because I'd have lost my job and my standing in the community. But that doesn't matter now.' He shrugs. 'They all think I'm a murderer.'

He babbles then, explaining about Boxing Day and what Cate did. He wishes he'd told them earlier about Cate's vindictive streak. It feels lost among the lies and the truth he's now giving them.

Questions fire back at him until he's exhausted, barely able to form replies. He hates that they think he's an idiot and a liar and a terrible husband. Being those things, and people knowing he is those things, are very different.

'So you now want us to believe that someone else has kidnapped your wife and child?' Pope asks. There's a slight mocking to her tone that grates on him. He thought telling the truth would get him out of this, but why does it feel like the hole he's in is getting deeper?

Oliver nods anyway, a vigorous movement that causes his headache to intensify. 'Yes,' he adds, remembering the recording. 'I swear, the last time I saw them was lunchtime at the school.'

Hacker leans forward in his seat, fixing his gaze on Oliver. 'I assume you suddenly have a perfectly reasonable explanation for the photos of Cate's bruised body now too?'

Oliver closes his eyes for a moment. He has an explanation, but it isn't reasonable. 'The photos... they're... they're not of Cate. I have no idea how she got them, but they're not her.'

The pinch of a frown forms on Pope's brow. 'How do you expect us to believe you?'

And here it is. The second can of worms. He bites down on the inside of his mouth, fighting to keep control as memories pound his head. 'They're of an ex-girlfriend,' he says, squeezing his eyes shut for a second; the memories of who he was add to the pounding pressure racing through him. 'I... Look, it was a long time ago. I was an angry person. I felt like the universe was always against me and that I'd never get the same opportunities I saw being given to other people. It made me lash out sometimes. I'm not proud of who I was and what I did then.

'I was in a very toxic relationship. We weren't good for each other. She'd wind me up and...' His voice trails off at the look of disdain crossing the detectives' faces. 'But I'm not that person anymore. I met Cate, and she helped me see that I needed to change if I wanted people to treat me better.' He searches for something else to say, a way to explain what he did, to excuse it somehow. But there's nothing, so he stops and he waits.

'The problem we have, Oliver,' Pope begins, 'is that you've lied to us throughout this investigation and now you're telling us an entirely different version of events.'

'But Gemma will tell you she was with me. Just ask her.' His voice rises to a squeak.

'I'm afraid' – Hacker pauses for another second – 'what

you've told us doesn't prove that you're innocent of the murder
of Cate and Archie. If anything, what it does is give us a strong
motive for why you'd want to harm your wife and child.'

'What?' The word comes out in an exhale of disbelief.

'It's entirely possible,' Hacker continues in a hard voice,
'that you arrived home on Friday, killed your wife and son, met
Gemma as you've described then returned to cover up the
murders. Or perhaps Gemma was in on it. Perhaps the two of
you decided to kill them together and drove up to Barton Woods
to bury the bodies.'

'That's not true. Please, you must look for my wife and son.
I didn't do this.'

Pope snatches up the folder on the table in front of her. 'We
will follow up on your story with Gemma Rowley. And while
we do so, we'd like you to remain in police custody.'

Philip clears his throat. 'You can only hold my client
without charge for twenty-four hours.'

'We're well aware of the rules. Thank you,' Pope replies.
She stops the recording, and Oliver slumps back in the chair as
a nauseating guilt floods his body. What has he done? The truth
was supposed to fix everything, but they still think he's guilty.

Tears throb at the back of his eyes. There are no words for
how much he misses his boy. He even misses Cate a bit too.
He's been a shit husband and rubbish dad, but he doesn't
deserve this.

Don't you?

The whispered voice isn't his. It belongs to someone from
long ago, someone he's worked every day for the last sixteen
years to forget ever existed. Even after all this time, the faint
memory of it is honey and sweet and fills him with desire.

The hairs on the back of his neck stand on end. He thought
he'd forgotten that voice and everything about that time in his
life.

The detectives are standing, but Oliver remains in the chair.

He can't move. His muscles, his body, they don't belong to him while that voice is in his head.

And then a veil lifts; a light switches on. That déjà vu feeling he gets when he sees Lexi; the scar on her arm. He knows exactly how she got it, and the memory of that time hits him so fiercely, it's a fight not to double over.

FORTY-SIX

LEXI

It's gone nine by the time he comes for me. The sun has set, and the sky is dusty black and scattered with stars like a spilled glitter pot. The fairy lights on the trellis in the pub garden cast the only light. It doesn't reach to where I've moved my car, away from the apartment and hidden behind a Land Rover – and where I've been sitting for the last three hours.

I knew the second I saw him watching me from the window last night that he'd come. And despite the pulsing terror catching with every breath of my lungs, I had to be ready.

He appears as a shady figure, skirting the edge of the car park, heading straight for my apartment. And even though I expected this, planned for it; even though he warned me I'd be next – not Oliver like I thought, but James Simpson, the funeral director – even though I've been waiting for it, my pulse still thrums at the same pace as my Tabata workout music: fast, pounding. I wonder if he'll knock on the apartment door, or if he's scooped up the key again from the corkboard in the pub and will let himself in. What will he do when he finds the place empty?

The moment the bell rang earlier and my class were

scooped up from the playground, I hurried back to my apartment. I changed, pulling on a pair of jeans and a T-shirt, and gathered my curls up and away from my face. I forced myself to eat a bowl of pasta before I packed my things – clothes, wash kit, blender. I stacked everything by the door, ready to leave. I don't know what the night will bring, but I need to be ready.

Then I grabbed a torch and a bottle of water, and I moved my car, before turning off the engine and sitting low in the seat. I watched cars come and go, people wanting a pub dinner or a quick drink. I passed the hours by searching on my phone for more missing women. I found another one from four years ago. I think of the body in the well from twenty years ago. Is it all connected? Is it possible that a serial killer has been living in somewhere like Leedham all this time and the police had no idea?

He reaches my front door and throws a glance over his shoulder. He's dressed in black, a hood pulled over his head. He pulls out a white envelope. Another threat. The realisation lands at the same time as the next one. I sit up in my seat. I lean forward, peering at the figure.

Something isn't right.

Why threaten me again? I was warned and I carried on. I even broke into his warehouse at the funeral home. I've seen his stash of photos.

Stop asking about the missing teacher or you'll be next.

The *next* moment has arrived, and yet the figure is already bending down to slip another note under my door.

There's something else wrong too. The figure. Even as a shadow, it's not the large frame of James Simpson but someone smaller. Every movement short and quick.

My mind leaps to Jeanie. That tight grip; nails digging into my skin. How is she connected to this? Why is she helping him take these women? Did he send her here?

I'm out of the car in seconds and halfway across the car park before the figure sees me. They freeze for a split second before darting in the direction of the road.

They're quick, but I'm quicker. Two strides, three, four, and I'm on them, my hand snatching at their shoulder. The hood falls from their head, and they stop running and turn to face me.

'You?' I gasp. 'What are you doing here?'

FORTY-SEVEN

GEMMA

Gemma's head spins. Everything has fallen apart.

It's been the worst day! She's bone-weary from a drawn-out interview with DC Hacker and DS Pope. They made her go to the police station and endure the humiliation of a recorded interview. She told them everything. The affair. Oliver. The lies. His promises of a future together. Their pact to keep their relationship secret.

Then she had to go home and tell it all again to her parents. She's not sure which was worse – DS Pope's pitying disdain or the way her parents talked about her like she wasn't there. Their disappointment and the plans she had no say in. She'd needed air. She'd needed to lash out at someone, and there was only one person she could think of.

'Why are you threatening me?' Confusion carries in Lexi's tone, and the truth is Gemma isn't sure anymore.

She always saw Cate as her rival. Beautiful, classy, popular and married to the head teacher, Cate was hard to compete with. It's one of the reasons she flirted back when Oliver made it clear he was interested. Even if no one else knew that Cate's life wasn't as perfect as she made out, Gemma knew. Then Cate disappeared and, with her, Gemma's rival at school. She'd felt sure, come September, she'd move from the snivelling noses of the Reception class to take Cate's Year Four class. She's paid her dues with the little ones for long enough, and waiting for Steve Bishop to retire was taking too long.

But then Lexi arrived, swooping in to her class and making everyone love her, just like Cate always did.

Gemma can feel the tremble in her hands spreading through her body. She isn't sure of anything anymore. Her gaze falls to the envelope she dropped. It's sitting on the gravel a metre back. Lexi spots it too and picks it up. She thinks about running again, wishing Ginger was with her. Like when she was little and she'd dreamed of her own horse and galloping across the fields, riding forever, never stopping.

She wants to say something, but words fail her. So she stands, silent, heat burning her face, as Lexi opens the envelope and reads the note Gemma wrote.

'Get out of Leedham now!' Lexi's eyes bore into her. 'What is this?'

She shakes her head. There are too many emotions battling for space. Her throat is tight. There's no way to wriggle out of this, to deny or lie. It feels like she's woken up from a dream – a nightmare – and nothing feels real.

'Gemma,' Lexi says, 'do you have any idea how scared I've been this week? Why are you threatening me?'

She shakes her head. 'I... I don't know. I... You... you came in from nowhere, and suddenly you were acting like you were part of this community. You have no right to be here, taking over from Cate and then snooping around. I thought you might want to stay at the school permanently. And Oliver – I saw the way he was looking at you—'

'What are you talking about?'

'He likes you. He was always watching you. And I—'

'You were jealous.' Lexi throws her hands in the air. 'Seriously? You wanted me gone because you didn't like that people thought I was nice? You didn't like the way your boss looked at me.'

Lexi's eyes widen. Gemma sees the realisation starting to dawn.

'He's not just my boss,' she says. 'Oliver and I, we were having an affair. We love each other.' *Loved*, she corrects in her mind, before wondering if that's even true. Did she really think he'd leave Cate and they'd make a go of it? That she'd step into Cate's shoes and be the queen bee? She's been such a fool.

She looks around her before stepping to a low brick wall at the edge of the car park and sinking down.

'How long has it been going on for?' Lexi asks, sitting down beside her.

'About a year. He told me he was going to leave Cate for me. Then Cate disappeared and you came, and I thought you were going to steal Oliver from me after everything I'd worked for.'

'Gemma, this' – she waves the note in the air – 'is not OK. You broke into my apartment. I was terrified. I thought someone was after me.'

'I know. I'm sorry.'

'How did you get in?'

Another wave of humiliation rushes through her, dragging her down with it. 'I'd had a few drinks in the pub, and I saw the key on the corkboard. I used to work behind the bar when I was eighteen. I know how it all works. When Paul went to refill the ice, I reached over and borrowed the key for a minute.

'I didn't mean for you to wake up,' she carries on, remembering the bolt of fear she'd felt in the apartment. The strike of lightning, the moment she'd realised she'd gone too far but it was too late to take back. 'I just wanted you to find the note on the table and for it to freak you out.'

'So I'd leave?'

She nods.

'And what about this one?'

'Things with Oliver are over. I was an idiot to think we had something special. The police know everything now; so do my parents. It's been a horrible day, and I just... I wanted to make someone else feel as crappy as I do. I'm sorry.'

'Where's Cate? What happened?' Lexi asks, and Gemma isn't sure if she's accepting the apology or ignoring it, and whether it makes any difference now.

'I don't know.'

'But you said in the first note that the same thing will happen to me. What thing? You told me they were dead.'

'Oh.' She shakes her head as the realisation dawns. 'No. You've got it all wrong. I had nothing to do with Cate going missing. I made up the threat to scare you into leaving. I swear, I have no idea where Cate is, and, quite frankly, I don't care. She was always belittling me in front of the other staff. She'd give these backhanded compliments, like, I wish I had your curves and the confidence to wear such tight clothes. It only stopped when she started acting really weird a few weeks before they went missing. She was always looking over her shoulder and on her phone. I wondered at one point if she was cheating on Oliver too. I know you think Oliver did something to them,' Gemma continues, 'but he was with me that Friday night.'

'The whole night?' Lexi makes a face, clearly unconvinced.

'No. Just the evening.'

'How sure are you he didn't hurt them later then?'

'I'm sure,' she replies with less conviction than she means. The questions from the detectives have got in her head. Seeing Oliver last night – he looked so different. He looked old. It made her wonder how well she really knew him. 'Oliver can be... he can be intense, he has a temper, but he always shuts down on himself when he gets mad, like he takes himself away until he's calmed down.'

After a pause, she asks, 'What are you going to do now?'

Lexi's gaze is fierce. 'About Cate?'

Gemma shakes her head.

'Oh.' Lexi rolls her eyes. 'You mean, what am I going to do about this?' She looks at the envelope in her hands.

'Please,' Gemma says, unsure what's she asking, 'you have no idea how hard my life is here. You have no idea what it's like living in a place like Leedham with parents who run the parish council. They expect so much from me.'

'Then leave Leedham,' Lexi replies like it's the easiest thing in the world. 'And for what it's worth, you have no idea what a hard life even looks like.'

There's a pause. For the first time, it feels like she sees beyond the smiling, peppy substitute teacher in her floaty skirts and baby pink. 'Who are you? Really?' Gemma asks.

Lexi closes her eyes for a second. 'I'm no one. When this is over, you can forget I ever existed.' She stands, handing the note to Gemma. 'I need to go.'

'Where?'

'To find Cate.'

'But how?'

'If you have any sense in you at all, Gemma, you'll go to the police station right now and tell them that it was you threatening me. Then you should think about getting some help for the jealousy.' Lexi spins away without waiting for a reply, jogging back in the direction of a row of cars.

Gemma doesn't move from the stone wall but sinks further down, dropping her head into her hands. Tears spill onto her cheeks, ruining her make-up again. Great!

She knows she's messed up, that her jealousy gets out of hand sometimes. She knows she shouldn't have threatened Lexi or had an affair with Oliver, and all she should be worrying about now is that a woman and a little boy are still missing. But really, all she can think about is the trouble she's in and how, and if, she'll get out of it.

Why does nothing ever go right for her?

There's a moment when Jeanie steps through the front door and kicks off her shoes when she thinks she might not lose it.

She's still here.

She hasn't been arrested.

They haven't connected her to Cate's disappearance. To little Archie, or even the body in the well. And Lord knows her hands are dirty on all of those things and more. But they will. In a week or a month, when they've processed the DNA, they'll get a hit from whatever database they hold these things in.

They'll discover the dead man was sent to prison for manslaughter for the death of his wife.

She steps into the kitchen and opens the fridge. Her hands shake with a nervous energy only wine will ease. She pours herself a large glass, drinking half of it back without tasting it. The edges of her thoughts soften. She slumps against the counter and wonders what else the police files will show about the dead man. The dead man who was once her father.

Will it tell them about the officer who left their new address on a notepad by the station phone after her mother had finally found the courage to report the abuse and leave? Or the desk sergeant – the one who'd got pally-pally with her father – nodding in agreement when he'd told him that the charges of domestic abuse against him were a misunderstanding?

And the police unit who didn't respond to the neighbour's emergency services call to report screaming from the new family next door, and the judge who thought seven years in prison was enough because even though her father went to the new house with a baseball bat clutched in his hands, he hadn't meant to kill her mother? And the parole board who released him after five years for good behaviour?

Jeanie had been sixteen when her mother was murdered and twenty-one when her father was released from prison. She'd known he'd come looking for her. She was surprised it had taken him seven years. If he'd thought time would heal old wounds, he'd been wrong. It hadn't mattered to Jeanie that the man on her doorstep was in his sixties, beaten down by prison and life on parole; homeless, broke and in need of help.

All she'd seen in those red, watery eyes were the years of beatings he'd given her mother, the life each punch had sapped from her until she was only ever half there. The man who'd tracked her down when she'd finally got the courage to leave him and had killed her.

Jeanie had known in that moment that she would kill him. But it wasn't something she could do on her own doorstep. She needed time to think and plan, so she'd invited him into her home and made him a cup of tea. And then she'd called James and told him their father was in her house.

Her brother had arrived less than five minutes later, red-faced from the rush or the same anger burning through Jeanie, she wasn't sure.

'What do you want from us?' James had asked with none of the pretend politeness Jeanie had felt compelled to show their father.

'Can't a man want to see his children?'

'A man can, but you're no man. Real men don't beat their wives to death.' His words had carried an electric shock that had zipped through the air between them.

In a split second, their father's hand had flown up and then down, smashing against the table, the sound loud and menacing. 'Enough,' he'd said, spitting the word. 'I've changed.'

Jeanie had felt herself cower, had felt the same emotions of her childhood rear up from a forgotten place, and then something else happened. The years of rage had exploded inside her, blinding her thoughts to all but the kitchen knife on the side. In a split second, it was in her hand. In another, it was stabbing into the flabby flesh of his gut and then into his chest before James could so much as think to stop her.

The shock had settled in fast. A tremor had taken over her body. She remembers stuttering an apology to James, but he'd shaken his head. 'It's what he deserved. He hadn't changed at all.'

They'd removed his wallet and wrapped him in an old sheet, and that night James had returned with his van and they'd taken him to the old Fairfield farm. She remembered the well. How deep it was, how it had scared her as a little girl, never wanting to get too close for fear she'd fall.

They'd dragged him across the ground together, hoisted him up and pushed him over the edge.

Not a day has gone by that Jeanie's regretted what she did. Blood on her hands, but justice too.

No, she doesn't regret killing her father, but she does worry about all that came afterwards and what their father's murder set in motion. Knowing what she knows now, and the path they turned down in that moment, she's not sure she'd do it again.

Their father's death unlocked a darkness in her. The temper she'd always struggled to keep at bay reared up more and more, until only alcohol could dull the fury.

She'd thought James had returned to life as normal, seemingly unaffected by what she'd done and all they'd seen as children. But she'd been wrong. He had the darkness in him too; worse, much worse than hers.

When James had told her about his plans a few years after their father's death, she'd had no choice but to agree to help him the way he'd helped her. Besides, James was her brother; they were the only family either of them had left. They had to stick together.

And so she's kept clothes and other items locked in her box room for years now, packing bags up when he tells her what he needs. She finds details for him too, when she's at work. Marriage certificates and deaths and addresses. Anything he asks for. And then there's the group he asks her to run. Finding all those women.

Her eyes fix on the draining board and the plate sitting there from her dinner last night. The plain white china gleams in the light.

She takes another gulp of wine. Memories swim through her head. Her heart races in her chest.

It's all over.

She's been so stupid.

Stupid. Stupid, stupid.

The rage builds, a quiet storm, a moment of still, before it bursts out in a vicious yell. 'Arrrghhh.' She's by the sink in one movement, snatching at the plate in both her hands and lifting it high above her head – so high, the tip scrapes against the ceiling. And then she's swinging it down, down, down, the breath leaving her lungs in a bellowing scream. At the last moment, she lets go and watches the plate smash to the floor.

There's a movement behind her. Buster shoots by and out the cat flap.

Already her eyes are roaming the kitchen, looking for more, for something to burn this anger out. The mug. Her last mug. She'll regret it in the morning, but it's in her hands in a second.

Down it goes with another scream, the blue china splintering alongside the white from the plate. A shard flies up, jumping into one of her slippers.

She grabs at the wine glass, gulping back the contents before that too crashes to the floor. She hasn't lost it like this since that dad screamed at her last year for nearly hitting him and his little girl while they were crossing the road. She'd been angry at him for shouting but angrier at herself for drink-driving. Another habit she'd picked up from her father.

On it goes. Jars and tins too, as blood races like hot lava through her body. Only when it's all gone – every cupboard empty, every last thing smashed or broken – does she stagger back, the anger gone, leaving in its wake the humiliation and regret she saw so many times on her father's face. The same look she's sure she sees on Oliver's sometimes too, when he's rushing from the house.

Tears build in her eyes. She's frustrated. Sad. Full of regret. She didn't hurt another person. She isn't like her father or any of them. But isn't that why she lives alone? Why she's never married or fallen in love? Because if someone was here, they would have felt that wrath. She might carry the same festering disease, but she won't be like them.

FORTY-NINE

LEXI

I try to make sense of what Gemma's told me as I run back to my car.

She was behind the threats because of jealousy? It's almost laughable that she would think something was going on with me and Oliver. It wasn't lust in his eyes; it was confusion. He was trying to figure out where he knew me from. I wonder if he's worked it out yet.

Gemma's jealousy is out of control. If she threatened me because of an imagined relationship, what would she do to Cate – the woman married to Oliver, and the only thing standing in the way of the life she wanted? She says she had nothing to do with the disappearance, but do I believe her?

And even if Gemma never meant her threats, and her reasoning was off, they still hit me with an all-encompassing fear I won't forgive her for. At some point, I'll have to decide what to do about that. But right now, my focus is on James.

I thought he was threatening me. I thought he took Cate and Archie. If the first is no longer true, then is the second? I start to doubt myself, but I can't erase the images of the women

I saw in the hidden drawer – Cate among them. I'm certain he's the key.

I start the engine and a plan starts to form. I can't sit around and wait any longer. Tomorrow it will be two weeks since Cate and Archie disappeared. I'm running out of time. Oliver has seen the scar. He'll figure out who I am if he hasn't done so already.

The moment the headlines broke – announcing Cate and Archie's disappearance for the first time – and I recognised Oliver's face, I'd known he was involved in his wife and son's disappearance. Just as I'd known Oliver would do all he could to play the victim. I couldn't let him convince everyone of his innocence like he did the last time. So I'd packed up my car and I'd phoned every substitute teaching agency in the area and told them I was available for any length of time. I got lucky. Karen must've called an hour after me, and they remembered.

I would've come to Leedham anyway, but this way I was injected into the heart of the community. Trusted. Approachable. I saw first-hand what Oliver was doing – that bumbling Hugh Grant act I remember from all those years back, when I was just ten years old. So I asked my questions, and I planted seeds, and I spread suspicion. Finding the photos in Cate's cupboard was serendipitous, but even without them, the tide was turning on Oliver. The photos just sped things up.

I watched his charm fade and the cracks appear. It seemed only a matter of time before he confessed. His life would've been over, just like mine was all those years ago. But then I met James. And now nothing is as it seems.

Is Oliver innocent after all?

I drive along the high street in the direction of the funeral director's. I could walk, but I might need a quick getaway this time.

I'll break in again. Just like before. I'll take photos –

evidence – and I'll search for more. I've been avoiding the detectives this week, and that's partly because they didn't believe me, and partly because I didn't want them to dig into my past and find out about Donna and learn of my connection to Oliver.

I wonder how much that matters now. I'll have to tell them about James. I'm certain now that Cate and Archie are dead, like all the other women must be. They deserve justice, and James needs to be stopped before it happens again.

I reach the funeral director's and pull into a space between two cars on the side of the road. The upstairs flat is in darkness, and I hope as I step out of my car that this means there's no one at home.

A car passes on the road, the bright headlights of a 4x4, and I instinctively drop into a crouch in the shadows. I let a moment pass, and I'm just about to stand when I see the nose of James's van pulling out of the driveway next to the funeral home. In the glow of the streetlights, I see him behind the wheel.

I freeze. The same fear from hiding in the warehouse clutches at my insides. Did he see me? I sink lower to the ground and wait for him to pull away. Where is he going this late on a Thursday night?

Indecision grips me. The funeral home and connecting warehouse will be empty. I can get the evidence I need to prove James is behind everything. But will the detectives believe me?

As the van drives along Leedham high street, another idea forms. Maybe James will lead me to other evidence. It's a risk I have to take. I jump behind the wheel and start the engine, following the van as close as I dare. The dark night and the twisty lanes hide me well. I'm just distant headlights in a wing mirror to him.

We hit the main road, heading towards the nearby town before turning off again, picking up speed as he winds through more narrow lanes.

I slow down, dropping back to keep myself hidden. He

rounds a corner, and by the time I get there, the van has disappeared.

I brake, half expecting to see the van dead ahead, lights off, James jumping out at me, but the road ahead is empty. I can see for at least a mile into the darkness, and there are no headlights.

I've lost him. Frustration kicks at me, sharp and hard.

I pull over into a lay-by and turn off the engine, killing my lights and waiting for my eyes to adjust to the dark. I step out of the car, scanning the horizon. There's nothing, and then in the bushes, to the right, a glint of light.

I step closer and notice for the first time an opening between the trees. Not a road but an unmade drive. I tread carefully in the dark, down the driveway. It's a steep path that twists to the left, coming out by a small cottage. The curtains are closed, but there's a soft glow from the edges of the window.

The blue van is parked outside. I've found him.

I keep close to the trees and watch James unlocking the front door and stepping inside. I hesitate. Torn. This could be nothing. This could be his home or the house of a girlfriend. It's dark and we're in the middle of nowhere. I pull out my phone. No signal.

Do I turn back? Or keep going?

The decision is made for me a second later when a scream pierces the air. The voice is anguished and cuts straight to my core.

FIFTY

LEXI

I reach the cottage wall and run my hands across the rough stone as I inch along in the darkness. I barely breathe as my eyes scan the windows, looking for a gap in the curtains, a sign of what's going on inside. The desire to turn back is a brick wall in front of me. But the scream... someone is in trouble. I can't leave. Is this where he takes them? A secluded cottage, no one for miles. Is his next victim already inside?

I slowly move towards the front door, like I'm on a cliff face and any second I'll fall to my death. My heart pounds in my chest. Nearly there. Then what? I check my phone again, but it's still showing no signal.

Another step closer. I'm half a metre from the door, almost there. Then it flies open. A scream catches in my throat. I think I gasp as I push myself against the wall. James strides out of the doorway. I'm so close, his size seems monstrous.

For a split second, as he strides through the door and I push myself against the wall, we're in touching distance from each other. There's nothing between us, nothing to stop him grabbing me and dragging me inside.

Every muscle in my body freezes. All I can do is wait.

The moment passes, and in the next one he's shutting the door and walking towards the van. The evening is dark, but there's a moon in the sky and slivers of light from the house. If he turns, if he looks, he'll see me.

Fear weakens my legs. My eyes dart to my surroundings. Brambles and bushes, trees, nettles. I'm younger and fitter, and if I can make a run for it, then I might get away, but I don't know this area. There could be fences and barbed wire, hidden fox holes I could break an ankle in. In the end, the fear keeps me frozen, and I stay where I am and hold my breath as James climbs into his van. The engine strains and then starts, and he disappears up the driveway.

I gulp in air; catch my breath. One deep inhale. Then two, then three. When I'm sure it's quiet, no engines, no running footsteps, I reach for the door handle. I don't expect it to open, but it does, easily – flying inwards and taking me with it. A deep unease spreads over my body. If the door is unlocked, then he isn't concerned someone will try to escape. I'm too late.

I listen to the silence and look at my surroundings. It's a small, run-down cottage with old carpets and bare walls. There's a staircase to the left, a kitchen straight ahead, and to my right is a closed door with a soft glow of light beneath it.

There's a noise. A shuffling scrape coming from inside the room. Someone is here. A dozen scenarios flash in my mind as I carefully open the door into a small living room, furnished with chunky floral sofas and overstuffed cushions. There are bookshelves around the walls but no TV, and an old-fashioned standing lamp on in the corner.

At first, I think it's empty. There's no one here. Then another sound echoes in the silence. A groan. My eyes draw to the sofa and the heap of what I first thought were cushions.

I'm across the room in seconds, my hands out. The closer I

get, the more human the shape becomes. Blonde hair, a hand, legs. I reach out, and they move, lurching up and staring at me with wide, panicked eyes.

FIFTY-ONE

LEXI

The woman blinks, pushing tangled hair away from her face. Her skin is pale, her eyes rimmed red and puffy. It takes me a moment to recognise her without the perfect make-up and the wide smile and the pretty dresses. I gasp.

'Cate?'

Confusion crosses her face. She nods. Her eyes dart around the room, landing on me and then the door before moving back to me. 'How do you know who I am?'

'You've been on the news. You've been missing for two weeks. I thought... you were dead.' I realise the moment I say it how awful it sounds. How wrong. I was basing my assumption on the threat slipped into my pocket on Saturday. But of course, that was just Gemma's cruel attempt to get me to leave Leed-ham. It had nothing to do with Cate's disappearance.

There's a pause. She seems stunned, unsure. Like she can't process what I'm saying.

'That man,' I continue, 'is James Simpson. He's kidnapped you. We have to leave before he comes back.' A niggle of worry worms through my mind. What is this I've walked into? I've been wrong about a lot of things this week, and there's some-thing off about this whole situation.

A wall of tears builds in Cate's eyes before spilling over in two lines down her face. She nods as a sob shudders through her body.

'Where's Archie?' A bolt of raw fear hits the pit of my stom-ach. It's me now looking around the room, searching for anything I've missed. But it's empty. He's not here.

Cate sobs again before lifting her head. 'He's... he's upstairs.'

Relief crashes through me. 'OK. We can get him. We need to get out of here before James comes back.'

'He's only gone to get some food. He likes to check on us first and see what we want to eat,' she whispers. There's a dazed look about Cate, and for a moment I think she might refuse to leave, but then she starts to stand. 'How did you find me?'

'I followed James here tonight. The rest is a long story, and there's no time to explain it all now.' The urgency in my voice seems to push through her fear and shock. 'Come on. Let's get Archie.'

'I... Yes... you're right.'

I hold my hand out, and she clasps it, fingers digging into me. 'Thank you.'

'It's OK. We're getting out of here.'

She walks slower than I'd like, her movements stiff as though she's forgotten how. 'Who are you?' she asks when we're halfway across the room.

'My name is Lexi Mills. I'm the substitute teacher who's taken over your class.'

'Oh.' I sense her thinking this through. 'So we don't know each other?'

It's my turn to pause, to think. How much should I say? Do I tell Cate that once upon a time, way back when I was a little girl only slightly older than Archie, I knew Oliver? That when I saw her face on the news, I had to come to Leedham to help, to make sure Oliver was punished, because I was certain he was behind their disappearance?

A noise startles me from my thoughts. An engine rattling. There's no time to unpick why or how I'm here. James is back.

Cate's feet stop dead, frozen, and I keep moving, so for a moment I'm dragging her.

'Stop,' she hisses. 'There isn't time. Just go before he finds you here.' She lets go of my hand, already moving back to the sofa.

The engine cuts out, and we both flinch at the sound of the car door banging.

A burst of adrenaline hits my bloodstream. My gaze flies around the room. I could hide behind the sofa or run for the stairs. I think of Archie somewhere else in the house, all alone. I could hide behind the doorway and leap out at James, take my chances in a fight.

But there's no time. The front door opens; floorboards creak. He's already in the cottage. And then, before I can move, he's in the living-room doorway, a carrier bag of food in one hand, his keys to the van in the other.

He stares at me and then Cate. Stunned at my presence. And in a flash, I see the darkness in his eyes and anger cross his face.

'What are you doing here?' he asks.

FIFTY-TWO

JAMES

It's your face I see first as I step through the doorway. The fear in your eyes, that horror. Even as I'm taking in the other woman standing before me, I worry about you first, and only second do I wonder what this means for me. For us.

Then I snap out of it and look to Lexi. For a moment, it feels like a fantasy. I've thought of this woman often over the last week. I've found myself drawn more and more to the pub car park to watch over her, to imagine what it would be like to take her, just as I took you. But she's not like us. Not like you. So watching and imagining is as far as I thought I'd go. Until now, seeing her here in my cottage.

I'm not surprised. She's a snoop, this one. Like Jeanie in a way. Maybe that's why I didn't mind when I saw her climbing the gate after digging around in my warehouse. She found the secret drawer and the photos of the other women that I keep to remember them by. It's morbid perhaps, to dwell, but there's comfort in knowing I've taken so many. You can understand that, can't you? I'll have to find a better hiding place for them. I can't keep them in my flat due to the prying eyes of my cleaner, but maybe somewhere in the cottage instead. Somewhere only I go.

'What are you doing here?' I repeat. My voice is gruff but not unfriendly, and yet still she flinches.

'I've called the police,' she says, hurried, fearful. 'They'll be here any second.'

The news hits me hard. I suppose I always knew it would end one day. It seems that day is today, but it doesn't make it any easier. I must let Jeanie know. She'll be angry. This was always my plan, not hers. She always said we were taking too many risks, taking too many women too often, but I couldn't help myself. Every time I thought I shouldn't, I remembered my mother. She used to be so fun, Cate. Like you and your boy. Dancing around and playing imaginary games, lifting his spirits when he's cried to go home, helping him pretend it's all a game, a holiday, instead of the end.

It reminds me of a Christmas one year when I was about your boy's age, when our father wouldn't spare the money for gifts. He really was a bastard. It didn't stop our mother trying though. She collected empty cardboard boxes from wherever she could – shops and supermarkets and neighbours. She painted them bright colours and built a fort in my bedroom from cardboard and duct tape while I was at school, covering it with sheets until Christmas morning so it would be a surprise.

Jeanie and I played in that fort for weeks; months even. We played in it until it was more duct tape than cardboard and there was no way to keep it upright any longer. In those months it became our secret den, where we'd play and where we'd hide too, when our father was in one of his moods.

I wonder sometimes if Jeanie hadn't lost her temper and killed him whether I would have done it. There's no way to know now, and all that matters is that I'm glad he's dead. There was something about that time, the help I gave Jeanie to cover up the murder, that awakened something in me that led me to

Bella Godwin and all the others, and to you of course. It's like my father's death gave me permission to do what I knew I had to do.

I shake the memory away. Thinking of my parents always muddies my decision-making. I need to think clearly. There might still be a way out. And so I step further into the room.

Lexi jumps back, guard up like I'm the sort to fly at her. That hurts, but I can't really blame her. She doesn't get who we are, does she?

I step to the empty sofa and sit, placing down the bag of food I've bought from the supermarket – bread and cereal and milk – the final breakfast we'd planned. Tomorrow you were going to die. You and Archie. I don't know what will happen now.

'What are you doing?' Lexi asks, her gaze moving from you to me. You sit down too, perching on the edge of a cushion as though you might leap up again at any moment.

'I'm waiting for the police to come,' I say.

Lexi's brow furrows in a cute kind of way. 'Come on,' she says to Cate. 'Get Archie – we should leave.'

We share a look, and I shake my head. 'No,' I say. 'Cate isn't going anywhere. We'll wait for the police.'

'Cate?' Lexi says, pleading now, and I realise she hasn't called them. The police aren't coming. I could almost laugh at my foolishness. Of course they're not coming. There's no phone signal here. It's one of the reasons I like this cottage. The peace and quiet. No one to interrupt us.

It was a bluff, and in my acceptance of the end, I called it.

'What... what's going on?' Lexi asks, backing away a little, putting herself closer to the door.

'Tell her,' I say. 'She knows most of it anyway.'

You nod. Timid. A little bird. Finally, you speak. 'I— James I mean... It's not what you think. I... I've not been kidnapped. James is helping me.'

'What? No.' Lexi shakes her head, and I realise that in all her snooping, her scrambling of the puzzle pieces, she's put it together so very, very wrong.

I stand. The power shifts between us. I see the look in her eyes. She doesn't believe you. She thinks I'm a monster. She has no idea.

FIFTY-THREE

LEXI

An alarm has been ringing in my head. Distant at first then louder. It started with the unlocked cottage door and finding Cate, not just alive but free to roam the cottage.

There's something not right here. There's a tension in the room I can't read. Why is he not trying to stop me from leaving? Why is Cate looking to him as though he'll help? Why is she trying to tell me he's not kidnapped her?

It has to be Archie. He must have him locked away, forcing Cate to do everything he says. No wonder she won't run out the door with me.

'Are you keeping Archie from her? Is that it?' I blurt the question out, forcing myself to stand my ground and stare into the darkness of his eyes.

'What? Of course not,' he says as though the very idea is ludicrous. 'Archie is asleep upstairs, isn't he, Cate? You can go check if you like.'

I don't move. It feels like a trap.

'It's true,' Cate says. 'I'm not being held against my will. I'm sorry if I made you think that a minute ago. I was just surprised to see you, that's all. James had just woken me up and made me jump, and I was still so sleepy. The truth is... James has helped me escape. I was—' She pauses; swallows. 'My husband, Oliver, was hitting me. I had to get away. James and his sister run a secret support group for abused women. Jeanie is my neighbour. Archie must have told her we were fighting, and she put two and two together. She told me about it, and I went.'

I think of the women in the hall. That mixed group. I see the nervousness of it now, that tension in the air. The fear. Things are clicking into place, and yet, they're not.

'I help women get a new life,' James says. 'I bring them here for a few days or however long. Jeanie helps with the documents a bit, and picks up clothes and household bits from charity shops to start a new life with. I'm not bad at making fake IDs. Not passports – I wouldn't go that far – but enough to get them set up. I've got connections in the North East, and when the time is right, they leave their old lives to die, and I take them to a new life.'

The women in the photos. The ones I found online. 'Bella Godwin,' I mutter.

James looks surprised but then nods. 'Cate and Archie would've gone sooner, but the attention in the news meant we had to wait. We couldn't risk someone spotting them and Oliver finding them.'

'But the police?' I say. 'Why didn't you report this to the police?' I ask Cate. 'Why didn't any of them?'

'The police are useless,' James says, a cold anger in his tone for the first time. 'My mother is dead because of that lot. She went to the police. Because of them, my dad found us and killed her. It's why Jeanie and I do what we do. We help these women in a way the police never can. I take them and keep them safe. Their old lives are dead. They can move on, and I give them new lives.'

His words settle in my mind, clicking into place, and I realise how wrong I've been. I thought Oliver had hurt his wife and son and came to Leedham to make sure he didn't get away with it. I thought he was threatening me, but that was Gemma. I thought James was a kidnapper and a serial killer. Wrong again. And even though there's something very off and very dark with this man, I believe him. He isn't a kidnapper or a serial killer; he's a vigilante.

I've been wrong about almost everything, I think. Almost – or all? I feel like I'm missing something as I focus on Cate. 'So Oliver was abusive to you, and you've left the community you loved, everything you know, your friends, your family, your job, to start over?'

I see a flash of discomfort in Cate's face before she nods. She flicks a glance at James. 'Yes, but actually, and I'm really sorry about this, James, but I think I need to go back. I've been thinking, and I don't want to throw my whole life away – or Archie's. It's not fair. I'm so grateful for all you've done.'

I wait for James to tell her she can't. That it's too late and she's agreed. I wait to see the darkness rise up in him, but his face is the same blank mask. 'He won't stop,' is all he says before getting to his feet. 'But I won't force you to go if you're not ready.' He looks between us before turning back to Cate. 'Think about it more tonight. I'll come back tomorrow, and whatever you decide is fine. Obviously, if you do go back, I'll need you to—'

'Of course,' Cate is quick to say. 'I won't tell anyone you helped me. I'll tell the police I left on my own and was in hiding for fear Oliver would find me and hurt me. I've... I've got some photos. I can prove what he did to me.'

'It's not what I'd have chosen, but I understand,' he says before he looks to me. 'Be careful, Lexi Mills. Snooping in places you don't belong can lead to a lot of trouble.' He strides out the door before I find the words to reply.

Cate leaps up, scooping her hair behind her ears. 'I'm so glad you came. I think I've been in some kind of trance these last weeks. I couldn't see a way forward, but you've reminded me of everything I'd be throwing away. Of course I have to go back. I know James doesn't trust the police, but I have evidence. They'll believe me.'

She smiles at me, and I see exactly what piece I'm missing.

'Everyone thinks Cate is this amazing woman, but she was a manipulative, controlling bitch.'

'But he wasn't hitting you, was he?'

'What?' She makes a face, and I see I'm right. 'Of course he was. I have proof.'

'No, you don't. Those photos of the bruises aren't of you.'

'Yes, they are,' she snaps back. 'Look, I don't know what you think you know—'

'Oliver is responsible for those bruises, but they're not of you, and I know this, because I took those photos, and I've kept them for over sixteen years. That's not you...' Emotion lodges in my throat. There's no relief in sharing the secret I've kept for so long. Only hurt and regret and guilt. 'It's Donna, my sister.'

FIFTY-FOUR

LEXI

It's Cate's turn to connect the dots. Her mouth opens as though she's going to say something, but she stops; tries again. 'You,' she says. 'You were sending me those emails about Oliver.'

I nod. 'I wanted to warn you,' I say before realising that isn't true, and by the way Cate raises an eyebrow and stares back at me, she probably sees that too.

Cate has been married to Oliver for long enough to know what kind of man he is. But it took me years to do anything about it. I think back to creating that fake account and the first email I sent ten months ago.

Do you know what kind of man your husband is? Do you know what he does to women?

I wasn't thinking straight about much back then. My grief for Donna had hardened into a jagged rock in my chest. I'd been accused of murder and chased out of my job at Haventhorpe Primary by gossiping parents and a weak head teacher. So I'd packed up my things and left. Without Donna, there was nothing for me in Brighton anyway.

But running away isn't the same as moving on, and whatever it was driving me forward – never settling in one place, never making friends or picking up the life I'd once had – it was the same thing that drove me to reach out to Cate.

And then she disappeared, and my first thought was to the emails I'd sent. I saw a world where Cate had confronted Oliver about the photos I'd shared and he'd lost his temper with her. I saw my plans backfiring, and instead of justice, I'd risked another woman's life. And so I came to Leedham. To do something, to find out what had happened to Cate and Archie, and make sure Oliver didn't get away with hurting someone again.

She pulls her hair back once more, this time twisting it up into a high bun and securing it with a hairband from on her wrist. 'How did you find me?'

'Facebook,' I reply. 'I searched Oliver's name and found you and your email on a flyer for a charity bake sale.'

Cate sighs. 'Fine. Well, you know the truth then, don't you? Oliver wasn't hitting me. When Jeanie knocked on my door one day and told me she knew all about Oliver hitting me, I thought... why not? Why not use the photos you'd already sent me and destroy his life the way he was trying to destroy our family?'

We've been moving down this path since I stepped into this cottage, but her admission is still a shock. This is a woman who's adored by everyone in Leedham. No one had a bad word to say about her, except Oliver and Gemma, and they had their own reasons for wanting to paint a different picture of Cate. It turns out their views are just the tip of a dark iceberg.

'You tricked everyone just to get back at your husband for having an affair?'

If Cate is surprised I know about Gemma, she doesn't show it. 'Don't act all high and mighty with me. Lexi, is it? You're not exactly Little Miss Honest.'

I back away and shake my head. 'I'm nothing like you.'

'Really.' She rolls her eyes. 'Let's see, shall we? Why did you send me those emails and those photos of your sister? It wasn't to warn me about Oliver. It was to try and stir something, wasn't it? You wanted to ruin our marriage. Well, guess what? It was already ruined. We're on the same side here. You want Oliver to pay for hurting your sister, and I want him to pay for sleeping with that little slut. If I go to the police tomorrow and tell them the photos are mine and that I've been in hiding for my life because Oliver threatened to kill me, then we'll both win.'

There's something triumphant about Cate in that moment. I see the layers of her thinking, like a game of chess, she's seeing three moves ahead. I hate that she's right about me. I did start sending her emails because I wanted to hurt Oliver, to destroy his life somehow, like he'd destroyed mine that night in the car all those years ago. Donna's too.

'I knew what you were doing the moment that first email arrived,' Cate continues. 'Although to be fair, I assumed you were Donna.'

'Donna is dead,' I say, choking on the word. 'She died a year ago. Tomorrow will be the anniversary of her death.'

'I'm sorry,' she replies.

I don't believe her, and I almost tell her what happened. All the ways I tried to save my sister and failed so epically. But I can't. That's my burden to carry and mine alone.

We fall silent, and I shift my feet a little, wondering where we go from here and what I should do. I came to Leedham to find Cate and Archie, to make sure Oliver was punished for whatever he'd done to them. I've done both of those things.

But somehow, it isn't enough.

'Look, it's getting late,' she says. 'You should go.'

'What?' Surprise carries in my voice. 'But we're not done here.'

'Yes, we are. Look, I'm grateful you came. It's sweet actually. But as you can see, I'm fine. The truth is, I was never going to go through with leaving. I was going to tell James tomorrow morning that I wanted to go home. So I'll be back at work on Monday. You can go back to wherever it is you came from. Revenge for Donna gained. Mission accomplished.'

I've been moving gradually across the room for the last few minutes and with one final step, I position myself between Cate and the door. 'No,' I say. 'You're not going back to Leedham. Not today, not tomorrow. Not ever. I won't let you.'

James, Jeanie, Oliver, Gemma, Cate – they're all messed-up, broken humans, but they're nothing compared to me. This isn't over until I say it's over.

FIFTY-FIVE

LEXI

A flicker of worry crosses Cate's face. Her eyes narrow, and it's like she's seeing me for the first time, taking in the set of my face and the muscles of my bare arms.

Her mouth twists into a grimace. 'What do you mean, no? You're the one who tracked me down.'

'When I thought you were in trouble, yes. When I thought you'd been kidnapped.'

A fury starts to burn in me – wildfire. It isn't enough. 'Of course I wanted to help you and Archie when I thought my emails might've caused Oliver to lash out and hurt you. But now... now I see everything clearly, and the funny thing is, Cate, I've always given you the benefit of the doubt about what kind of person you are, but silly me: wrong again.'

Cate's eyes narrow. I can see she's fighting to be indignant, but the worry has taken over. 'What do you mean?'

'You knew about Oliver's relationship with Donna back then, didn't you? He was twenty-six when they met. She was sixteen. Sixteen. They dated for a year when Oliver was teaching. You met at the school, right? You were young teachers together?'

'Yes. I knew he had a girlfriend and she was younger, but I didn't know how young,' Cate says, choosing her words carefully. I don't know if I believe her. 'We couldn't help how we felt about each other. It was wrong, but we fell in love.'

'While he was still dating my sister.'

It's not a question, but she nods anyway.

'You know, I've always wondered how Oliver could afford an expensive lawyer after the crash. I knew he didn't have family money, and on a teacher's salary. But you – you had a wealthy family. The mums of Leedham were so quick to tell me how lovely you are. Like how you donated the money for the roof repairs on the village hall. Just like how you helped Oliver all those years ago.'

'I was in love, and I didn't want one night to ruin the rest of our lives. Anyway, it was an accident. He wasn't even driving. I only asked my father to make sure he didn't get charged with anything.'

'Only,' I scoff. The room is hot, my face red, breath short. It's been sixteen years since the night Donna came to pick me up from dance class because our mother had a headache. She'd only passed her test the month before. Our parents didn't know about her relationship with Oliver. Donna was waiting to turn eighteen before telling them. It had been Oliver's idea. He'd thought the age gap wouldn't look so bad.

But I'd known. Oliver would come to the house when Donna was babysitting me and they'd sneak out to the garden or to sit in his car. And Donna would tell me things about him sometimes. At first it was flowers he'd bought her and romantic places he'd taken her. Then through tears she'd tell me about the fights and Oliver's anger. I saw the bruises he gave her. It was me that made her take photos on the digital camera Mum had given me for Christmas. Just in case. I'd only just turned ten, but I was mature for my age, and neither of us spoke about what 'just in case' meant.

'How old were you?' Cate asks.

'Ten. I was in the car that night too. Did you know that?'

She shakes her head.

'They were arguing. He was telling her about a teacher he'd met and was falling in love with.' I close my eyes as the memories pummel my mind. 'They thought I was listening to something on my headphones, but I was staring out the window at the dark night and the rain. I remember being so relieved when he told her that, because I thought it meant she'd be free of him.'

'You didn't really think I'd marry you, did you?' I can still remember the disdain in Oliver's voice. *'You're nothing. A nobody.'*

'Oliver, please, I... What about the baby?'

'Oh yeah, that. I was telling Cate all about it. She thinks you should get rid of it.'

'No. You know I don't want that.'

I open my eyes and look at the woman standing before me. 'You knew from the start Oliver already had a girlfriend, but you started a relationship with him anyway. He told you she was pregnant. Was he wavering? Was he thinking of doing the right thing? Until you suggested the abortion. The answer to your problems, right?'

'Of course I did. A baby would've ruined her life and Oliver's. Anyone would've suggested the same thing.'

'Except Donna didn't want that. She wanted to have the baby. She said she'd raise it on her own.'

'No, you won't.' The snipe of Oliver's words ring in my head. His hand had reached out then, grabbing at Donna's arm. She'd yelped in pain.

'Oliver, I'm driving.'

'It was an accident,' Cate says. 'The police even said so.'

'No, it wasn't. They were fighting. She told him she was keeping the baby and if he ever came near her again, she'd go to the police.'

He'd laughed at that. I still hear that hollow sound in my nightmares. *You wouldn't dare.*

'I would. For the baby.'

'There's not going to be a baby.' Then he'd moved so fast there wasn't time to scream before we were careening off the road, hurtling towards a tree. Donna tried to brake, but the grass was wet and we kept skidding.

'He grabbed the wheel,' I tell Cate. 'He caused the accident. The tree came out of nowhere. It hit the driver's side dead on.' Tears fall down my face. A lifetime of them.

'No. He told me it was an accident,' she says.

I wipe my face. 'Oliver got me out of the car, but I tried to go back. I cut my arm on the smashed window trying to get to Donna. He held me back. And when he told everyone it was a tragic accident, all charm and pathetic and tearful, they believed him. No one listened to the little girl who missed her big sister. If Donna could've spoken up, then maybe it would've made a difference. But the crash caused severe brain damage.'

'I knew she was hurt, but I didn't know it was bad. I just thought you all left town.'

'Well, it was. She never recovered. The damage to the frontal lobe was too severe. She was alive and breathing, but she never came back after that night. It destroyed my parents. They couldn't stand seeing her and sent her to a care home in Brighton. I moved there as soon as I was old enough and visited as often as I could.' I wipe my hand over my face and take a shuddering breath. There'll be time for tears later. Right now, I want to finish this.

'I'm sorry,' Cate says. 'I'm so sorry about Donna.'

I shake my head. The words are meaningless. Sorry she's been caught out. Sorry I've stepped in to ruin her little game.

'It was so long ago,' she continues. 'I didn't know Donna. It was nothing to do with me.'

'It was everything to do with you. If you hadn't been whispering in Oliver's ear about an abortion, he might not have crashed the car. If you hadn't asked Daddy to get him a good lawyer, maybe the police would've believed me. I used to think you were innocent. Doing what any girlfriend in love would do, but I bet anything that you knew back then that Oliver was the man you'd marry. I bet you saw a future together, and him having a baby with someone else didn't fit into your plans, did it?'

She says nothing, but I can see I'm right.

'What are you going to do?' she asks.

A floorboard creaks behind us. We both turn to the door, and even though I know James isn't a serial killer now, I can't forget the malice in his voice when he spoke to his sister or those dark eyes watching me. He may not be bad, but he's not good either. He's getting something out of this, feeding a darkness in him.

But it's not James standing in the doorway. It's a little boy with blond hair sticking up on one side where his head has been resting on a pillow. He's wearing green dinosaur PJs that are too short in the legs.

'Archie,' Cate says, rushing towards him, 'are you OK?'

'I'm thirsty.'

'Come on. I'll get you some water.'

'Is it morning?' he asks, looking from his mum to me and back again. 'Are we still going home? I miss Daddy.'

'He misses you too.' Cate drops a kiss on top of his head and guides him out of the room. 'Go get some water. I'll be right in.'

She turns back to me, her face pleading. If she thinks the sweetness of a little boy can change my path, she's wasting her time.

'If you go home tomorrow, I'll make sure everyone knows the truth about the last two weeks. I'll tell all those gossips in Leedham, and I'll tell the police all about how you used the photos I sent of Donna to fake the abuse. I'm assuming you deleted the emails I sent, but I didn't.'

'What am I supposed to do then?'

'Disappear. Tell James you're ready for your new life and leave and never come back.' The moment the words are out, I realise I mean them. I didn't know until tonight what I'd do if I ever got to confront Cate. But then I didn't know what kind of person she was either. Now, her life and everything she's known will be gone for her part in what happened to Donna.

'You'll be in trouble too,' she replies, but there's no conviction in her voice.

'For what? Sending you some emails? I don't think so. Besides, I've got nothing to lose, remember? You and Oliver already ruined my life sixteen years ago.'

'Mummy?' Archie's voice calls through the house. 'I can't reach the glasses.'

'I'm coming, darling.'

Guilt comes from nowhere. Archie is innocent in all of this. He doesn't deserve to be uprooted from his life, and yet isn't that what Cate's done to him? I can't let my feelings for this sweet little boy cloud my judgement; change my course. I've lived with the guilt of what happened to Donna. I'll live with this too. 'You brought this on yourself, Cate,' I say. 'Disappear. Take Archie and give him a good life. Never go back to Leedham, or I will ruin you.'

Tears build in her eyes, but she gives the briefest of nods before leaving the room.

I step out of the cottage. The night air is cool on my face. My mouth is dry and my thoughts are spiralling. Talking about Donna and my past hurts more than I can bear.

I wait for the relief to come. The sense of justice. But there's only raw hurt. The whispers of a new plan start to form. I think of the pouch tucked in my bag and my next destination, and I realise that justice will never be enough. I need more. I need vengeance. It's time to face Oliver.

FIFTY-SIX

OLIVER

Oliver sips at the whisky in his glass. His head is fuzzy. He's not eaten since a slice of toast this afternoon. It's nearly midnight. He should be in bed, asleep. And he definitely shouldn't be drinking on the antibiotics he's on, but right now he doesn't care. Six hours they held him in that police cell before letting him go home. Six hours of listening to a drunk in the next cell cry, and wondering if this was the rest of his life – alone in prison for a crime he didn't commit.

They only let him go because the witness who supposedly saw Cate and Archie running by the river retracted her statement. They discovered she'd already left for her holiday by the time Cate and Archie disappeared and couldn't have seen them. Apparently, she has a history of making things up. Another village busybody wanting to get involved.

But he's not off the hook. The detectives are coming for him again tomorrow morning. Philip called this evening with the heads-up. Another interview. He thinks an arrest this time too. Oliver wonders if they've found something. Another piece of evidence against him that isn't real.

His in-laws arrive tomorrow too. First thing. They'll come straight here. Angry and worried and accusing. God, he really hates those people. He can't think now why he put up with them treating him like shit for all these years. Was the money and the lifestyle really worth it? He looks around the empty living room and thinks it wasn't.

How has it come to this?

He knows the answer. Even with the alcohol swimming through his veins, he knows this is on him. He never should have started something with Gemma. Isn't that always the advice? Never crap on your own doorstep. But those skirts she wears, that arse – anyone in his position would've done the same.

It was only sex, for God's sake. Maybe he led her on, over-promised. Men do it all the time. They do a hell of a lot worse, and yet it's him being punished.

Karma.

He huffs a laugh at how ridiculous that thought is. He doesn't believe in karma. And yet his mind still snags on Lexi's scar. He corrects himself. Not Lexi. Her real name is Laura. Laura Gregg. Laura Alexis Gregg. He wonders when she changed it to Lexi Mills. The name suits her. Even as Donna's annoying little sister, who always got in the way of him seeing Donna, listening in to conversations that didn't concern her, she had something about her. A sparky edge that made her seem more than a Laura Gregg.

His stomach churns. The whisky, the hunger, the antibiotics, the impending arrest and the question he doesn't know the answer to – how is the little sister of a girl he dated a lifetime ago involved in this? It had to be Lexi behind the emails and the photos of the bruises. Which means her presence here isn't a coincidence, and whatever game she's playing, it started long before Cate and Archie disappeared.

Did she have something to do with their disappearance?

God, what is it with these women? What the hell happened to the subservient housewife types? Even Donna wouldn't listen to him about the abortion. If she'd just seen reason, they'd never have crashed.

A sound. Not from the living room where he's currently slouched on the sofa but from inside his head. The crunching of the car metal. So much louder than he could've thought possible. The jerking force of the impact as the car hit the tree; his neck whipping forward then back, and the sudden departure of his anger, leaving only horror and regret in its wake.

He'd scrambled out, dizzy and aching, before helping Lexi get free. Donna wasn't so easy to get at. A branch had pushed through the windscreen, pinning her body in place. He remembers thinking she was dead.

He did that.

Oliver's temper had been landing him in a world of trouble all his life. From tantrums with his parents to punch-ups in the school playground, to road rage and police warnings. He knew the way he treated Donna was off-the-charts wrong, but she always said or did something to rile him. She was so secretive. Never telling him where she was going or who with. She drove him to madness sometimes. He loved her too much; he can see that now.

Standing by the wreckage of the car, ears ringing, heart racing, he knew he'd gone too far. That this was the moment – a turning point in his life. He would get control of his anger. He would never again lash out. It was a promise he's kept.

He can still hear Lexi's screams, her pleading for him to let her go. The surprising strength of her as she'd thrown herself back towards the car, desperate to help her big sister. He'd tried to hold her back, but she'd wriggled free, cutting her arm on a shard of glass as she'd tried to reach Donna.

She'd looked from her arm to him with such anger, such malice, that he'd stepped back. Let her look, he'd thought, before replaying the last ten minutes in his head. Getting his story straight as the first wail of a siren sounded in the distance. A tragic accident. Him heartbroken. A victim.

The insides of his cheeks ache with the desire to vomit. He's not that person anymore. It feels like a lie, but he's not sure why.

He lifts the glass to his lips again, surprised to find the liquid gone. He stands, the room tilting with him. Where did he leave the bottle? The kitchen? The toilet when he went for a piss earlier?

He's drunk. Too drunk. He needs sleep not more whisky. He takes a breath, the nausea coming in a wave. He's moving slowly towards the stairs and his bed when the doorbell trills.

The police? Panic grips him. The urge to run. Ridiculous but still there.

Another trilling ring. Then a fist knocking. 'Oliver?' The voice is female, but it isn't DS Pope. 'Oliver, it's Lexi. I've found something. I know where Cate and Archie are.'

He forces his legs forward and shakes his head as though the movement will be enough to push away the fog of alcohol. The room tilts again. He has the feeling of trying to walk across a ship in a storm, and yet he keeps going, hope sparking.

And even though a part of him knows that Lexi is involved in this much more than she's saying, the thought of finding his wife and child is too great to ignore. He stumbles forward and throws open the door. 'Lexi. What's going on?'

She's on the doorstep. Stunning. Her red curls are pulled away from her face, and she's wearing a tight T-shirt and a pair of jeans, a bag slung over one shoulder. She looks nothing like the quaint substitute teacher he'd met in the hall on that Tuesday. She looks, in fact, like Donna. So much so that his breath snags with the sharp inhale, and he can't believe he didn't notice it before. It's why he's felt déjà vu when he's been near her, and why just looking at her face makes him feel so angry, just like Donna always used to make him.

'Can I come in?' she asks.

He nods, stepping back and pointing to the kitchen before closing the front door and following her in. 'Do you want a drink?'

She shakes her head. Her eyes find his, and he can see the calculations running through her mind. Is she wondering if he's figured out who she is or just questioning how drunk he is? He pulls his shoulders back and widens his eyes a little. Let her wonder.

'How are you?' she asks.

He waves the bandaged hand in the air. 'About to be charged with the murder of my wife and son. Missing them like crazy, worried about what's happened to them.' He shrugs. 'You said you know where they are.'

She nods, and he's suddenly sober, or alert at least. 'Where?' he asks. 'Are they OK?'

She nods again, and it's like a stone slab has been removed from his shoulders. Everything will be all right now. The police can't charge him with murder when his family are alive.

His legs feel suddenly weak. He moves to a stool at the island and drops onto it. Emotion builds up and up. Tears form in his eyes. He'll be OK. Archie and Cate are OK. There's still a way back from this, a way for them to be the happy family they're supposed to be.

'They're staying in a cottage about half an hour away.'

The relief morphs. Then realisation. A pulsing anger. The tears dry before they've had a chance to fall. 'So she did this then?' He shouldn't be surprised.

'Yes. She knows about Gemma.'

He sighs, the regret stinging.

'And Donna too,' Lexi adds, and he catches the bitterness in her voice. His gaze flicks up, catching her own. He's thought of little else but Donna since he made the connection to Lexi, but hearing her name causes his insides to squirm.

'Your sister,' he says.

'You figured it out.' She rubs a finger over the scar on her arm. The room sways at the edges again. It's all too much. Cate and Archie are safe. Alive. He'll be vindicated. But Donna, his past, it's come back to him. He should get himself a glass of water but feels too unsteady to move from the stool.

He waits for his mind to clear a little before speaking. 'You gave Cate the photos of Donna. Of those... bruises.' He forces the word out.

She nods.

'Why now?'

'Why not?'

'I mean, you must have had them all this time. You could've shown them to the police back then. After it all happened.'

'Don't be vague, Oliver.' Her words fire out, and he flinches and checks himself for it. There's a shift in the air between them, and he finds himself getting to his feet, stepping closer so they're barely a metre apart. He can feel his pulse beating in his head.

'You mean, why didn't I give them to the police after you tried to kill my sister and left her with severe brain damage? Well, for starters, if you'll remember – I was ten years old. You had everyone, my parents included, lapping up your lies about it being an accident. I showed the photos to my mum. She cried, but then she told me to delete them. She said it didn't make any difference to the outcome.'

He sighs, a 'sheesh' kind of noise. This is all nonsense. Cate and Archie are safe. They'll come home. He'll be off the hook. It won't be easy to rebuild his reputation and his marriage, but he will. As soon as he's dealt with whatever mess Lexi is trying to drag him into. 'So you and Cate have been working together in – what? A female pact of solidarity all this time? The pair of you out to destroy me – is that it?'

'No.' She smiles as though he's said something funny. She's

just like Donna. Pushing his buttons. The thought swirls on a gust of wind that carries through his mind and out again just as fast.

He's not that person anymore.

Is he?

'We need to tell the police,' he says. 'Whatever you and Cate have or haven't done, we need to let DS Pope know that she's safe.'

'Maybe we do, or maybe I get back in my car and drive away and leave you to your mess. Maybe Cate and Archie don't come back.'

He steps to the counter and reaches for the bottle of whisky, giving himself another moment to process her words. She's bluffing. She thinks she can play games with him, but deep down she's just a stupid little girl that needs to be put in her place.

'What do you want... Laura?' he asks, dragging out her real name as he sloshes another few inches of whisky into the crystal tumbler some aunt of Cate's bought them as a Christmas gift.

'I want you to pay for what you did to my sister,' she says. 'I want you to admit that you hit her and that you tried to kill her, and I want to take from you what you took from me.'

The venom in her words rings in his ears, and with it comes an anger so fierce, it steals his breath from his lungs; it takes over his body, and before he can think or process or stop, his hand is up, flying through the air and landing with a slap of stinging skin across Lexi's face.

He *is* that person.

She backs away, eyeing him with caution but not crying, not even angry as far as he can tell. 'And if you don't admit what you did,' she says as though the last thirty seconds haven't happened, 'I'll kill you.'

He scoffs at that. A half laugh of disbelief. 'Come off it,

Lexi. You're not the type. All you women are the same. You think you have all the power now, but you don't.'

The smile she gives unsettles him. 'Actually, I am the type. I've killed before. I'm a murderer, in fact.' Her eyes dart to the clock on the wall. 'In fact, it was a year ago today. I killed my sister. I murdered Donna.'

FIFTY-SEVEN

LEXI

His movements are fumbled, drunken, and the slap lands stinging but not hard. And yet still, an innate part of me wants to cup my hand to my face and cry. It's the shock, and I have to bite the inside of my lip to fight it back. Only when I'm sure I've got control do I tell him the truth about Donna. That I couldn't save her, so I killed her.

I watch the look of surprise dawning on his face as my words sink in. Then when he's least expecting it, I move. Rushing at him and crouching low, left foot stepping forward, right hand pulling back and rolling forward with the propulsion of my entire body until my fist sinks into Oliver's gut and he's dropping to his knees, coughing, gagging.

I could carry on. A jab cross to the face, a broken nose, missing teeth. I could keep going and not stop until this pathetic man is nothing more than mush. But already I'm stepping back, giving him space. That isn't part of the new plan that formed in my head as I drove to Leedham.

I keep my hands up – a fighting stance. Although there's really no need. He turns around, scrambles to his feet and rushes to the sink before throwing up.

The smell is putrid. Vomit and stale whisky that turns my stomach.

He runs the tap, splashes water on his face and slurps from his cupped hand. Only when he's upright does he turn back to me, face ashen. 'You bitch,' he says.

'You hit me first,' I reply, like my heart isn't racing so hard I think I'll pass out. It's the adrenaline of the fight and the fear I'm hiding, and that I'm here in a moment I've spent the longest time imagining.

I wait for him to move, but he keeps his distance.

'What do you mean, you killed Donna? Why are you here blaming me when you're just as bad?'

The wildfire of fury returns. Scorching. Memories flood my thoughts. The smell of the care home – overboiled vegetables and cleaning products fill my senses, only a fraction better than the smell of stale whisky and vomit in Oliver's kitchen.

My cheery '*Hello*' that was never answered. Saving up all the titbits of my day and the little things the children did to tell her.

'*Do you remember I told you Dominic finally got the courage to perform his ballet in assembly? Everyone clapped so hard, I could've cried.*'

'*You remember that mum I thought was pregnant? Well she is. Baby number five. She'll have her hands full there.*'

When I ran out of things to say, I'd read from the gossip magazines that Donna used to love. Hoping she didn't mind that neither of us had heard of half the names. The years passed, and I watched my big sister waste away.

'You know,' I tell Oliver, 'the doctors, the care-home staff, my parents – they all said I was projecting. That Donna's mind was gone. They said she had no idea who I was, but that wasn't true. There was a light in her eyes when I walked into her room.

'And they were just letting her waste away.' Hot tears roll down my face. I blink them away and see Donna in hospital, struggling to breathe through her third bout of pneumonia in eighteen months.

The light changed after that. No one else saw it because no one else wanted to look. My parents had grieved for the loss of their daughter long ago. To them, she was already gone. But she no longer had love in her eyes when I walked into the room. She had hate. She hated me, and I knew why. I was the only one that saw she was still there, hidden beneath a brain injury and a body that would never again respond to her commands. And I let her continue to rot in that care home day after day after day. Of course she hated me.

I swallow; force myself back to the room and to Oliver. 'I moved her out of the care home in the end. I rented a little house right on the seafront and made sure she could see the sea every day.

'Donna didn't deserve the life you'd trapped her in, but no amount of visits or sisterly love could save her. So I waited, and I learned all there was to learn about medication and morphine, and when I had all I needed, I gave her what she wanted...' My voice cracks. 'She wanted to die. And so I murdered her.'

It was easier than it should've been to kill Donna. I'd been rationing her morphine for a while after her recovery from pneumonia and the inevitable complications that came from a body that didn't move; giving 10mg instead of 15mg. When the day came, I added the extra to her canula, held her hand and looked into her pleading eyes until she slipped away.

The guilt and the grief hit me hard – a knockout punch. Sometimes the guilt I feel is because it took me so long, because I allowed Donna to hate me. I loved her too much to end it. And sometimes the guilt comes because I'm the reason she's gone.

The chance to process what happened, and to grieve, was ripped away from me by a carer at the home Donna had stayed in before I'd taken her out. He told the police he thought I'd killed her. The police knew it too. And the school, thanks to the wife of one of the officers spreading the news among the mums. But they just couldn't prove it. I'd made sure of that.

But Donna's death wasn't the end. It was the beginning.

'I might have helped her go, but you were the one who crashed that car, Oliver. You were the one that ruined Donna's life and mine that night sixteen years ago. *You* killed her.'

He sighs, and it takes every ounce of self-control not to deliver another gut punch, knocking the impatience right out of him. He still thinks there's a way out of this for him.

'All right. So I admit I caused the accident that injured Donna,' he says, 'and apologise, and you tell me where Cate is, and we all move on with our lives? Fine, I'm sorry. I made Donna crash the car, and I'm sorry for it. I've regretted it every day since. I never meant for her to get so badly hurt. It changed me too, you know?' he continues, emotion carrying in his voice. 'I knew my anger was out of control. It took that accident for me to stop. I've never hit a woman since.'

'Until a minute ago, you mean?'

He lets out a cry. An anguished moan of frustration. 'What more do you want from me?'

'The confession and the apology are very nice,' I say in a cool voice. 'Now you can pop along to the police station and tell them.'

'No.' The word is instant, and I see in that second that he's exactly who he's always been. He'll never confess to what he did. But that's OK; the confession was the old plan. I was just testing it out, seeing what kind of man he really is. The skin on my face burns from his hand, and I have my answer. I wonder for a moment if there was anything he could have said or done tonight that would've changed my mind. I doubt it.

When I left Cate at that cottage, I knew there was only one way I would ever stand a chance of moving on from Donna's death. The fact that he's proven without a shadow of a doubt that he's still exactly the same man I remember from all those years ago simply makes the next part of the plan easier.

I turn away from him, reaching into my bag.

'What are you doing?' he asks. 'Who are you calling?'

He moves quicker than I expect for someone so drunk. His hand is out, grabbing for my bag, but my rage makes me fast, and I sidestep until we're on opposite sides of the square island in the middle of the kitchen.

We shuffle, one way then the other, as he tries to outsmart me. A strange and pointless dance. I find what I'm looking for, and I drop my bag to the floor, keeping my hand hidden below the counter.

He moves again. Left, then a quick right, and this time I pretend he's outsmarted me. He rushes me, and I let him, until his hands are on me, grabbing at my neck. Tight. Hard. There's no air. My lungs burn. Panic rains across my thoughts. A second passes, and another, and he keeps squeezing, and I start to think I've made a mistake. And then the fury kicks in again, and I lift my hand and jab the needle into his stomach – pushing in the liquid I drew from the bottle in the pouch while I sat in the car.

The syringe is out before he's even realised. His hands loosen then drop. I cough as air hits my lungs once more. He looks from my face to my hand and the syringe, to his stomach. 'What was that?'

'Insulin,' I whisper as I double over and heave in breath after breath. 'A handy little find in the school fridge. Thanks to Sebastian.'

'It won't kill me. It's only insulin.' The anger is ugly on his face, and before I've caught my breath, he's leaping at me again, and I'm knocked from my feet and thrown to the floor. He lands on top of me, and his hands find my neck again.

I can't breathe once more. The world is going black at the edges. My hands slap at his, and I buck my body, but I don't scratch, and I don't bring my fist up to smack his head. I wait and wait, a gamble I might not win. Who will die first – him or me?

My thoughts drift away, the panic ebbing into the black. I'm half gone; half-dead. But then there's air again. I'm coughing and gagging and gasping all at once. My vision returns, blurry at first but clearing fast, enough for me to see that Oliver is no longer on top of me but by my side. His eyes are closing. He's sinking away.

I don't move. My pulse is still pounding in my ears. I'm shaking – a violent tremor. My throat is dry, and it throbs with the pain of Oliver's grip.

Tears fall, and I let them. The guttural sadness of grief returns, mixing with the relief that I've done it, that I'm alive.

Oliver is unconscious now. Soon his body will start to shut down, thanks to the insulin I injected into his stomach. A handy way to kill someone, which I stumbled across when I was looking for ways to end Donna's life peacefully.

It's a natural hormone in the body, and for diabetics like Sebastian who can't produce enough of their own, it's a lifesaver. But for someone like Oliver, who can produce insulin, the huge dose he's been given will send his body into shutdown. He's already slipped into a hypoglycaemic coma. He needs medical treatment immediately, or his organs will fail and he'll die.

Of course, Oliver doesn't deserve this kind of death. He deserves a long, drawn-out and painful death. But I don't have the time or the luxury for that, and there's no way I'm spending the rest of my life in prison for doing what was right.

A quiet falls across the kitchen. I sit for a while more before wiping my eyes and getting to work. His body is heavy, and I huff as I drag him as carefully as I can to the living room and hoist him onto the sofa.

My bag is where I left it on the kitchen floor along with the syringe. I pick them up and place the syringe next to Oliver's right hand. I position Sebastian's pouch and empty vial nearby and add the whisky bottle and glass to the table next to him. And then I wipe down the surfaces I've touched, loop my bag over my shoulder and step out into the night.

I've killed two people, and both of them deserved it. Donna to escape her brain damage, and Oliver for causing it. Scents of dewy grass and lilac carry in the night air as I walk through the dark streets of Leedham.

I wait for the relief, the sense of an ending, of this being enough for me to pick up the fractured pieces of my life and start again.

It doesn't come.

TWO MONTHS LATER

EPILOGUE

LEXI

Leedham high street is both empty and jam-packed. Cars and vans are parked across pavements and on yellow lines, but there are no people around. Green-and-white bunting hangs from every shop, and all of them are closed apart from the super-market on the corner.

I stroll towards the park as though I have no particular place to be. The summer sun warms the back of my neck. Beneath my baseball cap, my hair is a chestnut brown and deadly straight, and I'm quietly confident that if I keep my head down and stick to the outskirts of the village fete, no one will recognise me.

I'm already forgotten. A substitute teacher who worked at the school for two weeks before leaving. I waited for Anika to call the substitute teaching agency and unleash her promised fury at my desertion, but it never came. I'm sure, with the shock of Oliver's death, I was the least of her worries.

I checked the news hourly and breathed a sigh of relief when a story confirmed it was suicide and included an unnamed police source who claimed his death was believed to be the result of the guilt of killing his wife and child. There it was. My plan finished. Everything tied up with a neat little bow.

And I really did try to move on. I finally answered the phone to the Brighton number – it was Haventhorpe Primary. I'd been expecting more accusations of murder, but it was nothing like that. The head teacher wanted to apologise. They were down a teacher, and I was missed. Would I consider coming back? Of course I said no. I shouldn't have ignored the calls for so long, letting it build up in my head to be something it wasn't.

Then a week passed, and another news story broke.

MISSING CATE AND ARCHIE ALIVE AND WELL

She must've tried the new life out and decided to take her chances with me, returning to the village and telling the police her abuse story. Claiming she ran away with Archie in fear for her life and had only just learned of Oliver's suicide.

She wanted her life back, and I don't blame her for that. But like Oliver, she's underestimated me.

The park is a riot of colour. Rainbow bunting and bright marquees. The air smells of candyfloss and hot dogs. There's a huge red bouncy castle and inflatable slide in the centre of the park, surrounded by stalls selling crafts or games to play. I stick to the trees and smile when I spot Jessica pump her fist in the air after hooking a duck. I realise with a pang how much I miss working with the children. Teaching English to fourteen-year-olds at the high school two towns away isn't anywhere near as rewarding, but it pays well and means I'm close enough to Leedham to pop back when the urge takes me.

From across the park, I see another lone figure. Tall and broad. I sense his eyes on me and wait for that familiar bolt of fear, but it doesn't come this time. He gives a slow nod; an acknowledgement of sorts. Somehow, he's recognised me. Or perhaps it's the darkness he recognises, the one I'm sure he carries in him and acts on in his own way, just as I do. James might not be a murderer or a serial killer, but I can't forget the way he always seemed to be there, watching me. Doing bad things for good reasons doesn't mean you're not bad. I should know.

My gaze travels among the picnic blankets until I see Cate. She's sat among a group of mums, holding court. Her hair is shorter, a neat blonde bob that suits her face and matches the other mums around her. She's wearing a red linen dress I recognise from one of the photos used in the search.

She's holding a plastic glass of Prosecco and is laughing about something. I allow myself a moment of knowing. The calm before the storm that only I know is heading Cate's way. I wonder if she had sleepless nights at first, worrying whether I'd follow through on my promise to tell everyone what she did. I wonder how long it's taken her to settle into her old life, giving herself a good pat on the back, feeling oh so smug that she's won. Oliver is gone. Gemma has left too, according to the school website. Off to pursue a career in law apparently.

I watch Archie race up to her, pulling at her arm, pleading with her to come watch something or play something. She whispers in his ear, and he runs off alone. Seeing Archie gives me a moment's pause. He doesn't deserve any of this. He doesn't deserve to have a dead father or a mother who plays dark and troubling games.

But Donna didn't deserve to have her life stolen away either, so I crush the hesitation before it can take hold and pull out my phone. The fake news site was easy to create. It was only a matter of copying over the banner and the side bars and writing my own headline and story.

OLIVER WALKER DEATH RULED MURDER – WIFE SUSPECTED

I'm quite proud of the story that follows. Perhaps I missed my calling as a tabloid journalist, adding salacious details and unnamed sources.

It will only take one look at the website address or a search of the website itself to realise it's fake. That's OK though. I know these people, and I know that all they need is the whisper of gossip to start talking. In an hour, or a day, or however long it takes someone to realise the website isn't real, the damage will already be done.

I copy the link to the website and, using a fake profile I've been building up, pretending to be a sixty-something widower moving to the village, I post the link onto Leedham's Facebook page. I wait for it to load before dropping a second into the village WhatsApp group.

From my position by the treeline, I watch one of the mums check her phone, showing the screen to the woman next to her. Five minutes later, the atmosphere of the fete changes, like a storm cloud moving across the sun. Cate cries out, arms gesturing wildly in the air. Someone pats her on the back. Supportive, kind. For now.

Cate might not have grabbed the wheel and crashed the car Donna was driving that night, but she was the one whispering in Oliver's ear about abortions, painting a picture of a life they could have together. It was her family's money that paid for the solicitor that helped him wriggle out of any punishment, that twisted what I told the police into the deranged ramblings of a scared little girl, rather than the truth of an eyewitness.

It won't be long before the community Cate loves so much turns on her just like they did with Oliver. And if they don't, I'll be here with something else. Something more final.

This is just the beginning for Cate.

And for me.

A LETTER FROM LAUREN

Dear reader,

My eternal thanks for reading *The Teacher's Secret*. If you want to keep up to date with my latest releases and offers, you can sign up for my newsletter at the following link. Your email address will never be shared and you can unsubscribe at any time.

www.bookouture.com/lauren-north

I took a step away from my usual style with this book. Normally, my stories have two points of view, and normally those characters are both women. So it was great fun to tell this story from so many different perspectives, and to include Oliver's story as well. Points of view from Lexi, Gemma, Jeanie and Oliver made for quite a few red herrings, and I particularly loved Jeanie's character and some of her thoughts on her fellow villagers.

I always love to hear from you. Whether it's through reviews, tags in posts or messages, it never fails to make my day! My social media links are below, and I can be found most days popping in to X and Instagram.

If you enjoyed *The Teacher's Secret*, I'd be so grateful if you would leave a review on either Amazon or Goodreads, or simply share the book love by telling a friend.

With love and gratitude,

Lauren x

www.Lauren-North.com

instagram.com/Lauren_C_North

tiktok.com/@Lauren_C_North

facebook.com/LaurenNorthAuthor

x.com/Lauren_C_North

ACKNOWLEDGEMENTS

This feeling never gets old or boring. The feeling of having sat with a blank page, then word after word after word for days and weeks and months until it's alive somehow – a story. Then the edits and the many (many!) hours of hard work from me and all the team, making it not just a story anymore but the best story it can be. This feeling is pride and joy and the biggest smile, and I'm thankful every day that I have THE BEST job in the world.

I always like to start the acknowledgements by thanking the most important people in this process, and that's you! The reader. Thank you for taking a chance and spending your precious time falling into the world of my characters. I do hope you enjoyed this story as much as I enjoyed writing it.

For the bloggers, Bookstagrammers and NetGalley reviewers, thank you for the early reviews and the time you spend shouting about this book. I always say this, but you guys are total rock stars. A special mention to Vik at Vik's Book Haven (Little Miss Book Lover 87), for always being at the front of the queue for my books and being so generous with your time shouting about them. I'm so grateful! I hope my portrayal of a primary school is up to scratch!

A massive thanks to Lucy Frederick, my fabulous editor. You are so on it with everything! Your ability to shape my stories and elevate them to another level is beyond words. Plus, of course, you're so lovely and so much fun to work with.

I'm so grateful to Jenny Geras and the entire Bookouture team for their continual hard work and dedication. I'm absolutely delighted to be working with you again. It really is a team effort, and this isn't by any means an exhaustive list, but special mentions to Melissa Tran for her editorial input, Jess Readett in publicity, Mandy Kullar for overseeing all the magic from copy-edits and beyond, Kim Nash, Melanie Price, and the entire sales and marketing teams. I'd also like to thank Donna Hillyer for copyediting the novel, and Laura Kincaid for proofreading it. They are two skillsets (superpowers!) which are so incredible and so important.

Thank you to my amazing agent, Amanda Preston. Your energy, knowledge, ideas and hard work blow me away every time! Thanks also to the LBA team and everyone working behind the scenes with Amanda.

I was fortunate enough to have an author intern while I was working on this book, and I'd like to say thanks to Tara Woods for her focus and drive, not to mention her insights. Gemma's character is so much better because of your thoughts on her in the earlier draft. Keep writing and believing in yourself!

To Carla Kovach and Sue Bennet – thank you for your motivational support! To my besties – Nikki Smith, Zoe Lea and Laura Pearson. I'm so grateful to have you in my corner, as well as my In Suspense podcasting pals – Nikki and Lesley Kara. To Lottie, Tommy and Andy, thank you as always for the creative input, the constant and unwavering support, and a lot of laughter!

I'm absolutely certain that I'll have forgotten to thank a few people, so this one is for you. THANK YOU!

PUBLISHING TEAM

Turning a manuscript into a book requires the efforts of many people. The publishing team at Bookouture would like to acknowledge everyone who contributed to this publication.

Commercial
Lauren Morrissette
Jil Thielen
Imogen Allport

Data and analysis
Mark Alder
Mohamed Bussuri

Cover design
The Brewster Project

Editorial
Lucy Frederick
Imogen Allport

Copyeditor
Donna Hillyer

Proofreader
Laura Kincaid

Marketing

Alex Crow
Melanie Price
Occy Carr
Cíara Rosney

Operations and distribution

Marina Valles
Stephanie Straub

Production

Hannah Snetsinger
Mandy Kullar
Jen Shannon

Publicity

Kim Nash
Noelle Holten
Myrto Kalavrezou
Jess Readett
Sarah Hardy

Rights and contracts

Peta Nightingale
Richard King
Saidah Graham